英语应用能力考试
B级真题与模拟题解析

董淑英　主编

国防工业出版社
·北京·

内 容 简 介

本书严格按照《高等学校英语应用能力考试大纲》及其样题编写。共有14套试题，其中含有3套真题。其目的在于使学生在模拟训练的基础上，在不同的时间段用真题来测试自己对知识掌握的情况。本书具有内容新、题材广、应用问题覆盖面宽、试题难易程度适中等特点。本书由一线教师和长期从事辅导英语应用能力考试的教师编写。每套试题后面附有听力录音原稿和答案解析，同时还附有MP3格式听力光盘。

图书在版编目(CIP)数据

英语应用能力考试B级真题与模拟题解析/董淑英主编.

北京：国防工业出版社,2009.1

ISBN 978-7-118-05899-4

Ⅰ.英... Ⅱ.董... Ⅲ.英语 – 高等学校：技术学校 – 水平考试 – 解题 Ⅳ.H319.6

中国版本图书馆CIP数据核字(2008)第121071号

※

*国防工业出版社*出版发行

（北京市海淀区紫竹院南路23号 邮政编码100044）

北京奥鑫印刷厂印刷

新华书店经售

*

开本 787×1092 1/16 印张 14¼ 字数 328千字

2009年1月第1版第1次印刷 印数1—5000册 定价28.00元(含光盘)

（本书如有印装错误，我社负责调换）

国防书店：(010)68428422 发行邮购：(010)68414474

发行传真：(010)68411535 发行业务：(010)68472764

本书编委会

主　编　董淑英

副主编　常　识　戈　峰　法治安

参　编　（按姓氏笔画排列）

毛　芳　石　冉　朱丽娜　吴　燕　宋　颖

沙晓岩　陈钢涛　林澍峻　袁宝旺　郭贺彬

黄丽娜　焦晓希　窦爱燕　滕利君　潘　超

主　审　康占俊　翟天利

前　言

　　"高等学校英语应用能力考试"是教育部批准施行的教学考试,其考试对象为高等职业学校、普通高等专科学校、成人学校,以及本科办职业技术学院的学生。学生修完《高职高专教育英语课程教学基本要求》(简称《基本要求》)所规定的内容后,可以参加考试。本考试于 2000 年正式实施,分为 A、B 两个等级。A 级为标准级别,覆盖《基本要求》的全部内容;B 级略低于 A 级,对应《基本要求》的 B 级范围,为过渡级别。考试时间为 120 分钟。

　　本考试的目的是既测试考生的英语基础知识和技能又考核其掌握应用语言的能力。在语言基础方面,测试语言基础知识和听、读、写、译的技能,不包括口头表达能力;在语言能力方面,要求考生理解和运用《基本要求》所规定的日常交际和涉外业务交际的内容。

　　本书根据《基本要求》的内容,贯彻了"实用为主,够用为度"的教学方针;以《高等学校英语应用能力考试大纲》为依据,精选了部分真题供学生们检测使用。同时总结了近年来考生在考试中的实际困难和需要,编写了多套模拟试题并做了详细的解析。目的在于使学生通过练习,对每一种题型考什么、怎么考和难易度如何都能更加熟悉,从而提高应答的准确率。

　　本书由董淑英任主编,常识、戈峰、法治安任副主编,参加编写工作的还有毛芳、石冉、朱丽娜、吴燕、宋颖、沙晓岩、陈钢涛、林澍峻、袁宝旺、郭贺彬、黄丽娜、焦晓希、窦爱燕、滕利君、潘超。陈钢涛和黄丽娜负责录音工作。本书在编写过程中得到了北京京北职业技术学院、北京电子科技职业技术学院、枣庄科技职业学院、北京培黎职业学院的大力支持与帮助。本书在录音过程中得到北京豪典弘扬文化传播有限公司及其录音师李梓健的大力协助,在此表示衷心感谢!

　　由于编者水平有限,书中难免出现错误和疏漏,恳请读者谅解和指正。

编　者

目　　录

Test 1

（2007 年 6 月高等学校英语应用能力考试真题试卷）

Part I Listening Comprehension （15 minutes）

Directions：*This part is to test your listening ability. It consists of 3 sections.*

Section A

Directions：*This section is to test your ability to give proper answers to questions. There are 5 re-corded questions in it. After each question, there is a pause. The questions will be spoken two times. When you hear a question, you should decide on the correct answer from the 4 choices marked A）, B）, C）and D）given in your test paper. Then you should mark the corresponding letter on the Answer Sheet with a single line through the centre.*

Example：*You will hear：*

You will read：A) I'm not sure.

                 B) You're right.

                 C) Yes, certainly.

                 D) That's interesting.

From the question we learn that the speaker is asking the listener to leave a message. Therefore, **C**）**Yes, certainly** *is the correct answer. You should mark C）on the Answer Sheet.*

[A] [B] [C] [D]

Now the test will begin.

1. A. Yes, I am.   B. Yes, I do.   C. I'm sorry.   D. It's my pleasure.
2. A. Please do.   B. Not yet.   C. Yes, I know.   D. Most of the time.
3. A. It's early.   B. Eight hours   C. Yes, I'd love to.   D. At half past eight.
4. A. Nothing serious.   B. No, thank you.   C. Yes, I have.   D. It's terrible.
5. A. Yes, I often go.   B. Yes, I do.   C. No, not yet.   D. No, thanks.

Section B

Directions：*This section is to test your ability to understand short dialogues. There are 5 recorded dialogues in it. After each dialogue, there is a recorded question. Both the dialogues*

1

and questions will be spoken two times. When you hear a question, you should decide on the correct answer from the 4 choices marked A), B), C) and D) given in your test paper. Then you should mark the corresponding letter on the Answer Sheet with a single line through the centre.

6. A. Warm.   B. Cold.
   C. Hot.   D. Wet.

7. A. Go to Beijing.   B. Meet him tomorrow.
   C. Book a ticket.   D. Buy a book.

8. A. He's serious.   B. He's careless.
   C. He's kind.   D. He's polite.

9. A. They will stay at home.   B. They will be late.
   C. They won't go to the party.   D. They won't be late.

10. A. She doesn't need his help.   B. She doesn't like the man.
     C. She wants to work for the man.   D. She wants to ask for help.

Section C

Directions: *In this section you will hear a recorded short passage. The passage is printed in the test paper, but with some words or phrases missing. The passage will be read three times. During the second reading, you are required to put the missing words or phrases that you hear on the Answer Sheet in order of the numbered blanks according to what you hear. The third reading is for you to check your writing. Now the passage will begin.*

The world population today is about 6 billion. But only about 11 percent of the world's land is suitable for farming. However, the area of farmland is becoming smaller and smaller ____11____. So it will be difficult to feed so many mouths. There are several reasons why farmland is being ____12____. Firstly, a lot of the land is being used for the ____13____ of houses. Secondly, some of the land has become wasteland because wind and ____14____ have removed the top soil. Thirdly, some of the land has become too salty to ____15____. Therefore, a big problem that we face today is hunger.

Part II Vocabulary & Structure (15 minutes)

Directions: *This part is to test your ability to use words and phrases correctly to construct meaningful and grammatically correct sentences. It consists of 2 sections.*

Section A

Directions: *In this section, there are 10 incomplete sentences. You are required to complete each statement by choosing the appropriate answer from the 4 choices marked A), B), C)* *and D). You should mark the corresponding letter on the Answer Sheet with a single line through the centre.*

16. I didn't answer the phone _____ I didn't hear it ring.

    A. if   B. unless   C. although   D. because

17. In his report of the accident he _____ some important details.

    A. missed   B. wasted   C. escaped   D. failed

18. _____ a wonderful trip he had when he traveled in china.

    A. Where   B. How   C. What   D. That

19. We're going to _____ the task that we haven't finished.

    A. take away   B. carry on   C. get onto   D. keep off

20. She didn't receive the application form; it _____ to the wrong address.

    A. sent   B. be sent   C. was sent   D. being sent

21. She gave up her _____ as a reporter at the age of 25.

    A. career   B. interest   C. life   D. habit

22. It is necessary to find an engineer _____ has skills that meets your needs.

    A. whom   B. which   C. whose   D. who

23. Time _____ very fast and a new year will begin soon.

    A. takes off   B. goes by   C. pulls up   D. gets along

24. This new style of sports shoes is very popular and it is _____ in all sizes.

    A. important   B. active   C. available   D. famous

25. The general manager sat there, _____ to the report from each department.

    A. to listen   B. listen   C. being listened   D. listening

Section B

Directions: *There are also 10 incomplete statements here. You should fill in each blank with the proper form of the word given in the brackets. Write the word or words in the corresponding space on the Answer Sheet.*

26. She managed to settle the argument in a (friend) _____ way.

27. I would rather you (go) _____ with me tomorrow morning.

28. If I (be) _____ you, I wouldn't ask such a silly question.

29. You should send me the report on the program(immediate) _____.

30. As soon as the result (come) _____ out, I'll let you know.

31. If you smoke in this non-smoking area, you will (fine) _____ $50.

32. It is quite difficult for me (decide) _____ who should be given the job.

33. The new flexible working time system will enable the (employ) _____ efficiently.

34. The more careful you are, the (well) _____ you will be able to complete the work.

35. I'll put forward my (suggest) _____ now so that he can have tome to consider it before the meeting.

3

Part III　Reading Comprehension　(40 minutes)

Directions: *This part is to test your reading ability. There are 5 tasks for you to fulfill. You should read the reading materials carefully and do the tasks as you are instructed.*

Task 1

Directions: *After reading the following passage, you will find 5 questions or unfinished statements, numbered 36 through 40. For each question or statement there are 4 choices marked A), B), C), or D). You should make the correct choice and mark the corresponding letter on the Answer Sheet with a single line through the centre.*

Some cities have planned their transportation systems for car owners. That is what Los Angeles did. Los Angeles decided to build highways for cars rather than spending money on public transportation.

This decision was suitable for Los Angeles. The city grew outward instead of upward. Los Angeles never built many tall apartment buildings. Instead, people live in houses with gardens.

In Los Angeles, most people drives cars to work. And every car has to have a parking space. So many buildings where people work also have parking lots.

Los Angeles also became a city without a Central Business District (CBD). If a city has a CBD, crowds of people rush into it every day to work. If people drive to work, they need lots of road space.

So Los Angeles developed several business districts and built homes and other buildings in between the districts. This required more and more roads and parking spaces.

Some people defend this growth pattern. They say Los Angeles is the city of the future.

36. According to the passage, Los Angeles is a city where _____.

　A. there is no public transportation system

　B. more money is spent on highways for cars

　C. more money is spent on public transportation systems

　D. public transportation is more developed than in other cities

37. "The city grew outward instead of upward" (Sentence 2, Para 2) means _____.

　A. the city became more spread out instead of growing taller

　B. there were fewer smaller houses than tall buildings

　C. rapid development took place in the city center

　D. many tall buildings could be found in the city

38. According to the passage, if a city has several business districts, _____.

　A. people won't have to drive to work every day

　B. there have to be more roads and parking spaces

　C. companies would be located in between the districts

　D. there would be no need to build parking spaces within the districts

39. According to the growth pattern of Los Angeles, homes were mainly built _____.

A. in the city center

B. along the main roads

C. around business districts

D. within the business districts

40. The passage is mainly about _____ .

A. the construction of parking spaces in Los Angeles

B. the new growth pattern of the city of Los Angeles

C. the public transportation system in Los Angeles

D. the problem of traffic jams in Los Angeles

Task 2

Directions: *This task is the same as Task 1. The 5 questions or unfinished statements are numbered 41 through 45.*

We've found that eating habits vary so much that it does not make sense to include meals in the price of our tours. We want to give you the freedom of choosing restaurants and ordering food that suits your taste and budget(预算).

As our hotels offer anything from coffee and toast to a full American breakfast at very reasonable prices, it will never be a problem for you to start the day in the way you like best. At lunch stops, your tour guide will show you where you can find salads, soups, and sandwiches.

Dinner time is your chance to try some local food. Sometimes the tour guide will let you have dinner at a restaurant of your own choice. At other times he or she will recommend a restaurant at your hotel. Years of research have taught us which restaurants reliably serve a good choice of delightful dishes at down-to-earth prices.

In Mexico, Alaska, and the Yukon, where your restaurant choice may be limited, we include some meals. The meals provided are clearly stated on the tour pages.

41. According to the passage, most meals are not included in the price of tours mainly because _____ .

A. meals make up a large part of the tour budget

B. meal prices vary a lot from place to place

C. people dislike menus offered by tour guides

D. people have different eating habits

42. We can learn from the passage that _____ .

A. the hotels where you stay will offer you free breakfast

B. dining information can be obtained from your tour guides

C. you can have a complete choice of local dishes at the hotel

D. a full list of local restaurants can be found on the tour pages

43. Which of the following statements is TRUE? _____

A. tour guides are supposed to arrange dinner outside the hotel.

B. tour guides' recommendations on food are unreliable.

C. tourists must have lunch in the hotels they stay in.

D. tourists may taste local dishes during dinner time.

44. The word "down-to-earth" (Sentence 4, Para. 3) most probably means _____.

    A. changeable

    B. expensive

    C. reasonable

    D. fixed

45. Meals are included in the tour price in some places where _____.

    A. restaurant choice may be limited

    B. there are many nearly restaurants

    C. delightful dishes are not served

    D. food may be too expensive

Task 3

Directions: *The following is an instruction of writing a trip report. After reading it, you should complete the information by filling in the blanks marked 46 through 50 **in not more than 3 words** in the table below.*

Trip Reports

Many companies require their employees to hand in reports of their business trips. A trip report not only provides a written record of a business trip and its activities, but also enables many employees to benefit from the information one employee has gained.

Generally, a trip report should be in the form of a memorandum (内部通知), addressed to your immediate boss. The places and dates of the trip are given on the subject line. The body of the report will explain why you made the trip, whom you visited, and what you did. The report should give a brief account of each major event. You needn't give equal space to each event. Instead, you should focus on the more important events. Follow the body of the report with a conclusion.

A Trip Report

Reported by: an employee back from a business trip

Addressed to: his or her immediate _____46_____

Used for:

    1. serving as a written record

    2. giving helpful _____47_____ that can be shared by others

written in the form of: a _____48_____

information to be included in the report:

    1. the places and dates of the trip on _____49_____

    2. major events during the trip in the _____50_____ of the trip

    3. conclusion

Task 4

Directions: *The following is a list of terms used in railroad services. After reading it, you are required to find the items equivalent to（与……等同）those given in Chinese in the table below. Then you should put the corresponding letters in the brackets on the Answered Sheet, numbered 51 through 55.*

A——information desk

B——ticket office

C——half fare ticket

D——waiting room

E——excess baggage charge

F——baggage check-in counter

G——security check

H——platform underpass

I——ticket agent

J——departure board

K——railroad track

L——traffic light

M——railroad crossing

N——soft sleeping car

O——hard sleeping car

P——hard seat

Q——baggage-claim area

Examples：（Q）行李认领处　　　　（E）超重行李费

51.（　）硬座	（　）软卧
52.（　）开车时间显示牌	（　）信号灯
53.（　）站台地下通道	（　）候车室
54.（　）问询处	（　）安全检查
55.（　）半价票	（　）售票处

Task 5

Directions: *The following is the Trouble-shooting Guide to a microwave oven. After reading it, you are required to complete the statements that follow the questions (No. 56 through No. 60). You should write your answers in no more than 3 words on the corresponding Answer Sheet.*

Problems	**Probable causes**	**Suggested solutions**
The display is showing the sign " **:** ".	There has been a power interruption.	Reset（重新设置）the clock.

Problems	Probable causes	Suggested solutions
·The fan seems to be running slower than usual.	The oven has been stored in a cold area.	The fan will run slower until the oven warms up to normal room temperature.
The display shows a time counting down but the oven is not cooking.	The oven door is not closed completely.	Close the door completely.
	You have set the controls as a kitchen timer(定时器).	Touch OFF/CANCEL to cancel the Minute Timer.
The turntable will not turn.	The support is not operating correctly.	Check the turntable support is properly in place, and restart the oven.
The microwave oven will not run.	The door is not firmly closed.	Close the door firmly.
	You did not touch the button "START".	Touch the button "START".
	You did not follow the directions exactly.	Follow the directions exactly.

56. What should you do if the display is showing the sign " : "?

Reset _____.

57. What is the probable cause if the fan seems to be running slower than usual?

The oven has been stored in a _____.

58. What are you advised to do if you have set the controls as a kitchen timer?

Touch OFF/CANCEL to cancel _____.

59. What is the cause for the turntable to fail to turn?

_____ is not operating correctly.

60. What will happen if you do not touch the button "START"?

The microwave oven _____.

Part IV Translation—from English to Chinese   (25 minutes)

Directions：*This part, numbered 61 through 65, is to test your ability to translate English into Chinese. Each of the four sentences (No. 61 through No. 64) is followed by four choices of suggested translation marked A), B), C) and D). Make the best choice and write the corresponding letter on the Answer Sheet. Write your translation of the paragraph (No. 65) in the corresponding space on the Composition/Translation Sheet.*

61. Mr. Smith demands that all reports be carefully written and above all based on the facts.

A. 史密斯先生要求把所有的报告都写好,还要求全部都应该是事实。

B. 史密斯先生需要的报告都应该写得详尽,而且全部都只能是事实。

C. 史密斯先生所需要的报告都写得很完整,而且包括了所有的事实。

D. 史密斯先生要求认真写好所有的报告,最重要的是应以事实为根据。

62. Candidates should be given the company brochure to read while they are waiting for their interviews.

A. 求职者应帮助公司散发有关的阅读手册,同时等后面试。

B. 在阅读了公司所发给的手册之后,求职者才能等待面试。

C. 在求职者等待面试时,应该发给他们一本公司手册阅读。

D. 求职者在等待面试时,可要求得到一本公司手册来阅读。

63. The manager tried to create a situation in which all people present would feel comfortable.

A. 经理在设法创造条件,让所有的人都得到令人满意的礼物。

B. 经理试图营造一种氛围,让所有在场的人都感到轻松自在。

C. 经理在设法创造一种条件,让所有人都能够显得心情舒畅。

D. 经理想努力营造一种氛围,让所有的人到场时都觉得畅快。

64. Obtaining enough food is the first concern for every nation; in some countries food shortages have become a serious problem.

A. 生产足够的粮食是各国的首要国策;有些国家已面临粮食减产这一重大问题。

B. 能否获得充足的粮食关系到每个国家的生存;有些国家粮食短缺的问题日趋严重。

C. 获得足够的粮食是所有国家的头等大事;粮食短缺已成为一些国家的严重问题。

D. 首先每个国家对生产足够的粮食都会关心;有些则已经解决了粮食短缺的重大问题。

65. The new Holiday Inn has everything you need for a weekend of family fun or business travel. Conveniently located, the Holiday Inn is within walking distance to the hot springs and downtown shopping area. Each room has a refrigerator, coffee maker, Western or Chinese breakfast every morning.

Part V Writing (25 minutes)

Directions: *This part is to test your ability to do practical writing. You are required to write an email according to the information given below in Chinese. Remember to write the email on the composition/Translation Sheet.*

说明:假定你是王军。根据以下内容以第一人称发一封电子邮件。

内容:

1. 发件人:王军

2. 收件人:Anna

3. 发件人电子邮箱地址:wangjun11007@ hotmail. com

4. 收件人电子邮箱地址:anna11008@ hotmail. com

5. 事由：

王军在网站 www. ebay. com. cn 上卖出了一本书,书名《电子商务导论》。买家是美国客户 Anna Brown。

6. 邮件涉及内容：

   1）感谢对方购买《电子商务导论》；

   2）书已寄出,预计一周内到达；

   3）希望收到书后在网站上留下反馈意见；

   4）如果满意,希望向其他客户推荐；

   5）最近还会推出一些新的图书,欢迎选购；再次购买可以享受折扣。

Words for reference：

反馈意见 feedback

电子商务导论 Introduction to E-commerce

注意:e-mail 的内容要写成一个段落,不得逐条罗列。

E-mail Message

From：_____

To：_____

Subject：Feedback of transaction

Dear Miss Anna Brown：_____

Sincerely,

Wang Jun

答 案 解 析

Part I   Listening Comprehension

听力原文

Section A

1. Are you going to buy a house?

2. Have you read today's newspaper?

3. What time do you usually go to work?

4. Have you received my letter?

5. Do you often go shopping at weekends?

Section B

6. M: It's very cold this morning.

W：You are right. It's much colder than yesterday.

Q：What's the weather like this morning?

7. M：I am going to Beijing tomorrow morning. Would you please book a ticket for me?

W：Sure, with pleasure.

Q：What will the woman probably do?

8. M：What do you think of your new boss?

W：I don't like him. He is too serious.

Q：What does the woman think of her new boss?

9. W：I'm afraid we'll be late for the party.

M：Don't worry; there is still 20 minutes to go.

Q：What does the man mean?

10. M：Is there anything I can do for you?

W：Thank you very much, but I can do it all by myself.

Q：What does the woman mean?

Section C

The world population today is about 6 billion. But only about 11 percent of the world's land is suitable for farming. However, the area of farmland is becoming smaller and smaller **11 every year** . So it will be difficult to feed so many mouths. There are several reasons why farmland is being **12 lost** . Firstly, a lot of the land is being used for the **13 building** of houses. Secondly, some of the land has become wasteland because wind and **14 rain** have removed the top soil. Thirdly, some of the land has become too salty to **15 grow crop** . Therefore, a big problem that we face today is hunger.

答案详解

Section A

1. ［答案］A

［解析］本句问题是"你打算买房吗"回答应该是针对一般疑问句的肯定或否定回答。只有 A 项与其助动词一致，所以答案为 A。

2. ［答案］B

［解析］本句问题"你看了今天的报纸吗"是现在完成时的一般疑问句。回答必须用现在完成时的简略形式。

3. ［答案］D

［解析］问题是"你通常什么时间上班"，"what time 问句"要求用具体时间来回答，只有选项 D 符合要求。

4. ［答案］C

［解析］本句问题"你收到我的信了吗"是现在完成时的一般疑问句。它要求用肯定或否定的简略形式回答。只有 C 选项与其时态相符。

5. ［答案］B

[解析]本句问题"周末你经常去买东西吗"是一般现在时的一般疑问句。要求用"Yes,I do"或"No,I don't"回答。只有 B 选项符合题意。

Section B

6. [答案]B

[解析]对话中男士说"今天早上真冷",女士说"没错,今天比昨天冷得多",问题"今天天气如何"。双方都用"cold"这个词形容天气,所以答案应该是 B。

7. [答案]C

[解析]对话中男士说"我明天要去北京,麻烦你给我订一张票",女士说"没问题,很乐意为您效劳",从问题"这位女士可能做什么"可以推断出 C 选项为正确答案。

8. [答案]A

[解析]对话中男士问"你觉得新老板如何",女士回答"我不喜欢他,他太严肃了",问题是"这位女士认为她的老板如何"。根据女士的回答可知 A 选项为正确答案。

9. [答案]D

[解析]对话中女士说"恐怕我们参加聚会要迟到了",男士说"别担心,还有 20 分钟",问题是"男士的话意味着什么"。根据男士的回答推断出 D 选项为正确答案。

10. [答案]A

[解析]对话中男士问"我能为您效劳吗",女士说"非常感谢,不过我能独自完成",问题是"这位女士的话意味着什么"。根据女士的回答推断出 A 选项为正确答案。

Section C

11. every year   12. lost   13. building   14. rain   15. grow crops

Part II   Vocabulary & Structure

Section A

16. [答案]D

[解析]本题考查的是状语从句连词的用法。if 和 unless 引导的是条件状语从句;although 引导的是让步状语从句;because 引导的是原因状语从句。根据上下文的意思,这里选用 because 表示原因。

17. [答案]A

[解析]本题考查的是词义辨析。miss 翻译为"错过,遗漏";waste 翻译为"浪费,使荒芜";escape 翻译为"逃脱,溜走";fail 翻译为"失败,不及格,使失望"。根据句意,只有选项 A 符合题意。

18. [答案]C

[解析]本题考查的是感叹句的用法。How 是副词,后面通常接形容词;what 是感叹词,后面接名词。所以本题答案为 C。

19. [答案]B

[解析]本题考查的是固定短语的用法。take away 翻译为"带走,消失";carry on 翻译为"完成";get onto 不是固定短语;keep off 翻译为"让开,不接近"。根据句子意思答案为 B 选项。

20. [答案]C

[解析]本题考查的是时态和语态。因为前面分句用的是一般过去时,所以此句也应该用一般过去时。it 和谓语动词 send 之间是被动关系,要用被动语态结构。所以本题答案为 C。

21. [答案]A

[解析]本题考查的是词义辨析。career 翻译为"事业,职业";interest 翻译为"兴趣,关心";life 翻译为"生命,生活";habit 翻译为"习惯,习性"。根据句意和 as 引导的介词短语判断,答案应选 A。

22. [答案]D

[解析]本题考查的是定语从句的内容。whom 修饰的先行词是人,在从句中作宾语;which 修饰的先行词是物,在从句中作主语或宾语;whose 修饰的先行词既可是人也可是物,在从句中作定语;who 修饰的先行词是人,在从句中作主语。根据句子结构和先行词确定答案应该是 D 选项。

23. [答案]B

[解析]本题考查的是短语词义辨析。take off 翻译为"起飞,匆忙离去";go by 翻译为"时间的过去或消失";pull up 翻译为"拔起,停下";get along 翻译为"相处,进展"。根据句子意思 B 为正确答案。

24. [答案]C

[解析]本题考查的是词义辨析。important 翻译为"重要的,重大的";active 翻译为"积极的,活跃的";available 翻译为"可用的,可得到的";famous 翻译为"著名的,出名的"。根据句子意思答案 C 最合适。

25. [答案]D

[解析]本题考查的是非谓语动词的用法。根据句子结构和意思判断,"listen 与 manager"之间是能动关系。所以本句用现在分词作状语表示伴随情况。

Section B

26. [答案]friendly

[解析]冠词之后,名词之前应用形容词。friend 是名词,要变成形容词形式。

27. [答案]went

[解析]本题考查 would rather 的用法。would rather 后面接名词性从句,但从句要求用虚拟语气即"动词过去时"。

28. [答案]were

[解析]本题考查的是虚拟语气的用法。根据主句结构判断,句意表达的是与现在事实相反的情况。主句用"should/would/could + 动词原形";从句用"动词过去时"。但是 be 动词没有人称变化,都用"were"。

29. [答案]immediately

[解析]本题考查的是词性转换。副词在句中修饰动词和形容词。题中需要副词修饰谓语动词 send。因此将形容词变成副词 immediately。

30. [答案]comes

[解析]本题考查的是时间状语从句中时态的用法。由 as soon as 和 when 引导的时间状语从句,主句用将来时,从句用一般现在时表示将来。所以本题只能用 comes。

31. [答案]be fined

[解析]本题考查的是时态和语态的用法。根据句子意思"你将会被罚款"。will 后面用动词原型,即 be fined。

32. [答案]to decide

[解析]本题考查的是不定式的用法。It + be + 形容词 + for + 名/代词 + 不定式。此结构中,it 是形式主语,真正主语是不定式复合结构"for + 名/代词 + 不定式"。根据本题结构应该用 to decide。

33. [答案]employees

[解析]本题考查词性转换。句中动词短语 enable somebody to do something 是"某人能够做某事",因此可以判断此处应该用名词。employ 有两个派生名词:employee 翻译为"雇员";和 employer 翻译为"雇主"。根据全句意思应该用 employees。

34. [答案]better

[解析]本题考查的是比较级的用法。比较结构 the more... the more... 翻译为"越……越……",表示两个比例同时递增。more 代表的是比较级形式。

所以此处用 better。

35. [答案]suggestion

[解析]本题考查的是词性转换的用法。根据短语 put forward something 判断,此处用名词形式;另外根据形容词性物主代词 my 判断,此处也应该用名词形式。所以,此处用 suggestion。

Part III Reading Comprehension

Task 1

36. [答案]B

[解析]根据文章第一段中"Los Angeles decided to build highways for cars rather than spending money on public transportation."判断 B 为正确答案。

37. [答案]A

[解析]首先要理解 the city grew outward instead of upward 在文章中的意思;再根据后面这句话"Los Angeles never built many tall apartment buildings. Instead, people live in houses with gardens."判断 A 为正确答案。

38. [答案]B

[解析]本题考查考生的生活常识。如果一座城市拥有几个商业区将意味着什么。根据文章倒数第二段的最后一句"This required more and more roads and parking spaces."可以判断正确答案为 B。

39. ［答案］C

［解析］本题考查学生的综合判断能力。根据文章倒数第二段的第一句话"So Los Angeles developed several business districts and built homes and other buildings in between the districts."判断正确答案为C。

40. ［答案］B

［解析］本题考查学生的综合理解能力。根据全文的内容判断出正确答案应该是B。

Task 2

41. ［答案］D

［解析］根据第一段第一句"We've found that eating habits vary so much that it does not make sense to include meals in the price of our tours."可以判断原因是eating habits vary so much，所以正确答案是D。

42. ［答案］B

［解析］本题可以用排除法做。根据第二段第一句中的at very reasonable prices判断A项错误；根据第三段第二、第三句判断C项错误；根据最后一段"some meals we include（我们提供的食物）"可知D项也是错误的，因此只有B项是正确的。

43. ［答案］D

［解析］根据第三段第一句"Dinner time is your chance to try some local food."判断D为正确答案。

44. ［答案］C

［解析］第三段最后一句话"Years of research have taught us which restaurants reliably serve a good choice of delightful dishes at down-to-earth prices."中down-to-earth prices翻译为"价格合理的"。而选项中与其意思相近的是C选项reasonable。

45. ［答案］A

［解析］根据最后一段可以判断出A选项为正确答案。

Task 3

46. ［答案］boss

［解析］根据第二段第一句话"…addressed to your immediate boss."可得到答案。

47. ［答案］information

［解析］根据第一段第二句话"A trip report…, but also enables many employees to benefit from the information one employee has gained."可得到答案。

48. ［答案］memorandum

［解析］根据第二段第一句"Generally, a trip report should be in the form of a memorandum, addressed to your immediate boss."可得到答案。

49. ［答案］the subject line

［解析］根据第二段第二句"The places and the dates of the trip are given on the subject line."可得到答案。

50. ［答案］body

［解析］本题考查学生对文章中履行报告内容的理解。根据第二段第三句话"The body of the report will explain why you made the trip, whom you visited, and what you did. The report should give a brief account of each major event. "可得出答案。

Task 4

51. (P)(N)　52. (J)(L)　53. (H)(D)　54. (A)(G)　55. (C)(B)

A——问询处

B——售票处

C——半价票

D——候车室

E——超重行李费

F——行李过磅处

G——安全检查

H——站台地下通道

I——检票口

J——开车时间显示牌

K——铁轨

L——信号灯

M——铁路道口

N——软卧

O——硬卧

P——硬座

Q——行李认领处

Task 5

56. [答案]the clock

[解析]依据第一条信息,解决故障的方法是 Reset the clock

57. [答案]cold area

[解析]依据第二条信息里的故障原因"The oven has been stored in a cold area. "中可找到答案。

58. [答案]the Minute Timer

[解析]依据解决故障方法的第四栏可以找到答案。

59. [答案]the support

[解析]在故障第五栏中可以找到答案。

60. [答案]will not run

[解析]在故障第五栏中可以找到答案。

Part IV Translation—English into Chinese

61. [答案]D

[解析]注意几个要点的翻译。demand 后面引导的是定语从句;above all 翻译为"最重要,首先";based on 翻译为"基于,以……为基础"。

62. [答案]C

[解析]注意几个要点的翻译。should be given 为被动结构;while 翻译为"与……同时";candidates 翻译为"求职者";interview 翻译为"面试,接见"。根据全句的意思 C 选项最准确。

63. [答案]B

[解析]注意几个要点的翻译。in which 是介词提前的定语从句关系代词,修饰先行词 situation;comfortable 翻译为"舒适的"。feel 是系动词,翻译为"感觉,觉得"。根据句子意思,B 选项最准确。

64. [答案]C

[解析]在本题翻译时需要注意句子结构。这是并列句。第一个分句是动名词作主语,后面是系表结构;第二个分句中地点状语提前了,后面是一个现在完成时的句子。obtain 翻译为"获得";concern 翻译为"关心,关系";shortage 翻译为"不足,缺乏"。根据句子意思,C 选项为最佳答案。

65. [译文]新建的假日酒店能够满足全家欢度周末的家庭型客人或商务旅行客人的一切所需。酒店距离温泉和商业区购物中心仅一步之遥,很方便。每套客房都配备冰箱和咖啡机。客人也可免费享用中西式早餐。

Part V　Writing

E-mail Message

From：　wangjun11007@hotmail.com

To：　　anna11008@hotmail.com

Subject：Feedback of transaction

Dear Miss Anna Brown,

Thank you for ordering the book *Introduction to E-commerce*. We have mailed the book to you and it may reach you in a week. We will be very grateful if you feedback on our website. And we will be more than happy if you could recommend to your friends our satisfactory services. We guarantee you discounts on future purchase of our latest new offers.

Sincerely,

Wang Jun

Test 2

Part I Listening Comprehension (15 minutes)

Directions: *This part is to test your listening ability. It consists of 3 sections.*

Section A

Directions: *This section is to test your ability to give proper answers to questions. The question will be spoken two times. When you hear a question, you should decide on the correct answer from the 4 choices.*

1. A. I like it very much.　　　　　B. I am very busy.
   C. I had no time.　　　　　　　D. I was an actor.
2. A. I'm afraid I don't know.　　　B. Yes, I did.
   C. No, it isn't.　　　　　　　　D. You are on the ground floor.
3. A. Thank you very much.
   B. If possible, I'd like to be a salesman.
   C. I lost my job last month.
   D. I am a manager.
4. A. It's five miles away.
   B. We drive fast.
   C. By plane.
   D. Walking through the park.
5. A. June 23.
   B. Last week.
   C. Yes, they all go there.
   D. Every Monday and Friday.

Section B

Directions: *This section is to test your ability to understand short dialogues. Both the dialogue and the question will be spoken two times. When you hear a question, you should decide on the correct answer.*

6. A. 4826343　　　　　　　　B. 4286433
   C. 8426343　　　　　　　　D. 4286343
7. A. It's cloudy.　　　　　　　B. It's fine.

18

C. It's cold.   D. It's raining and cold.

8. A. Half   B. Four-fifths

   C. One-fifth   D. Fifty-one

9. A. The woman is busy working.   B. The woman can't take the message.

   C. Mr. Jackson is on his holiday.   D. Mr. Jackson will be back soon.

10. A. Books about Chinese history   B. Some shelves

    C. Some books   D. Some books on computers

Section C

Directions: *In this section you will hear a recorded short passage. The passage is printed on the test paper, but with some words or phrases missing. The passage will be read three times. You are required to put the missing words or phrases on the blanks.*

A man was at the dentist's. After the painful _____11_____, the patient asked the dentist how much the _____12_____ was.

"Five dollars," _____13_____ the dentist.

"What! Five dollars?" the patient cried in _____14_____. "Why? You _____15_____ to charge only one !"

"Yes," answered the dentist , smiling, "That was the regular charge, but you cried so loudly that you frightened away four other patients. "

Part II   Vocabulary & Structure   (15 minutes)

Directions: *This part is to test your ability to use words and phrases correctly to construct meaningful and grammatically correct sentences.*

Section A

Directions: *There are 10 incomplete statements here. You are required to complete each statement by choosing the appropriate answer from the 4 choices.*

16. My teacher is very handsome and has a _____ of humor.

    A. bit   B. kind

    C. sense   D. from

17. What the manager suggested at the meeting was that we _____ cancel the original plan.

    A. should   B. could

    C. would   D. must

18. Hardly _____ entered the classroom when the bell began to ring.

    A. he has   B. has he

    C. he had   D. had he

19. It was not until she went home _____ she remembered her appointment with the clerk.

    A. when   B. while

    C. that   D. as soon as

20. The dinning hall needs _____.

    A. paint   B. to paint

    C. to be painted   D. being painted

21. There was so much noise that the speaker couldn't make herself _____.

    A. heard   B. to hear

    C. hearing   D. being heard

22. I was _____ to find his article on such an _____ topic so _____.

    A. surprised... excited... bored   B. surprising... exciting... boring

    C. surprised... exciting... boring   D. surprising... excited... bored

23. I will graduate from college; I haven't got a suitable job. But I haven't decided to _____ my father's company in the small town.

    A. hand in   B. take over

    C. put on   D. lead to

24. Your mother is looking forward to _____ you soon. You should write it back as soon as possible.

    A. hearing from   B. hearing of

    C. hearing about   D. hearing for

25. That is the course of studies _____.

    A. what I'm interested in   B. I'm interested in

    C. that I'm interested   D. in that I'm interested

Section B

Directions: *There are also 10 incomplete statements here. You should fill in each blank with the proper form of the word given in the brackets.*

26. When will the computer (repair) _____?

27. It's too late now. It is time you (go) _____ back home.

28. If we had had his telephone number, we (call) _____ him.

29. The performance of students in this contest made the teacher fell rather (excite) _____.

30. His (think) _____ about the article is important, which affected a lot of young readers.

31. The doctor suggested that she (drink) _____ more water.

32. It's important for you to make yourself (understand) _____ when you explained the questions to others.

33. When I walked past his window, I heard him (sing) _____ the song.

34. You should avoid (make) _____ noisy during the meeting.

35. (fortunate) _____, he has passed the test and had the help of a learned teacher.

Part III Reading Comprehension (40 minutes)

Task 1

Directions: *After reading the following passage, you will find 5 questions or unfinished statements. You should make the correct choices.*

Mr. Peter Johnson, aged twenty-three, battled for half an hour to escape from his trapped car yesterday when it landed upside down in three feet of water. Mr. Johnson took the only escape route—through the boot(行李箱).

Mr. Johnson's car had finished up in a ditch(沟渠) at Romney Marsin, Kent after skidding on ice and hitting a bank. "Fortunately, the water began to come in only slowly," Mr. Johnson said. "I couldn't force the doors because they were jammed against the walls of the ditch and dared not open the windows because I knew water would come flooding in."

Mr. Johnson, a sweet salesman of Sitting Home, Kent, first tried to attract the attention of other motorists by sounding the horn and hammering on the roof and boot. Then he began his struggle to escape.

Later he said, "It was really a half penny that saved my life. It was the only coin I had in my pocket and I used it to unscrew the back seat to get into the boot. I hammered desperately with a hammer trying to make someone hear, but no help came."

It took ten minutes to unscrew the seat, and a further five minutes to clear the sweet samples from the boot. Then Mr. Johnson found a wrench and began to work on the boot lock. Fifteen minutes passed by. "It was the only chance I had. <u>Finally it gave</u>, but as soon as I moved the boot lid, the water and mud poured in. I forced the lid down into the mud and scrambled clear as the car filled up."

His hands and arms cut and bruised(擦伤), Mr. Johnson got to Beckett Farm nearby, where he was looked after by the farmer's wife, Mrs. Lucy Bates. Huddled in a blanket, he said, "That thirty minutes seemed like hours." Only the tips of the car wheels were visible, police said last night. The vehicle had sunk into two feet of mud at the bottom of the ditch.

36. What is the best title for this newspaper article? _____

    A. The Story of Mr. Johnson, A Sweet Salesman.

    B. Car Boot Can Serve As The Best Escape Route.

    C. Driver Escapes Through Car Boot.

    D. The Driver Survived A Terrible Car Accident.

37. Which of the following objects is the most important to Mr. Johnson? _____

    A. The hammer.   B. The coin.

    C. The screw.   D. The horn.

38. Which statement is true according to the passage? _____

    A. Mr. Johnson's car stood on its boot as it fell down.

    B. Mr. Johnson could not escape from the door because it was full of sweet jam.

C. Mr. Johnson's car accident was partly due to the slippery road.

D. Mr. Johnson struggled in the pouring mud as he unscrewed the back seat.

39. "Finally it gave" (Paragraph 5) means that _____.

    A. Luckily the door was torn away in the end

    B. At last the wrench went broken

    C. The lock came open after all his efforts

    D. The chance was lost at the last minute

40. It may be inferred from the passage that _____.

    A. the ditch was along a quiet country road

    B. the accident happened on a clear warm day

    C. the police helped Mr. Johnson get out of the ditch

    D. Mr. Johnson had a tender wife and was well attended

Task 2

Directions: *After reading you should make the correct choices.*

My father was a foreman of a sugar-cane plantation in Rio Piedras, Puerto Rico. My first job was to drive the oxen that ploughed the cane fields. I would walk behind an ox, guiding him with a broomstick. For $ 1 a day, I worked eight hours straight, with no food breaks.

It was very tedious work, but it prepared me for life and taught me many lasting lessons. Because the plantation owners were always watching us, I had to be on time every day and work as hard as I could. I've never been late for any job since. I also learned about being respectful and faithful to the people you work for. More important, I earned my pay; it never entered my mind to say I was sick just because I didn't want to work.

I was only six years old, but I was doing a man's job. Our family needed every dollar we could make because my father never earned more than $ 18 a week. Our home was a three-room wood shack with a dirty floor and no toilet. Nothing made me prouder than bringing home money to help my mother, father, two brothers and three sisters. This gave me self-esteem(自尊心), one of the most important things a person can have.

When I was seven, I got work at a golf course near our house. My job was to stand down the fairway and spot the balls as they landed, so the golfers could find them. Losing a ball meant you were fired, so I never missed one. Some nights I would lie in bed and dreamt of making thousands of dollars by playing golf and being able to buy a bicycle.

The more I dreamed, the more I thought. Why not? I made my first golf club out of guava limb(番石榴树枝) and a piece of pipe. Then I hammered an empty tin can into the shape of a ball. And finally I dug two small holes in the ground and hit the ball back and forth. I practiced with the same devotion and intensity. I learned working in the field—except now I was driving golf balls with club, not oxen with a broomstick.

41. The writer's first job was _____.

    A. to stand down the fairway at a golf course

    B. to watch over the sugar-cane plantation

C. to drive the oxen that ploughed the cane fields

D. to spot the balls as they landed so the golfers could find them

42. The word "tedious" in Paragraph 2 most probably means _____.

   A. difficult   B. boring   C. interesting   D. unusual

43. The writer learned that _____ from his first job.

   A. he should work for those who he liked most

   B. he should work longer than what he was expected

   C. he should never fail to say hello to his owner

   D. he should be respectful and faithful to the people he worked for

44. _____ gave the writer serf-esteem.

   A. Having a family of eight people

   B. Owning his own golf course

   C. Bringing money back home to help the family

   D. Helping his father with the work on the plantation

45. Which of the following statements is true according to the passage? _____

   A. He wanted to be a successful golfer.

   B. He wanted to run a golf course near his house.

   C. He was satisfied with the job he got on a plantation.

   D. He wanted to make money by guiding oxen with a broomstick.

Task 3

Directions: *After reading the passage, you should complete the correct answers.*

The Uniqueness of Finger-prints (指纹的唯一性)

Every human being has a *unique* arrangement of the skin on his fingers and this arrangement is unchangeable. Scientists and experts have proved the uniqueness of finger-prints and discovered that no exactly similar pattern is passed on from parents to children, though nobody knows why this is the case.

The ridge structure on a person's fingers does not change with growth and is not affected be surface injuries. Burns, cuts and other damage to the outer part of the skin will be replaced in time by new one, which bears a reproduction of the *original* pattern. It is only when the inner skin is injured that the arrangement will be destroyed. Some criminals make use of this fact to remove their own finger-prints but this is a dangerous and rare step to take.

Finger-prints can be made very easily with printer's ink. They can be recorded easily. With special methods, *identification* can be achieved successfully within a short time. Because of the simplicity and economy of this system, finger-prints have often been used as a method of solving criminal case. A suspected man may deny a charge but this may be in vain. His finger-prints can prove who he is even if his appearance has been changed by age or accident.

When a suspect leaves finger-prints behind at the scene of a crime, they are difficult to detect with the naked eye. Special techniques are used to "develop" them. Some of the marks found are incomplete but identification is possible if a print of a quarter of an inch square can be obtained.

46. Scientists and experts have proved that the pattern of a human being's finger skin _____.

    A. is similar to his mother's

    B. is valuable to himself only

    C. is like that of others with the same type of blood

    D. is different from that of all others

47. If your fingers are wounded by knife, fire or other means, the structure of skin will _____.

    A. be changed partly

    B. be replaced by a different one

    C. be the same when the wound is recovered

    D. become ugly

48. Some criminals remove their own finger-prints by _____.

    A. using printer's ink

    B. injuring the inner skin

    C. damaging the outer skin

    D. damaging the colour

49. Finger-prints have often been used as a method of solving criminal case because it _____.

    A. is complicated but reliable

    B. is simple and not expensive

    C. is expensive but easy to do

    D. can bring a lot of money

50. Finger-prints are used for solving criminal by _____.

    A. the naked eye   B. special techniques

    C. some of the marks   D. identification of a criminal's print

Task 4

Directions: *After reading the following list, you are required to find the items equivalent to those given in Chinese in the list below.*

A. ——4th ring Rd

B. ——Foggy Area

C. ——Ticket changing

D. ——Emergency vehicle lane

E. ——Ticket office

F. ——Two way traffic

G. ——Dangerous Area

H. ——Non-motor vehicle

I. ——Side Rd

J. ——Group tour entrance

K. ——Guide sign

L. ——Roundabout

M. ——Crosswalk

N. ——Crossroad

Example: （H）非机动车　　　　　（J）团队入口

51. （　）应急车道	（　）环岛
52. （　）多雾地段	（　）危险路段
53. （　）四环路	（　）辅路
54. （　）双向交通	（　）指路标志
55. （　）换票处	（　）售票处

Task 5

Directions：*After reading the passage, you are required to complete the statements that follow the questions.*

We are going to describe one way to build a rooftop garden that does not even require soil. Four things are needed for a small rooftop garden. One thing is a roof that can support the weight, another is grass cutting. The third thing is a sheet of plastic in which to spread the cut grass. And the last thing is a box about eight centimeters deep and made out of four pieces of wood.

Once you are sure the roof is good cut and collect some grass. Then lay down the plastic where the garden box will go. The four-sided box can be as long and as wide as needed. Place the box on top of the sheet of plastic. Then fill it with the cut grass. Next add water and walk on the cuttings to press them down.

After about three weeks, the rooftop garden is ready for planting. Put the seeds directly into the wet grass cuttings. This garden is a good place to grow peas, tomatoes, beans, onions and lettuce. If the box is deep enough, potatoes and carrots will also grow.

It is important to keep the grass wet until the plants begin to grow. When the plants are growing, they will need watering every day, unless there is rain. And they will need some liquid fertilizer. Also, seeds and new plants must be protected from insects and birds.

Rooftop gardens are increasingly popular, and not just to grow vegetables. They keep buildings cooler in the sun, so they save energy. They can also extend the useful life of a roof. Rooftop gardens also reduce the runoff of storm water and help clean the air. Plus they add beauty, and give birds and insects in the city a nice place to live.

56. Four things are needed for a small rooftop garden. One thing is a roof that can _____.

57. After about three weeks, the rooftop garden is ready for planting. Put the seeds directly into the _____.

58. It is important to _____ until the plants begin to grow.

59. When the plants are growing, they will need some liquid fertilizer. Also, seeds and new plants must be _____ and birds.

60. They keep buildings cooler in the sun, so they _____. They can also extend the useful

life of a roof.

Part IV　Translation—English into Chinese　（25 minutes）

Directions: *This part is to test your ability to translate English into Chinese. Each of the four sentences is followed by four choices of suggested translation. Make the best choice. Write your translation of the paragraph in the corresponding space.*

61. You are too careful to do anything.

　　A. 做任何事情你都太小心了。

　　B. 你太小心了,不能做任何事情。

　　C. 你小心做任何事情。

　　D. 你不能太小心做任何事情。

62. It is quite common that people don't complain about the weather in that city.

　　A. 常见的是城市的人们不抱怨天气。

　　B. 那个城市的人们不抱怨天气,这是常见的。

　　C. 人们不大会弄清楚那个城市的天气情况。

　　D. 那个城市的人们不谈论天气,这时很普遍的。

63. There is not quite so much activity in the fund exchange.

　　A. 基金交易活动不是很多。

　　B. 因为气候的改变,几乎没有活动了。

　　C. 因为活动太多了,没有基金了。

　　D. 没有活动就没有基金交易。

64. Most of us, from earliest school days, have been told that daydreaming is a waste of time.

　　A. 我们大多数人从刚上学就知道,空想就是浪费时间。

　　B. 我们中许多人在学校里很早就知道,白日梦就是浪费时间。

　　C. 我们中的大多数人在学校里早就知道,每天作白日梦都是浪费时间。

　　D. 我们绝大多数早上学的人都知道,上课时开小差是浪费时间。

65. Every country has its own peculiar dining customs. Americans feel that the first rule of being a polite guest is to be on time. if a person is invited to dinner at six-thirty, the hostess expects him to be there at six-thirty or not more than a few moments later.

Part V　Writing　（25 minutes）

Directions: *This part is to test your ability to do practical writing. You are required to finish the following writing according to the information.*

说明:商务信件

发信人:马明

收信人:张先生

内容:贵方从悉尼运往大连的空运货物已发出,航班号是 JL772。预计到达时间是 06 年 3

月 1 日。提单号是 NEA85904,货重 46.5 公斤。我将传真给你发票和提单。望查收。

答 案 解 析

Part I   Listening Comprehension

听力原文

Section A

1. Why not go to the party last night?

2. Where do you know is the office of the English department?

3. What kind of job do you want to apply for?

4. How far is the way to get to your house from here?

5. How often does Class A have listening classes in the language lab?

Section B

6. W: I'm sorry, sir. Would you repeat your telephone number?

   M: Yes. It's four-eight-two-six-three-four-three.

   Q: What's the man's telephone number?

7. M: Is the weather fine today?

   W: No, it isn't. It's raining and cold.

   Q: What's the weather like today?

8. M: Haven't you finished the book yet?

   W: Almost. I've only one-fifth of the pages left.

   Q: How many pages has the woman read?

9. M: Would you please give Mr. Jackson a message?

   W: Sorry. Mr. Jackson is having a holiday in Chicago.

   Q: What can we learn from the conversation?

10. M: Excuse me, have you got any books on Chinese history?

    W: Yes, they are on the shelf over there.

    Q: What does the man want?

Section C

A man was at the dentist's. After the painful **11 operation**, the patient asked the dentist how much the **12 charge** was. "Five dollars," **13 replied** the dentist.

"What! Five dollars?" the patient cried in **14 surprise**. "Why? You **15 promised** to charge only one!"

"Yes," answered the dentist, smiling, "That was the regular charge, but you cried so loudly that you frightened away four other patients. "

答案详解

Part I Listening Comprehension

Section A

1. [答案]C

   [解析]问题是"昨天晚上为什么没参加晚会"。回答 A 选项"我非常喜欢它";B 选项"我很忙(用的是一般现在时)";C 选项"我没有时间(一般过去时)";D 选项"我是一名演员"。根据问句,只能选 C。

2. [答案]A

   [解析]问题是"你知道英语系在哪儿吗"选项 A"对不起,我不知道";选项 B"是的,我知道(过去时)";选项 C"不,不是";选项 D"你在第一层"。根据时态和句意,所以选 A。

3. [答案]B

   [解析]问题是"你想申请什么样的工作"。选项 A"非常感谢";选项 B"如果可能的话, 我愿意当一名销售人员";选项 C"上月我失业了";选项 D"我是一名经理"。所以选 B。

4. [答案]A

   [解析]问题是"从这到你家有多远"。选项 A"五英里";选项 B"我们开得很快";选项 C"乘飞机";选项 D"穿过这个公园"。所以选 A。

5. [答案]D

   [解析]问题是"二班每隔多久在语音室上听力课"。选项 A"6 月 23 日";选项 B"上周";选项 C"是的,他们都去那";选项 D"每周周一和周五"。所以选 D。

Section B

6. [答案]A

   [解析]问题是"男士的电话号码是多少",回答是"It's four-eight-two-six-three-four-three. "所以选 A。

7. [答案]D

   [解析]问题是"今天天气好吗",回答是"不好,下雨还很冷",所以选 D。

8. [答案]B

   [解析]对话中男士问"你还没有读完这本书吗",女士回答"快了,还剩五分之一",问题是"女士读了多少页了"。选项 A"一半";选项 B"五分之四";选项 C"五分之一";选项 D"一分之五"。所以答案选 B。

9. [答案]C

   [解析]对话中女士问"请你给杰克先生留个信,好吗",回答说"对不起,杰克先生在度假",问题是"我们从对话中可以了解到什么"。选项 A"女士在忙工作";选项 B"女士不能留这个口信";选项 C"杰克先生在度假";选项 D"杰克先生很快就回来。"所以答案选 C。

10. ［答案］A

　　［解析］对话中男士说"请问,你们这有有关中国历史的书吗? 问题是"这个男士要什么",所以选 A。

Section C

11. operation　　12. charge　　13. replied　　14. surprise　　15. promised

Part II　Vocabulary & Structure

Section A

16. ［答案］C

　　［解析］a bit of 翻译为:"一点";a kind of 翻译为:"一种";a sense of 翻译为"一种感觉";a from of 没有这种搭配。根据句子意思"一种幽默感"。所以选 C。

17. ［答案］A

　　［解析］suggest 后面的从句应该用虚拟语气结构(should)do something,所以本句选 A。

18. ［答案］D

　　［解析］hardly,seldom 等含有否定意义的副词放在句首时,主句部分的谓语倒装。从句用的是过去时,主句就应该用过去完成时。因此选 D。

19. ［答案］C

　　［解析］本句是强调句结构"it + be + 强调部分 + that + 其他成分"或"it + be + 强调部分(人) + whom + 其他成分"。所以本题选 C。

20. ［答案］C

　　［解析］本题考查的是词的用法。need 前面是"物"作主语时,后面用动名词或不定式,即 need doing 或 need to be done。所以本题选 C。

21. ［答案］A

　　［解析］make oneself done 结构的意思是"使某人被怎么样"。根据句子意思,本题选 A。

22. ［答案］C

　　［解析］分词作表语时,过去分词形容人;现在分词形容物。根据题的第一个空和选项只能考虑 A 和 C;根据最后一空,只能选 C。

23. ［答案］B

　　［解析］词组辨析题。hand in 翻译为"上交";take over 翻译为"接管,接任";put on 翻译为"穿上,戴上";lead to 翻译为"导致某种结果"。所以选 B。

24. ［答案］A

　　［解析］look forward to 后面跟动名词作介词宾语。根据句子意思"母亲盼望收到来信。"所以选 A。

25. ［答案］B

　　［解析］定语从句。I'm interested in 是定语从句修饰前面的先行词 the course of studies。省略了关系代词 that。A 选项不应该用 what;C 选项没有介词 in;D 选项 that 不能提前。

29

Section B

26. [答案]be repaired

[解析]"计算机什么时候修完?"计算机是被修理,应该用被动态。前面有情态动词,所以用 will + be repaired。

27. [答案]went

[解析]"时间很晚了,你该回家了。"在 it's time …句型中,从句用过去时表示虚拟。

28. [答案]would have called

[解析]"如果我们知道他的电话号码,会给他打电话的。"虚拟语气中表示与过去事实相反,主句用 would have done 结构。

29. [答案]excited

[解析]"学生们在这次比赛中的表现使老师感到很激动。"考点主要是词性转换,to feel excited"感到激动",形容词作表语。

30. [答案]thoughts

[解析]"他对这篇文章的看法很重要,影响了很多年轻人。"形容词性物主代词后面用名词。

31. [答案]should drink

[解析]"医生建议她要多喝些水。"在 ask,demand,insist,advice,request,order,suggest 等表示"命令,愿望,建议"等动词后,宾语从句的谓语动词要用虚拟语气(should) + 动词原形。

32. [答案]understood

[解析]"当你向别人解释问题时,把自己的意思表达清楚很重要。"make oneself understood 使自己被人理解。

33. [答案]singing

[解析]"我走过他窗前时,听到他在唱这首歌。"在 make,let,have,see,hear,watch,notice,feel 等感官动词后面,可以用分词或不带 to 的不定式,前者表示部分动作;后者表示动作全过程。用现在分词还是用过去分词,要根据句子意思而定。本句用 singing 是因为宾语 him 与宾补 sing 表示能动关系。

34. [答案]making

[解析]"会议期间应该避免发出噪音。"在某些动词之后只能用动名词。这些动词有 mind,avoid,consider,finish,keep,enjoy 等。

35. [答案]Fortunately

[解析]"幸运的是,它通过了这次考试并得到了一位有经验的老师的帮助。"副词修饰整个句子。

Part III   Reading Comprehension

Task 1

36. [答案]C

[解析]主旨题。根据第一段中"Mr. Peter Johnson…escape from his trapped car…through the boot."可归纳出文章的标题为答案 C。

36. [答案]B

[解析]细节题。根据第四段 Mr. Johnson 所说的话及他后面所做的事情可推知此题答案为 B。

38. [答案]C

[解析]细节题。根据第二段第一句…skidding on ice and hitting a bank 可推知答案为 C。

39. [答案]C

[解析]词句理解题。根据其上文…work on the boot lock 及下文 but as soon as I moved the boot lid,the water and mud poured in 可推知此题答案为 C。

40. [答案]A

[解析]推断题。根据第四段最后一句 but no help came 及最后一段的第一句 Mr. Johnson got to Beckett Farm nearby 可推知地点是在寂静的农村,此题答案为 A。

Task 2

41. [答案]C

[解析]语义理解题。第一段第二句话"My first job was to drive the oxen that ploughed the cane fields."和题干几乎完全相同,所以选 C。

42. [答案]B

[解析]词义猜测题。从第二段第二句话中的 I had to be on time every day and work as hard as I could 可以推知 tedious 的正确词义。

43. [答案]D

[解析]语义理解题。看到文章第二段第四句话"I also learned about being respectful and faithful to the people you work for."便可知答案为 D。

44. [答案]C

[解析]语义理解题。从文章第三段最后两句话"Nothing made me prouder than bringing home money to help my mother,father,two brothers and three sisters. This gave me self-esteem."可以判断出答案为 C。

45. [答案]A

[解析]判断题。从最后一段内容可知他想当一名高尔夫球员的迫切之心。

Task 3

46. [答案]D

[解析]细节理解题。从第一段最后一句可知"人的指纹是独一无二的"。

47. [答案]C

[解析]推理判断题。从第二段第二句"Burns,cuts and other damage to the outer part of the skin will be replaced in time by new one,which bears a reproduction of the original pattern."可以推断正确答案为 C。

48. [答案]B

[解析]推理判断题。从第二段最后两句可知"罪犯要想改变以前的指纹,必须把内部的皮肤损害掉"。

49. [答案]B

[解析]细节理解题。从第三段第四句 Because of the simplicity and economy of this system 可知"指纹鉴别的方法简单而且经济"。

50. [答案]D

[解析]推理判断题。从第四段最后一句"Some of the marks found are incomplete but identification is possible if a print of a quarter of an inch square can be obtained."即"一些被发现的痕迹是不完全的但是如果能获得四分之一英寸的手印,就可以辨别出罪犯。"可判断答案为 D。

Task 4

51. (D)(L)　　52. (B)(G)　　53. (A)(I)　　54. (F)(K)　　55. (C)(E)

A——四环路

B——多雾地段

C——换票处

D——应急车道

E——售票处

F——双向交通

G——危险路段

H——非机动车

I——辅路

J——团队入口

K——指路标志

L——环岛

M——人行横道

N——十字路口

Task 5

56. [答案]support the weight

　　[解析]依据第一段的第二行,可得出答案。

57. [答案]wet grass cuttings

　　[解析]依据第三段的第二行,可得出答案。

58. [答案]keep the grass wet

　　[解析]依据第四段的第一行,可得出答案。

59. [答案]protected from insects

　　[解析]依据第四段的第三行,可得出答案。

60. [答案]save energy

　　[解析]依据第五段的第二行,可得出答案。

Part IV Translation—English into Chinese

61. ［答案］B

    ［解析］本题关键在于 too…to 句型结构的翻译。"太……而不能"。

62. ［答案］B

    ［解析］本题的关键是对 complain about"抱怨某事";还有"it's quite common that"句型的理解。It 是形式主语,that 引导的从句是真正的主语,翻译为"……是常见的"。

63. ［答案］A

    ［解析］本题的关键是分清几个词的翻译。activity 翻译为"活动";not quite so much 翻译为"没有多少活动";fun exchange 翻译为"基金交易"。

64. ［答案］A

    ［解析］本题翻译时注意,most of us 翻译为"我们中许多人";have been told 虽然是被动结构,但翻译成中文习惯上用主动结构;a waste of time 翻译为"浪费时间";from earliest school days 翻译为"从早期学校开始即刚上学时"。

65. ［译文］每个国家都有自己的聚餐习惯。美国人认为,作为一名有礼貌的客人,第一条规矩就是要守时。如果一个人被邀请参加六点半的宴会,女主人希望他在六点半或稍后几分钟到。

Part V Writing

Dear Sir,   March 18,2007

    I wish to inform that your goods have been shipped on board the Jl772 flight from Sydney to Dalian on the estimated arrival time of March 1,2006. B/L number: NEA 85904,46.5kg. I will send you by fax a copy of our invoice and B/L.

Yours truly,

Ma Ming

Test 3

Part I Listening Comprehension （15 minutes）

Directions: *This part is to test your listening ability. It consists of 3 sections.*

Section A

Directions: *This section is to test your ability to give proper answers to questions. The question will be spoken two times. When you hear a question, you should decide on the correct answer from the 4 choices.*

1. A. It's such bad news.   B. Yeah, I get a lot of exercises.
   C. It doesn't matter.   D. Really, I can't believe it.
2. A. It's my pleasure.   B. Don't mention it.
   C. What a waste of time.   D. Yes, it cost me a lot of time.
3. A. I won't go.   B. With my uncle.
   C. Shopping center.   D. This afternoon.
4. A. Yes, it is.   B. No, it isn't.
   C. About 10 hours.   D. About 10 o'clock.
5. A. I'd like to try some Sichuan food.   B. No, I won't order.
   C. There's nothing special for you to do.   D. I'm not your boss.

Section B

Directions: *This section is to test your ability to understand short dialogues. Both the dialogue and the question will be spoken two times. When you hear a question, you should decide on the correct answer.*

6. A. The man   B. The woman
   C. Both of them   D. Neither of them
7. A. Tea   B. Juice
   C. Coffee   D. Milk
8. A. Three days   B. A week
   C. Ten days   D. Not settled
9. A. A lot of things   B. Nothing special
   C. Reading   D. Sports
10. A. At a shop   B. At a restaurant
    C. At a cinema   D. At the post office

Section C

Directions: *In this section you will hear a recorded short passage. The passage is printed on the test paper, but with some words or phrases missing. The passage will be read three times. You are required to put the missing words or phrases on the blanks.*

Since the reform and _____11_____ policy in 1978, great changes have _____12_____ in China. In the past, people's life was almost the same and quite _____13_____. People worked 6 days a week and stayed at home or went to the movie at leisure. They had no other places to go for _____14_____. But now people have more free time and more choices to _____15_____. They can make use of public and natural sports resources. Besides, they can make use of public sports facilities in the neighborhood or go to the health center.

Part II Vocabulary & Structure (15 minutes)

Directions: *This part is to test your ability to use words and phrases correctly to construct meaningful and grammatically correct sentences.*

Section A

Directions: *There are 10 incomplete statements here. You are required to complete each statement by choosing the appropriate answer from the 4 choices.*

16. The final plan is supposed to _____ before December.

    A. hand in　　　　　　　　B. be handed in

    C. hand over　　　　　　　D. be handed over

17. He asked me some questions relative _____ my plans.

    A. on　　　　　　　　　　B. about

    C. with　　　　　　　　　D. to

18. The boss ordered that the workers _____ unless they finish the work.

    A. would not be paid　　　B. be not paid

    C. would not pay　　　　　D. not pay

19. "You'd better _____ some money for emergency", she told me.

    A. set back　　　　　　　B. set about

    C. set down　　　　　　　D. set aside

20. Not until midnight _____ .

    A. did the noise stop　　　B. the noise stopped

    C. the noise did stop　　　D. stopped the noise

21. _____ he goes, he'll meet someone begging for money.

    A. No matter wherever　　B. Wherever

    C. Where　　　　　　　　D. Somewhere

22. It'll _____ him a lot to further his education in Paris.

A. spend   B. take

C. cost   D. expend

23. He _____ the final exam if he had wasted less time on computer games.

     A. must pass   B. would pass

     C. would have passed   D. must have passed

24. She is _____ girl that everyone will like her at the first sight.

     A. such a lovely   B. so a lovely

     C. such lovely a   D. how lovely a

25. His suggestion that the meeting _____ to next month was accepted.

     A. was put off   B. be put off

     C. put off   D. would be put off

Section B

Directions: *There are also 10 incomplete statements here. You should fill in each blank with the proper form of the word given in the brackets.*

26. New Year's Eve is the world's oldest (celebrate) _____ .

27. Her father's words (encourage) _____ her, and she decided to give up her plan.

28. The waiting time (short) _____ dramatically from eight weeks to just one week since the new rule was set.

29. The (type) _____ is quite familiar with office software.

30. By the end of next year, the bridge (build) _____ .

31. I'd love to come, but (fortune) _____ , I have to work that day.

32. _____ (take) the financial difficulties into consideration, the plan seems to the impractical.

33. His dream is to live a (peace) _____ life in a small village with his family.

34. Tom's (understand) _____ of the world is quite beyond his age.

35. People are (confuse) _____ by a lot of information on internet.

Part III   Reading Comprehension   (40 minutes)

Task 1

Directions: *After reading the following passage, you will find 5 questions or unfinished statements. You should make the correct choices.*

A recent reality TV program called "Metamorphosis (Bian Xingji)" has stirred up debate.

The program, which <u>aired</u> on Human Satellite TV, offers two primary school students a chance to exchange life roles. For one week, Gao Zhanxi, a poor country boy from Qinghai, and Wei Cheng, a rich city boy from Hunan, <u>walked in each other's shoes.</u>

Many people praised the program because it changed the kids in good ways. Wei has decided to throw away his former extravagant lifestyle and keep away from Internet games. Gao opened his eyes to see a wonderful world outside the mountains.

But others don't agree. They think the program actually hurt Gao a lot. He actually wept when he first tasted modern life. People doubt whether he will turn to his poor family willingly without feeling the inequality of life after experiencing the colorfulness of city life.

Someone says, "Gao is just too young to experience the huge gap between his country life and the far-too-good modern city life. He may think that life hasn't treated him fairly. He may even hate society's inequality. The program hurts him, for sure. "

36. What does the word "air" in the first line mean? _____
    A. To put a piece of clothing in a place that is warm or has a lot of air, so that it smells clean.
    B. To let fresh air into a room.
    C. To broadcast a program on television or radio.
    D. To pump something.

37. What does the phrase "walked in each other's shoes" in the first paragraph mean? _____
    A. To exchange shoes with each other.
    B. To be in each other's situation.
    C. To make choices for each other.
    D. To feel quite uncomfortable.

38. Some changes happened to Wei Cheng. Which of the following is not true? _____
    A. He decided to live a saving life.
    B. He decided not to waste money.
    C. He decided to give up Internet games.
    D. He decided to stay in Qinghai Province.

39. The following are opinions against this program. Which one is not mentioned in the passage? _____
    A. Gao is so young that it is hard for him to accept the gap between the rich and the poor.
    B. Gao will be unwilling to return to his poor family after he tasted this new lifestyle.
    C. The inequality might lead to Gao's hatred of the society.
    D. Gao may have a sense of jealousy.

40. Which of the following is not true according to the passage? _____
    A. This program brought a heated debate among audience.
    B. Wei Cheng was addicted to Internet games before he took part in the program.
    C. Gao Zhanxi will never feel satisfied with his family after he tasted the rich life.
    D. Gao Zhanxi lives in mountainous area in Qinghai.

Task 2

Directions: *After reading you should make the correct choices.*

Ten years after the birth of the world's first cloned(克隆)animal, Dolly the Sheep, America appears to become the world's first country to introduce meat and mild form cloned cattle.

Last week, the US Food and Drug Administration (FDA), which oversees food safety, announced that the cloned products were safe to eat and could be put on the market.

However, Americans remain considerably uneasy about eating cloned food. A national poll last year found 64 percent of Americans uncomfortable with the idea of eating cloned food.

It is estimated that there are already several hundred cattle among America's 9 million that have been cloned. The FDA will accept comments from the public for the next three months before announcing its final decision.

41. What does the US Food and Drug Administration think of cloned products? _____

    A. It thinks it not safe to eat cloned products.

    B. It thinks it safe to put cloned products on the market.

    C. It suggests American people to eat cloned products instead of traditional food.

    D. It is not sure whether it's safe to eat cloned products.

42. What's the function of FDA? _____

    A. To ensure the safety of food and drugs.

    B. To promote the sales of food and drugs.

    C. To supply people with new food.

    D. To control the production of food and drugs.

43. How do most Americans feel about having cloned food? _____

    A. They are glad to have cloned food.

    B. They are not interested in cloned food.

    C. They declare they'll never eat cloned food.

    D. They are uneasy about eating cloned food.

44. What will the FDA do before announcing its final decision? _____

    A. They'll do more research.

    B. They'll consider public opinion.

    C. They'll ask experts for advice.

    D. They'll wait for government's decision.

45. Which of the following is the best title for this passage? _____

    A. The Function of FDA

    B. New Technology

    C. Cloned Food

    D. The Best Food in the World

Task 3

Directions: *After reading the passage, you should complete the correct answers.*

For BEC Vantage, candidates are required to produce two pieces of writing:

An internal company communication; this means a piece of communication with a colleague or colleagues within the company on a business-related matter, and the delivery medium may be a note, message, memo or e-mail. And one of the following:

A piece of business correspondence; this means correspondence with somebody outside the company (eg. A customer or supplier) on a business-related matter, and the delivery medium may be letter, fax or e-mail.

A report; The report will contain an introduction, main body of findings and conclusion.

A proposal; this has a similar format to a report, but unlike the report, the focus of the proposal is on the future, with the main focus being on recommendations for discussion; it is possible that the delivery medium may be a memo or an e-mail.

For BEC Vantage, an internal company communication and a piece of business correspondence, or

     a report, or _____46_____ are required.

A piece of business correspondence means correspondence with _____47_____.

A report will contain an introduction, _____48_____ and conclusion.

Somebody outside the company refers to a customer or _____49_____.

The delivery medium of a proposal may be a memo or _____50_____.

Task 4

Directions: *After reading the following list, you are required to find the items equivalent to those given in Chinese in the list below.*

A. ——management functions

B. ——bank account

C. ——resolve conflicts

D. ——cash management

E. ——set a goal

F. ——interest-free loan

G. ——formulate plans

H. ——controlling function

I. ——annual sales

J. ——motivate subordinates

K. ——credit rating

L. ——communication channel

M. ——bottom price

N. ——savings account

O. ——potential candidates

P. ——human resources

Q. ——job hunter

R. ——job responsibility system

Examples: (B) 银行账户 　　　　　　　 (F) 无息贷款

51. (　　) 潜在求职者	(　　) 制定计划
52. (　　) 岗位责任制	(　　) 沟通渠道
53. (　　) 求职人员	(　　) 设立目标
54. (　　) 控制职能	(　　) 管理职能
55. (　　) 解决矛盾	(　　) 人力资源

Task 5

Directions: *After reading the passage, you are required to complete the statements that follow the questions.*

A Letter of Appointment

Dear Sir or Madam:

We refer to your application for employment with us and are pleased to offer you the position of Room Attendant (Housekeeping) on the following terms and conditions:

(01) Date of Commencement

Your commencing date of employment shall be on September 17th, 2007.

(02) Salary

You will be paid a basic salary of $1,500. This will be credited to your account with a bank designated by the Hotel on 7th and 20th of each month.

(03) Probation

You will be required to serve a probationary period not exceeding three months effective from the date you report for work.

(04) Duties

You will be required to carry out such duties and job functions as assigned by the Hotel.

(05) Transfer

You may be transferred or assigned to any department/section within the Hotel when the Management deems it necessary.

If you agree to the terms and conditions of service stated herein, kindly sign in the appropriate space below.

Yours faithfully,　　　　　　　　　　　　 Agreed and Accepted by

Wachai Hotel

———————————　　　　　　　　　　 ———————————

Simon Drone　　　　　　　　　　　　　　 Name:

　General Manager　　　　　　　　　　　　 Date:

56. When will the employment begin?

————————————————————————

57. What's the basic salary?

————————————————————————

58. How will the salary be paid?

The salary will _____ the applicant's account.

59. How long will a probationary period last at most?

_____

60. How many terms and conditions are mentioned in the letter.

_____

Part IV Translation—English into Chinese   (25 minutes)

Directions: *This part is to test your ability to translate English into Chinese. Each of the four sentences is followed by four choices of suggested translation. Make the best choice. Write your translation of the paragraph in the corresponding space.*

61. She has satisfied the conditions for entry into the college.

A. 她已满足这所学院的要求。

B. 她已符合进入这所学院的条件。

C. 她对这所学院的条件很满意。

D. 她已具备进入这所学院的资格。

62. Our school is looking for a few young people interested in teaching.

A. 我们学校招收了几个对教书感兴趣的年轻人。

B. 我们学校在为一些年轻人提供有趣的教师工作。

C. 我们学校只招到很少几个年轻人来做教师工作。

D. 我们学校在招收一些对教师工作感兴趣的年轻人。

63. Sometimes students cheated by bad people get less money than they have been promised or no money at all.

A. 有时学生上当受骗,从而得到了比预计少的钱或者得不到钱。

B. 通常学生欺骗了坏人,从而得到了比预计少的钱或者得不到钱。

C. 有时受坏人欺骗的学生得到的钱要比许诺的少,甚至一分钱都拿不到。

D. 有时学生上当受骗,得到的钱只比没有多一点。

64. Given the government's record on unemployment, their chances of winning the election look poor.

A. 鉴于政府在解决失业问题上成绩不佳,他们在选举中获胜的机会不大。

B. 考虑到政府以往处理失业问题的态度,他们在选举中不太可能获胜。

C. 如果政府以往处理失业问题成绩不佳,他们将无法做出选择。

D. 政府在以往处理失业问题的态度决定了他们在选举中不太可能获胜。

65. The Shangri-La is destined to become the focal point for dining and entertaining in Beihai. The Coffee Garden serves excellent Asian and international dishes. The Xiang Palace with its magnificent sea view offers outstanding Cantonese food, including fresh seafood from the surrounding waters. The Lobby Lounge serves snacks and a wide selection of beverages during the day, and offers live music in the evenings.

Part V　Writing　(25 minutes)

Directions：*This part is to test your ability to do practical writing. You are required to finish the following writing according to the information.*

说明：根据下列信息写一张借据。

时间：7 月 25 日

内容：英语系学生会向系办公室借 SANYO 牌录音机一台，言明 7 月 29 日归还。

答 案 解 析

Part I　Listening Comprehension

听力原文

Section A

1. Oh, Mary. You've lost a lot of weight. You're in great shape.

2. Thank you so much for your time.

3. Where would you like to go?

4. For how many hours is the public library open on weekdays?

5. May I take your order, Sir?

Section B

6. M：Oh, finally we got here.

　 W：I go to get the tickets and you park the car, OK?

　 Q：Who will buy the tickets?

7. M：What would you like to drink, tea or coffee?

　 W：Well, I prefer juice.

　 Q：What drink does the woman want?

8. M：How long will you stay at London?

　 W：I had planned to stay there for 3 days, but my friend insisted we stay for a week, then I agreed with her.

　 Q：How long will they stay at London?

9. M：What do you do in your spare time?

　 W：A lot of things, but reading is my favorite.

　 Q：What does the woman often do in her spare time?

10. M：Good morning, may I help you?

　　 W：Yes, I'm looking for a light blue sports jacket.

Q: Where does the conversation take place?

Section C

Since the reform and **11 opening-up** policy in 1978, great changes have **12 taken place** in China. In the past, people's life was almost the same and quite **13 boring**. People worked 6 days a week and stayed at home or went to the movie at leisure. They had no other places to go for **14 entertainment**. But now people have more free time and more choices to **15 enjoy** life. They can make use of public and natural sports resources. Besides, they can make use of public sports facilities in the neighborhood or go to the health center.

答案详解

Section A

1. ［答案］B
［解析］题干是"你瘦了很多。现在身材真好"。对此,应给予的正确回应为 B。

2. ［答案］A
［解析］只有 A 是对对方表示感谢的正确回应。

3. ［答案］C
［解析］对于 where 提问应该给予具体地点,所以 C 为正确答案。

4. ［答案］C
［解析］题干问的是"公共图书馆开放多少个小时",所以 C 为正确答案。

5. ［答案］A
［解析］题干的意思是"您点菜吗,先生",这是发生在餐馆里的对话,故选 A。

Section B

6. ［答案］B
［解析］细节题。在对话中,女士说"我去买票你去停车好吗",故选 B。

7. ［答案］B
［解析］细节题。对话中,女士已经明确表示"更喜欢果汁",所以选 B。

8. ［答案］B
［解析］推断题。男士问女士会在伦敦呆多久,女士回答她自己想待三天,但是朋友坚持待一周,而且她同意了,所以 B 为正确答案。

9. ［答案］C
［解析］推断题。女士回答她在业余时间做很多事情,但最喜欢阅读。据此可以推断出她最常做的事情就是阅读。故选 C。

10. ［答案］A
［解析］推断题。"May I help you?"是服务行业常用来招待顾客的话。根据顾客的回答"我想买一件淡蓝色的运动衣",可以推断出这个对话发生在商店。故选 A。

11. opening-up   12. taken place   13. boring   14. entertainment   15. enjoy

Part II   Vocabulary & Structure

Section A

16. ［答案］B

［解析］考查被动语态和 hand in 这个短语。最后的计划应该"被上交",所以选择 B。

17. ［答案］D

［解析］考查与 relative 搭配的介词。relative to 翻译为"与……相关"。

18. ［答案］B

［解析］考查虚拟语气和被动语态。order 这个词后面的从句应该用虚拟语气,形式为 "(should) + 动词原型",本句还采用了被动语态。

19. ［答案］D

［解析］考查和 set 有关的短语。其中 set aside 翻译为"留出,拨出"的意思,符合题意, 故选 D。

20. ［答案］A

［解析］倒装句。not 这样的否定词放在句首,引起句子的部分倒装。

21. ［答案］B

［解析］句子的意思是"无论他走到哪儿,都会碰到有人乞讨",所以 B 是正确答案。

22. ［答案］C

［解析］考查和"花费"有关的词的用法。此句中测试 It takes somebody some time to do something. 这一句型。

23. ［答案］C

［解析］考查虚拟语气。对过去事情的虚拟,主句采用 would have done 结构。

24. ［答案］A

［解析］考查 such 和 so 的用法。

25. ［答案］B

［解析］考查虚拟语气。suggestion 表示"建议"时,后面的 that 从句需采用虚拟语气。 形式为"(should) + 动词原型",本句还采用了被动语态。

Section B

26. ［答案］celebration

［解析］此处需要名词,故将 celebrate 改成它的名词形式,即 celebration。

27. ［答案］discouraged

［解析］从句子的意思可以判断出"她父亲的话使她灰心",所以应改为 encourage 的反 义词 discourage。并且因为后半句用了过去时,所以正确答案是 discouraged。

28. [答案]has been shortened

[解析]从句由 since 引导,故主句应为现在完成时,并且需要采用被动语态。首先将 short 变成它的动词形式 shorten,再改为现在完成时的被动语态,所以正确答案为 has been shortened。

29. [答案]typist

[解析]根据题意"这位打字员熟悉办公软件",所以改为 typist。

30. [答案]will have been built

[解析]考查时态和语态。与 by the end of 相对应的时态为完成时,而 next year 要求将来时,所以应该填入的是将来完成时的被动语态形式。

31. [答案]unfortunately

[解析]根据题意,应为"不幸",并且此处要求副词,所以填入 unfortunately。

32. [答案]taken

[解析]take 与句子的主语 the plan 构成被动关系,所以填入 take 的过去分词 taken。

33. [答案]peaceful

[解析]修饰名词 life 需要用 peace 的形容词形式,所以将 peace 改成 peaceful。

34. [答案]understanding

[解析]of 前面要用的是名词,所以将 understand 改成名词形式 understanding。

35. [答案]confused

[解析]confused 翻译为"感到迷惑",符合题意。

Part III Reading Comprehension

Task 1

36. [答案]C

[解析]词汇猜测题。从文章中可以猜测出,air 的意思与播放节目有关,故选 C。

37. [答案]B

[解析]词汇猜测题。walk in each other's shoes 翻译为"处于对方的位置上",所以选 B。

38. [答案]D

[解析]细节题。在四个选项中,只有 D 在文章中没有提到,所以选 D。

39. [答案]D

[解析]细节题。反对这一节目的意见体现在文章的最后两段。其中并未提到高会嫉妒,所以选 D。

40. [答案]C

[解析]推断题。D 可以从第二段"Gao Zhanxi,a poor country boy…"推断出来。B 可以从第三段"Wei has decided to throw away his former extravagant lifestyle…"推断出来,而 A 可以从人们表示的不同意见推测出来。所以选 C。

Task 2

41. [答案]B

[解析] 细节题。可以根据第二段"……宣布克隆产品食用安全并且可以投放市场"选择 B。

42. [答案] A

[解析] 细节题。FDA 的作用在第二段提到了。FDA 的作用是 oversee food safety, 即管理食物安全, 所以选 A。

43. [答案] D

[解析] 细节题。文章第三段提到美国人对食用克隆食物依然感到不安, 所以选 D。

44. [答案] B

[解析] 细节题。文章最后一段提到 FDA 在宣布最后决定之前会听取公众的意见, 所以选 B。

45. [答案] C

[解析] 主旨题。作者通篇都在讨论克隆食物的问题, 所以选 C。

Task 3

46. [答案] a proposal

[解析] 从文章第四段第一句话可找到答案。

47. [答案] someone outside the company

[解析] 从文章第二段第一句话可找到答案。

48. [答案] main body of findings

[解析] 从文章第三段可找到答案。

49. [答案] supplier

[解析] 从文章第二段第一句话可找到答案。

50. [答案] an e-mail

[解析] 从文章最后一段最后一句话可找到答案。

Task 4

51. (O)(G)   52. (R)(L)   53. (Q)(E)   54. (H)(A)   55. (C)(P)

A——管理职能

B——银行账户

C——解决矛盾

D——现金管理

E——设立目标

F——无息贷款

G——制定计划

H——控制职能

I——年度销售额

J——激励下属

K——储蓄账户

L——沟通渠道

M——底价

N——储蓄账户

O——潜在求职者

P——人力资源

Q——求职人员

R——岗位责任制

Task 5

56. ［答案］September 17th,2007.

　　［解析］在(01)中提到开始的日期是 September 17th,2007。

57. ［答案］$1,500

　　［解析］在(02)中提到基本工资是 $1,500。

58. ［答案］be credited to

　　［解析］在(02)中提到工资将存入账户。

59. ［答案］Three months

　　［解析］在(03)中提到试用期不超过三个月。

60. ［答案］5

　　［解析］在这封信中共列明 5 个条款。

Part IV　Translation—English into Chinese

61. ［答案］B

　　［解析］satisfy 在此句中的翻译为"符合"最为恰当。condition 翻译为"条件"。

62. ［答案］D

　　［解析］该句翻译的重点是现在进行时的翻译。其次是对 interested 和 interesting 的辨析能力。

63. ［答案］C

　　［解析］该句考查的重点是被动语态和比较级的翻译方法。

64. ［答案］A

　　［解析］该句考查的重点是 given,在句中翻译为"鉴于"最为恰当;其次是 selection 和 election 的分辨。

65. ［译文］香格里拉已成为北海市著名的宴会聚会地。咖啡座特备亚洲风味和环球美食。面对美丽海景的香宫提供精美的粤式点心,以及附近海域的新鲜海鲜。酒店大堂白天提供快餐和各种饮品,夜间有现场演奏的音乐。

Part V　Writing

July 25th

Borrowed from the office of the Department a SANYO tape recorder and

promised to return at July 29th.

The Student Union of the Department of English

Test 4

Part I Listening Comprehension （15 minutes）

Directions：*This part is to test your listening ability. It consists of 3 sections.*

Section A

Directions：*This section is to test your ability to give proper answers to questions. The question will be spoken two times. When you hear a question, you should decide on the correct answer from the 4 choices.*

1. A. That's a good idea .   B. One month.

    C. Once a week.   D. Go to their house.

2. A. Of course not.   B. I don't think it's so good.

    C. Oh, Yes.   D. It's over there.

3. A. She's an English student.   B. She's interested in music.

    C. She's a friend of mine.   D. The tall girl with dark hair.

4. A. I don't like button and beef.   B. A bag of fruit and some vegetables, please.

    C. My favorite food isn't bread and butter.   D. I don't like this meal.

5. A. Cotton.   B. They are not so nice.

    C. They are dear.   D. They are beautiful.

Section B

Directions：*This section is to test your ability to understand short dialogues. Both the dialogue and the question will be spoken two times. When you hear a question, you should decide on the correct answer.*

6. A. At the bookstore.   B. At the nursery.

    C. In the school office.   D. In the park.

7. A. A shop assistant and a customer.   B. A teacher and a student.

    C. A boy and a girl.   D. Wife and husband.

8. A. To have a meeting.   B. To travel by car.

    C. To go to the movies.   D. To want a car.

9. A. He does not like to ask personal questions.

  B. He is not willing to answer the woman's questions.

  C. He has promised to answer the questions.

  D. He doesn't know the answers to the questions.

10. A. He wants but he has no time now.

   B. He is leaving now, for he's not willing.

   C. He is reluctant.

   D. It is possible for him to do that now.

Section C

Directions: *In this section you will hear a recorded short passage. The passage is printed on the test paper, but with some words or phrases missing. The passage will be read three times. You are required to put the missing words or phrases on the blanks.*

   Do you know what lungs (肺) are like? _____11_____ are in the upper part of our bodies. We have two of them. There are thousands of little pipes (管子) going through them. The _____12_____ are like the branches of a tree and they go through every part of each lung. When we breathe in, air goes through the nose and mouth and travels down a large pipe. The other end of this pipe becomes two smaller pipes and each goes into one lung. _____13_____ passes through those pipes and is carried around the body.

   When you _____14_____, your upper body moves in and out. To breathe in, air rushes into your lungs. To breathe out, air is forced out of your lungs. The air we breathe goes into every part of the lungs through the branching pipes. They take it to the _____15_____ which is moving all the time through the lungs and round to every part of our bodies. The blood goes around our body and back to the lungs in a very short time.

Part II Vocabulary & Structure (15 minutes)

Directions: *This part is to test your ability to use words and phrases correctly to construct meaningful and grammatically correct sentences.*

Section A

Directions: *There are 10 incomplete statements here. You are required to complete each statement by choosing the appropriate answer from the 4 choices.*

16. Hardly _____ his parents in such good mood (心情) since he fell into ill.

   A. he saw   B. he have see

   C. has he seen   D. does he see

17. You'd better _____ the paper today, because you need do some correcting work.

   A. not to hand in   B. not handing

   C. to not hand in   D. not hand in

18. —"How about _____ dinner at Roast Duck Restaurant?"

   —"Wonderful."

   A. to have   B. have

   C. having   D. have had

19. Let's go and wash our hands because dinner will be ready <u>right away</u>. Here "right away" means _____.

    A. at all   B. at least

    C. just now   D. at once

20. Students will continue to make the same mistakes _____ we teachers tell them why they shouldn't do so.

    A. unless   B. when

    C. if   D. because

21. You will improve your life quality a lot if you _____ your bad habits.

    A. gave up   B. give up

    C. had given up   D. will give up

22. We are often told by our parents never to _____ till tomorrow what we can do today.

    A. give out   B. come up

    C. put off   D. turn on

23. All the Chinese people are getting more and more excited when Spring Festival is _____ near.

    A. joining   B. drawing

    C. operating   D. taking

24. The university has two branch colleges, _____ are in coasted cities.

    A. both of them   B. both of which

    C. both two   D. they both

25. All is not gold _____ glitters.

    A. that   B. in that

    C. which   D. of which

Section B

Directions: *There are also 10 incomplete statements here. You should fill in each blank with the proper form of the word given in the brackets.*

26. The host required that every lecturer (give) _____ three minutes in their speeches.

27. You are supposed (lock) _____ the room before you leave the language lab.

28. It needs a long time to be used to (drive) _____ on the left after you arrive in Britain.

29. Bill Gates is famous for his Microsoft which is his greatest (achieve) _____.

30. Charlie is the (diligent) _____ postgraduate I have ever taught.

31. His theory turned out to be very (effect) _____ to improve our experiment.

32. A few cleaners (hire) _____ in the company next year.

33. It is difficult for a (speak) _____ to speak loudly enough without a microphone.

34. Both of the twin brothers (be) _____ capable of doing technical work at present.

35. A new start means Victor is (self-confidence) _____ again after he has got several times of failure.

Part III Reading Comprehension (40 minutes)

Task 1

Directions: *After reading the following passage, you will find 5 questions or unfinished statements. You should make the correct choices.*

There are a number of phrases built on the word "put", among which is the expression "putting one on". When one finds it difficult to believe what you said, he may look at you more closely and ask, "Are you putting me on ?" He doesn't think you are serious. Perhaps, you are joking with him, laughing at him, trying to test his reaction. People who try to put you on are more often just joking, having some pleasant friendly fun. There are people who like to play jokes on friends, to put them on in strange ways, some funny, some not. This is especially true on April 1st, April Fool's Day. Year after year, a number of people let themselves be fooled by the same joke. They just forget what happened to them the year before.

One of these often repeated jokes is about a telephone call. The caller changes his voice and tells his friend a certain Mr. Tiger calls him and asks him to make a quick reply to the given number, which is the telephone number of the National Zoo. Unthinkingly, the friend quickly makes his call and asks for Mr. Tiger.

The man on the other end says, "who ?"

"Mr. Tiger, I don't know his full name. Please hurry. "

The man at the other end answers, "We have no Mr. Tiger here". Then he realizes it is a joke and he has heard it before. And he begins to laugh and says, "Look, friend, this is the zoo. Somebody is putting you on".

"How foolish I am!" But he thinks about it and can't help having a good laugh over it.

36. According to this passage, "put one on" means _____.

   A. to dress somebody

   B. to give someone a phone

   C. to lift somebody onto a higher place

   D. to joke with someone to see what he will react to it

37. Why are people repeatedly fooled on April Fool's Day? _____

   A. Because they are also fond of fun.

   B. Because they are forgetful.

   C. Because they don't take the same joke seriously.

   D. Because their legs are pulled by someone.

38. The friend can't speak to Mr. Tiger because _____.

   A. this Mr. Tiger turned out to be an animal

   B. Mr. Tiger happened to be out at that time

   C. he called the wrong number and the wrong place

   D. the one who answered the phone didn't know Mr. Tiger

39. Which of the following statements is NOT true? _____

    A. People like playing jokes on others on April 1st.

    B. The popular joke is about a phone call on April 1st.

    C. The man who is joked on is a fool.

    D. Some of the jokes are funny, some are not.

40. This text is mainly about _____.

    A. the jokes people are likely to make on April Fool's Day

    B. the meaning of "putting one on" and how to use it

    C. why people play jokes on others

    D. April 1st is a day when people look for Mr. Tiger

Task 2

Directions: *After reading you should make the correct choices.*

As we know, it is not easy to build a satellite. Building a traditional satellite normally takes years. The costs can be as high as $250 million or more. Most members of the design teams have worked in the field for a long time. They hold advanced degrees in math, science, or engineering.

But things are changing. High costs, unusual educational requirements and long start-up times are no longer an obstacle to space exploration. The scientists at Stanford University have developed a new type of tiny, inexpensive earth-orbiting satellites that go from ideas to launch in a year.

So far, college students have built and launched several cube-shaped satellites, or Cube-Sats. At least 15 more are ready to go. Those already in orbit take pictures, collect information and send it back to the earth, just as regular satellites do.

But you might not even have to wait until you get to college to start designing and building your own satellite. A new program called KatySat aims to get teenagers to take part. Once kids understand what satellites can do, says Ben Yuan, an engineer at Lockheed Martin in Menlo Park, Calif. , the kind of applications they'll come up with may be countless.

"We'd like to put this technology in your hands," he tells kids. "We're going to teach you how to operate a satellite. Then we want to turn it over to you as a sandbox for you to play in. We want you to take the technology into new directions that we haven't thought of yet. "

Education isn't the only goal of CubeSats. Because these tiny, technology-filled boxes are relatively inexpensive to build and can be put together quickly, they're perfect for testing new technologies might one day be used on major tasks.

The biggest challenge now is to find ways to bring the satellites back to the earth after a year or two. Otherwise, major highways of space junk could gradually increase as CubeSats become more common.

Nowadays, college and high school students are getting a chance to learn what it takes to explore in space. Someday—perhaps a lot sooner than you imagine—you might get to design, build and launch your own satellite. If you do, you're sure to have fun. And you might also get crazy about science for life.

41. Compared with the traditional ones, the new satellites _____.

    A. need long start-up times   B. are low-cost and small-sized

    C. are very hard to operate   D. collect more information in orbit

42. What does the underlined word "obstacle" probably mean? _____

    A. An aim to achieve in the near future.

    B. An imagination that kids usually have.

    C. Something dangerous to terrify people.

    D. Something difficult that stands in the way.

43. According to the passage, which of the following is true? _____

    A. CubeSats could possible cause pollution in space.

    B. A few kids will send applications for the project.

    C. Scientists designed CubeSats for kids to play with.

    D. Students can't design satellites without college education.

44. What's the purpose of the author writing the passage? _____

    A. To show that high technology brings a big change in kids' life.

    B. To show that kids lead the space research into a new direction.

    C. To tell us that satellite technology can also be learned by kid.

    D. To tell us kids must study hard to learn satellite technology. ·

45. Why is it the biggest challenge now to find ways to bring the satellites back to the earth after a year or two?

    A. Because it is too hard.

    B. Because there are no such scientists that can do so.

    C. Because major highways of space junk could gradually increase as CubeSats become more common.

    D. Because kids can't do that.

Task 3

Directions: *After reading the passage, you should complete the correct answers.*

    When you want to call a store or an office that you don't call often, you look the number up in the telephone book. You dial the number, and then you forget it! You use short-term memory to remember the number. Your short-term memory lasts about 30 seconds. However, you don't need to look it up in the telephone book if it is your best friend's number. This information is in your long-term memory. Your long-term memory has everything that you remember through the years.

    When you call a store or an office that don't call often, you ___(46)___ the number in the ___(47)___ . You dial the number, and then you forget it! According to the passage you forget the telephone number that you don't call often because you use your ___(48)___ to remember it. A person's short-term memory lasts about ___(49)___ . However you needn't look up your best friend's number because it is in your ___(50)___ .

Task 4

Directions: *After reading the following list, you are required to find the items equivalent to those given in Chinese in the list below.*

A. ——traffic volume

B. ——traffic jam

C. ——annual budget

D. ——traffic regulations

E. ——traffic control

F. ——traffic signal

G. ——Olympic mascots

H. ——traffic sign

I. ——Olympic flame

J. ——double-decker

K. ——police box

L. ——collision

M. ——one way traffic

N. ——Tibetan antelope

Example: (L) 撞车　　　　　　　　　　(J) 双层公共汽车

51. ( ) 交通量	( ) 交通规则
52. ( ) 奥运吉祥物	( ) 奥运火焰
53. ( ) 交通信号	( ) 警察岗亭
54. ( ) 藏羚羊	( ) 年度预算
55. ( ) 单行道	( ) 交通堵塞

Task 5

Directions: *After reading the passage, you are required to complete the statements that follow the questions.*

What Will You Do for Your Mum on Mother's Day?

Does your mother know how much you appreciate her? Well, Mother's Day is the time to show her. It's the time to say "thank you", or to tell your mum how much you love her.

In Britain, Mother's Day, or Mothering Sunday, falls on a different day each year, because it takes place a few weeks before the festival of Easter. But it is always in the early springtime. In the USA, Mother's Day comes in May.

So what do we do now to celebrate Mother's Day? The easiest and cheapest way is to send a greeting card. Small children might make their mother a hand-made card or draw a picture, which their mother will treasure even more.

Other presents such as boxes of chocolates are also popular. But what mothers would enjoy most is a visit from their grown-up children, especially if you live a long way away. Whatever you do, it should show your mother how much she means to you.

56. From the text, we can know something about _____.

57. The easiest and cheapest way is to send _____.

58. If you live far from your mother, the best way is to pay _____.

59. What do you say to your mother on Mother's Day?

It's the time to say _____ or to tell your mum how much you love her.

60. When does Mother's Day come in the USA. ? _____.

Part IV   Translation—English into Chinese   (25 minutes)

Directions: *This part is to test your ability to translate English into Chinese. Each of the four sentences is followed by four choices of suggested translation. Make the best choice. Write your translation of the paragraph in the corresponding space.*

61. The number of personal computer users will be at least fivefold by the year 2000.

A. 到 2000 年个人计算机的用户数将至少增加四倍。

B. 到 2000 年个人计算机的用户数将至少增加五倍。

C. 到 2000 年个人计算机的用户数将至少是五折。

D. 到 2000 年个人计算机的用户数将至少是现在的四倍。

62. Plastics account for about 3% of the industrial waste.

A. 塑料说明有工业垃圾百分之三。

B. 塑料占工业垃圾的百分之三。

C. 工业垃圾占塑料的百分之三。

D. 塑料这一个数字是工业垃圾的百分之三。

63. Urban poverty and poor housing became more and more serious.

A. 郊区贫困化以及住房紧张问题日益严重。

B. 城市贫困化以及破旧的房子日益严重。

C. 城市贫困化以及住房紧张问题日益严重。

D. 都市贫困化以及住房紧张问题日益严重。

64. You ought to have told me the plan in advance.

A. 你应该告诉我这个计划的。

B. 你本该已经告诉我这个计划的。

C. 你早应该告诉我这个计划的。

D. 你本该事先告诉我这个计划的。

65. Have a happy attitude. Your attitude decides the way you see things. Is your cup half full or half empty: learn to think more positively about the difficulties you face.

Part V   Writing   (25 minutes)

Directions: *This part is to test your ability to do practical writing. You are required to finish the following writing according to the information.*

发信人：Harry Bennett

收信人：Market Section of Watermill inn

发信时间：2007 年 4 月 12 日

内容：因行程改变，取消 4 月 8 日以 Harry Bennett 的名义在贵酒店预定的 4 月 15 日到 17 日的双人房间。

询问是否需要支付违约金，并表示歉意。

Notes：双人房间 double room；以……的名义：in the name of…；违约金 Cancellation penalty

---

Message

To：Market Section of Watermill inn

From：_____

Date：_____

Subject：Cancellation of Hotel Booking

Dear Sir or Madam,

    I am writing the message to inform you that _____

_____

_____

_____

Yours sincerely,

Harry Bennett

答 案 解 析

Part I Listening Comprehension

听力原文

Section A

1. How often do you visit your aunt and uncle?

2. Tony, would you mind passing me the milk, please?

3. Jim, which is your girlfriend among the girls?

4. What can I do for you, Madam?

5. What are these pants made of?

Section B

6. M: What did the headmaster tell you just now?

   W: He required us teachers to finish the book before this weekend.

Q: Where does the conversation probably happen?

7. M: I am wondering where to spend our winter holiday, dear.

W: I prefer to have it in a coasted city to celebrate our wedding anniversary.

Q: What is the relationship between the man and the woman?

8. M: I have been wanting a free vacation by car for a long time.

W: So you are to travel by car.

Q: What is the man's plan?

9. W: May I ask you some personal questions?

M: Yes, of course. But I refuse to answer.

Q: What does the man mean?

10. W: Will it be possible if I ask you to accompany me to the hotel?

M: Certainly yes. But I am busy now.

Q: What does the man mean?

Section C

Do you know what lungs (肺) are like? __11 Lungs__ are in the upper part of our bodies. We have two of them. There are thousands of little pipes (管子) going through them. The __12 pipes__ are like the branches of a tree and they go through every part of each lung. When we breathe in, air goes through the nose and mouth and travels down a large pipe. The other end of this pipe becomes two smaller pipes and each goes into one lung. __13 Air__ passes through those pipes and is carried around the body.

When you __14 breathe__, your upper body moves in and out. To breathe in, air rushes into your lungs. To breathe out, air is forced out of your lungs. The air we breathe goes into every part of the lungs through the branching pipes. They take it to the __15 blood__ which is moving all the time through the lungs and round to every part of our bodies. The blood goes around our body and back to the lungs in a very short time.

答案详解

Section A

1. [答案]C

[解析]"That's a good idea"翻译为"那是个好主意";"One month."翻译为"一个";"Once a week"翻译为"一周一次";"Go to their house"翻译为"去他们家"。问题句是"你多久看望一次你的叔叔和婶婶",所以根据题意应选 C。

2. [答案]A

[解析]"Of course not"翻译为"当然不";"I don't think it's so good."翻译为"它不太好";"Oh, yes"翻译为"噢,是的";"It is over there"翻译为"它在那边"。对话中说"托尼,请把牛奶递给我好吗?",所以根据题意应选 A。

3. ［答案］D

　　［解析］"She's an English student" 翻译为"她是一名英国学生"；"She's interested in music"翻译为"她对音乐感兴趣"；"She's a friend of mine"翻译为"她是我的一位朋友"；"The tall girl with dark hair"翻译为"那位黑头发的高个儿女孩"。问题是"这群女孩里哪个是你的女朋友,吉姆",所以根据题意应选 D。

4. ［答案］B

　　［解析］"I don't like button and beef"翻译为"我不喜欢羊肉和牛肉"；"A bag of fruit and some vegetables ,please"翻译为"请给我称一袋水果和一些蔬菜"；"My favorite food is not bread and butter"翻译为"我最喜欢的食品不是面包涂黄油"；"I don't like this meal"翻译为"我不喜欢这餐饭"。所以根据题意应选 B。

5. ［答案］A

　　［解析］"Cotton"翻译为"棉布"；"They are not so nice"翻译为"裤子不太好看"；"They are dear"翻译为"裤子很贵"；"They are beautiful"翻译为"裤子很漂亮"。所以根据题意应选 A。

Section B

6. ［答案］C

　　［解析］"At the bookstore"翻译为"在书店"；"At the nursery"翻译为"在托儿所"；"In the school office"翻译为"在学校办公室"；"In the park"翻译为"在公园里"。所以根据题意应选 C。

7. ［答案］D

　　［解析］"A shop assistant and a customer" 翻译为"一位商店售货员和一位顾客"；"A teacher and a student"翻译为"一位老师和一位学生"；"A boy and a girl"翻译为"一名男孩和一名女孩"；"Wife and husband"翻译为"夫妻"。所以根据题意应选 D。

8. ［答案］B

　　［解析］"To have a meeting"翻译为"开个会"；"To travel by car"翻译为"驾车旅行"；"To go to the movies"翻译为"去看电影"；"To want a car"翻译为"想买辆车"。所以根据题意应选 B。

9. ［答案］B

　　［解析］"He does not like to ask personal questions"翻译为"他不喜欢问个人问题"；"He is not willing to answer the woman's question"翻译为"他不愿意回答这位女士的问题"；"He has promised to answer the question"翻译为"他已经答应回答这个问题"；"He doesn't know the answer to the question"翻译为"他不知道这个问题的答案"。所以根据题意应选 B。

10. ［答案］A

　　　［解析］"He wants but he has no time now"翻译为"他想去,但他现在没有时间"；"He is leaving now,for he's not willing"翻译为"他现在要走了,因为他不愿意去"；"He is reluctant"翻译为"他不情愿(陪她去旅馆)"；"It is possible for him to do that now"翻译为"对于他来讲现在陪她去旅馆是可能的"。所以根据题意应选 A。

11. Lungs   12. pipes   13. Air   14. breathe   15. blood

Part II   Vocabulary & Structure

Section A

16. ［答案］C

［解析］这道题测试的是部分倒装的用法,当句子的开头出现了 seldom,hardly,never 等否定词汇,句子要采用部分倒装,即助动词提前。本句的意思是"自我生病以来,我很少见到我的父母有这样好的心情。",是个现在完成时态的句子,所以助动词是 have,正确答案为选项 C。

17. ［答案］D

［解析］根据句型"had better not do something(最好不做某事)"选择答案 D。

18. ［答案］C

［解析］how about 后接 doing,翻译为"做……怎么样",所以正确答案为选项 C。

19. ［答案］D

［解析］right away 在此翻译为"立即,马上";at all 翻译为"根本";at least 翻译为"至少";just now 翻译为"刚才";at once 翻译为"立即,马上"。所以根据题意应选 D。

20. ［答案］A

［解析］连词 unless 为"除非"之意,本句的意思为"学生们将会继续犯同样的错误,除非我们老师告诉他们为什么不应该犯这样的错误"。所以根据题意应选 A。

21. ［答案］B

［解析］根据 if 连词的用法"主句一般将来时 + 从句一般现在时"句型,B 为正确答案。

22. ［答案］C

［解析］give out 翻译为"分发,精疲力竭";come up 翻译为"走近,上来";put off 翻译为"推迟";turn on 翻译为"打开电源"。本句的意思为"我们的父母经常告诉我们今天能做的事情不要推迟到明天"。所以根据题意应选 C。

23. ［答案］B

［解析］joining 翻译为"连接";drawing 翻译为"向…移动,挨近";operating 翻译为"操作";taking 翻译为"带,拿"。本句的意思为"随着春节的临近,所有的中国人都愈加兴奋"。所以根据题意应选 B。

24. ［答案］B

［解析］后半句为 college 的非限制性定语从句,必须用引导词 which,故选 B。

25. ［答案］A

［解析］A 选项为固定用法。本句意思为"闪光的不一定都是金子"。

Section B

26. [答案]be given

[解析]require 后边的宾语从句用虚拟语气(should)do,而 lecturer 作主语时动词用被动语态,(should) be done,因此答案可以是 (should) be given。本题考查的是在表示愿望、请示、建议、命令等意义的动词后的宾语从句中要用虚拟语气的用法"(should) + 动词原形"。同样用法的动词还有 demand,insist,suggest,command,request,order,propose,desire,require,urge,maintain,deserve,recommend,intend,move,ask,prefer,advise,decide 等。例如:He demanded that he be given the right to express his opinion. (他要求给予他表达自己意见的权利。)

27. [答案]to lock

[解析]be supposed to do 为不定式用法,意思是"应该"。类似的词语还有 be expected to do,be meant to do。

28. [答案]driving

[解析]be used to doing 是固定表达法,翻译为"适应做某事,习惯于做某事",所以填 driving。同时注意区分 used to do sth 是"过去常常做某事"。be/become/grow accustomed to doing 也表示习惯于做某事。

29. [答案]achievement

[解析]最高级 greatest 后接名词,所以把动词 achieve 变成 achievement。

30. [答案]most diligent

[解析]根据前面的定冠词 the 推断出多音节形容词 diligent 使用其形容词最高级形式 most diligent。

31. [答案]effective

[解析]effect 翻译为"效果",是名词。此外需变成形容词作 be 的表语,与前面的 be 一起构成系表结构。

32. [答案]will be hired

[解析]时间状语 next year 决定将来时态,a few cleaners 作主语是 hire 动作的承受者,所以用将来时被动语态 will be hired。

33. [答案]speaker

[解析]for sb to do sth 是动词不定式的复合结构,speak 是动词,应该变成名词 speaker。

34. [答案]are

[解析]both of the twin brothers(两个双胞胎兄弟)是复数,at present(目前)决定此句为一般现在时,所以动词用 are。

35. [答案]self-confident

[解析]self-confidence(自信)是名词,根据系表结构句型 be self-confident 需用形容词 self-confident 作 is 的表语。

Part III   Reading Comprehension

Task 1

36. ［答案］D

　　［解析］put one on 在短文中的意思是"开某人的玩笑看他对此的反应"，只有 D 符合。

37. ［答案］C

　　［解析］问题是"人们为什么在愚人节反复被愚弄"，根据第一段推断出"因为人们对同样的玩笑没当真"。

38. ［答案］D

　　［解析］从第五段看出"这个人无法与 Tiger 先生说话，是因为接电话的人不认识 Tiger 先生"。所以答案为 D。

39. ［答案］C

　　［解析］根据各选项的意思，只有 C"被开玩笑的人是个傻瓜"这点文中没有提到，因此选 C。

40. ［答案］B

　　［解析］这篇文章主要讲 put one on 这个词语的意思及其用法，所以选 B。

Task 2

41. ［答案］B

　　［解析］从第六段的这句话"Because these tiny，technology-filled boxes are relatively inexpensive to build"（因为这些小小的有技术含量的盒子相对来说建造起来不贵），可以看出答案为 B。

42. ［答案］D

　　［解析］obstacle 意为"障碍"，所以选 D。

43. ［答案］A

　　［解析］从第七段此句"Otherwise，major highways of space junk could gradually increase as CubeSats become more common"（否则随着立体卫星变得越加普遍，主要轨道上的太空垃圾可能会逐渐增加）可以判断 A 正确。

44. ［答案］C

　　［解析］细读第四段"A new program called KatySat aims to get teenagers to take part."（一项叫凯逊卫星的新计划目的是使青少年也参与。），根据此句可以分析出答案为 C。

45. ［答案］C

　　［解析］答案在第七段"因为随着立体卫星变得越加普遍，主要轨道上的太空垃圾可能会逐渐增加。"，故 C 正确。

Task 3

46. ［答案］look up

　　［解析］答案在原文第一句话中可以得出。

47. ［答案］telephone book

　　［解析］答案句同 46 题。

48. ［答案］short-term memory

　　［解析］"You dial the number, and then you forget it! You use short-term memory to re-member the number"（你拨这个号码，然后你就把它忘了！你使用了短期记忆来记忆这个号码）。从此句可以看出答案是短期记忆。

49. ［答案］30 seconds

　　［解析］从原文第四句可以得出答案。

50. ［答案］long-term memory

　　［解析］"This information is in your long-term memory"（这个信息在你的长期记忆里），这句话给出了答案。

Task 4

51. (A) (D)　　52. (G) (I)　　53. (F) (K)　　54. (N) (C)　　55. (M) (B)

A——交通量

B——交通堵塞

C——年度预算

D——交通规则

E——交通控制

F——交通信号

G——奥运吉祥物

H——交通标志

I——奥运火焰

J——双层公共汽车

K——警察岗亭

L——冲突

M——单行道

N——藏羚羊

Task 5

56. ［答案］Mother's Day

　　［解析］答案在第一段。

57. ［答案］a greeting card

　　［解析］答案在第三段。

58. ［答案］a visit

　　［解析］答案在第四段。

59. ［答案］thank you

　　［解析］答案在第一段。

60. ［答案］It comes in May

　　［解析］答案在第二段。

Part IV　Translation—English into Chinese

61.　［答案］A

　　［解析］注意 fivefold—增加四倍,是原来的五倍。

62.　［答案］B

　　　［解析］account for 是词组“(数量)占……”。

63.　［答案］D

　　［解析］注意 more and more(越来越……)比较级的用法。

64.　［答案］D

　　［解析］“ought to ＋ 完成时”表示过去应做而未做的事情,如 You ought to have done something to help him. (你本应该做些事情去帮助他。)Should 也有这样的用法:At the age of thirty-five,I should have understood. (35 岁那年,我本应该懂得了。)

65.　［译文］有一个乐观的态度。你的态度决定你看问题的方式。你的杯子是半满还是半空:学会更加积极地看待你面对的困难。

　　［解析］注意两个定语从句的翻译:the way you see things(你看问题的方式)和 the difficulty you face(你面临的困难)。

Part V　Writing

Message

To:Market Section of Watermill inn

From：Harry Bennett

Date：April 12th,2007

Subject：Cancellation of Hotel Booking

Dear Sir or Madam,

　　I am writing the message to inform you that owing to the change of the trip route,I'd like to cancel the room from April 15th to 17th that I reserved at Watermill inn in the name of Harry Bennett on April 8th. I am terribly sorry about the trouble and I wonder if I need to pay the cancellation penalty.

　　I am looking forward to your reply.

Yours sincerely,
Harry Bennett

Test 5

Part I　Listening Comprehension　(15 minutes)

Directions: *This part is to test your listening ability. It consists of 3 sections.*

Section A

Directions: *This section is to test your ability to give proper answers to questions. The question will be spoken two times. When you hear a question, you should decide on the correct answer from the 4 choices.*

1. A. Yes, I am.
   C. OK, I'll take the notes.
   B. So I can remember all the new information.
   D. No, thank you.

2. A. New York.
   C. Last week.
   B. For two months.
   D. Two weeks later.

3. A. It is not good at all.
   C. The history book is very interesting.
   B. No, I borrowed it.
   D. Yes, I will.

4. A. You have to buy it.
   C. On the third floor of the library.
   B. This afternoon, I think.
   D. It's 10:30.

5. A. Pretty well, thanks.
   C. Nice to meet you.
   B. Yes, thanks.
   D. How do you do.

Section B

Directions: *This section is to test your ability to understand short dialogues. Both the dialogue and the question will be spoken two times. When you hear a question, you should decide on the correct answer.*

6. A. She broke the bicycle herself.
   C. She was able to get the bicycle fast.
   B. She fixed the broken bicycle.
   D. She hurt herself on the broken bicycle.

7. A. He had two classes yesterday.
   C. His class begins at 9:00 o'clock.
   B. He will have classes all morning.
   D. His class lasts two hours.

8. A. Swimming is also a good exercise.
   C. She prefers hiking to swimming.
   B. She likes swimming better.
   D. Hiking is not a good exercise.

9. A. He is amused.
   C. He is calm.
   B. He is happy.
   D. He is upset.

10. A. He left his notes in classroom.
    C. He had an exam.
    B. He couldn't write his notes.
    D. A classmate borrowed his notes.

64

Section C

Directions: *In this section you will hear a recorded short passage. The passage is printed on the test paper, but with some words or phrases missing. The passage will be read three times. You are required to put the missing words or phrases on the blanks.*

Nancy walked out into the yard and took a deep ____11____ of cool, fresh air. She was eager to begin work. This time of year, with the new growth everywhere, always made her feel that she had to help things ____12____. She gathered her tools and went to the patch of freshly turned earth and began to ____13____ rows of holes. Then she carefully picked up one fragile plant and ____14____ it in a hole. Over and over she performed this same task and then gently patted the earth around each plant. Her growling stomach and the sun high overhead told her when it was time to ____15____.

Part II Vocabulary & Structure (15minutes)

Directions: *This part is to test your ability to use words and phrases correctly to construct meaningful and grammatically correct sentences.*

Section A

Directions: *There are 10 incomplete statements here. You are required to complete each statement by choosing the appropriate answer from the 4 choices.*

16. What he said _____ reasonable this time.

    A. tastes   B. sounds   C. looks   D. feels

17. Seldom _____ my neighbor in such good mood(心情) since I moved here.

    A. I saw   B. I have seen   C. have I seen   D. Do I seen

18. He is going to pick up his parents, so we _____ with him.

    A. needn't to go   B. don't need go   C. needn't go   D. needn't going

19. The situation will continue to become worse _____ we take some measures.

    A. when   B. because   C. if   D. unless

20. It is said that this medicine is _____ against fever.

    A. economic   B. easy   C. expensive   D. effective

21. He has changed his _____ about spending so much money on the book.

    A. brain   B. head   C. mind   D. thought

22. While _____ in Paris, the old artist picked up some French.

    A. staying   B. stay   C. stayed   D. to stay

23. Please wait me for a moment. I will be ready _____.

    A. by the way   B. right away   C. at last   D. in that case

24. If you travel in a strange place, a tour _____ may save you a lot of time.

    A. director   B. helper   C. guide   D. assistant

25. If you don't _____ smoking and drinking, she will break up with you.

    A. gave up   B. give up   C. had given up   D. will give up

Section B

Directions: *There are also 10 incomplete statements here. You should fill in each blank with the proper form of the word given in the brackets.*

26. Please remember (turn) _____ off the light when you leave.

27. Tom's parents are very (friend) _____ to his girlfriend.

28. He suggested that I (visit) _____ my teacher the next day.

29. I can jump (far) _____ than Tom.

30. He is asked to (short) _____ his thesis to 2,000 words.

31. Hardly had we get home when it (begin) _____ to snow.

32. Going out to have a picnic will be an (excite) _____ experience for us.

33. All the guests (invite) _____ at the part yesterday have been killed.

34. The broken bike needs (repair) _____.

35. Zhang Yimou, our favorite film (direct) _____, is becoming worldwide famous.

Part III   Reading Comprehension   (40 minutes)

Task 1

Directions: *After reading the following passage, you will find 5 questions or unfinished statements. You should make the correct choices.*

For the last hundred years the climate has been growing much warmer. This has had a number of different effects. Since the beginning of the 20th century, glaciers (冰河) have been melting very rapidly. For example, the Muir Glacier in Alaska has retreated 2 miles in 10 years. Secondly, rising temperatures have been causing the snowline to retreat on mountains all over the world. In Peru, for example, it has risen as much as 2,700 feet in 60 years.

As a result of this, vegetation has also been changing. In Canada, the agricultural crop line has shifted 50 to 100 miles northward. In the same way cool-climate trees like birches and spruce have been dying over large areas of Eastern Canada. In Sweden the tree line has moved up the mountains by as much as 65 feet since 1930.

36. According to the passage, the Muir Glacier has retreated because _____.

    A. glaciers have been melting very gradually

    B. the climate has been growing much warmer

    C. the snowline has retreated on mountains

    D. vegetation has been changing

37. The snowline's retreat means that it is getting _____.

    A. higher   B. lower   C. wider   D. narrower

38. Vegetation in Canada has shifted northward because _____.

A. there isn't enough water in southern Canada

B. the temperature is stable in northern Canada

C. there are much more fields in northern Canada

D. the temperature is much lower in northern Canada

39. What is the cause of all these phenomena? _____

    A. Melting glaciers.   B. Rising temperature.   C. Snow line.   D. Dying trees.

40. The passage is convincing because there are a lot of _____.

    A. descriptions   B. examples   C. arguments   D. conclusions

Task 2

Directions: *After reading you should make the correct choices.*

Nowadays, cities are becoming more and more crowded. Some pessimists (悲观者) are deeply worried about the serious problems caused by the huge populations. They believe that the public services are already overloaded and near the verge of collapse. Especially in some developing countries, the metropolis (大城市) are overcrowded all the time. Crowded streets, stuffed buses and jammed subways continuously affect people's lives. Some optimists, however, see the current problems as merely part of an evolutionary process. They argue that London and New York had similar problems but were able eventually to establish an orderly and safe environment for their citizens. It seems that people become the controversial factor here. Either they themselves as inhabitants cause inconvenience to each other, or they participate together in city developing plans and contribute efforts to facilitate city life. Human elements are therefore the center for determining the future of big cities.

41. According to the passage, _____ causes the most serious problem.

    A. pollution   B. noise   C. population   D. traffic jam

42. If the pessimists are to give examples, _____ serves as the best one.

    A. Tokyo   B. Singapore   C. New York   D. Sydney

43. "Controversial" has the similar meaning with _____.

    A. important   B. key   C. disputing   D. unusual

44. The last sentence implies that _____.

    A. good management systems are essential

    B. a great leader is all important

    C. the more people, the better

    D. big cities have no bright future

45. Why do optimists mention London and New York? _____

    A. There are a lot of people in London and New York.

    B. They are developing countries.

    C. They are crowded.

    D. Because of the orderly and safe environment in London and New York.

Task 3

Directions: *After reading the passage, you should complete the correct answers.*

When we talk about intelligence, we do not mean the ability to get good scores on certain kinds of tests or even the ability to do well in school. By intelligence we mean a way of living and behaving, especially in a new or upsetting situation. If we want to test intelligence, we need to find out how a person acts instead of how much he knows what to do. For instance, when in a new situation, an intelligent person thinks about the situation, not about himself or what might happen to him. He tries to find out all he can, and he acts immediately and tries to do something about it. And if he cannot make things work out right, he doesn't feel ashamed that he failed; he just tries to learn from his mistakes. An intelligent person, even if he is very young, has a special outlook on life, and how he fits into it. If you look at children, you'll see great differences between what we call "bright" children and "not bright" children. They are actually two different kinds of people, not just the same kind with different amount of intelligence.

46. According to the passage, what is intelligence?

    The ability to cope with _____.

47. In a new situation, what does an intelligent person usually try to do?

    To _____ what to do about the situation.

48. How can we find out whether a person is intelligent or not?

    We should see _____.

49. What will an intelligent person do if he fails?

    He will _____.

50. What does an intelligent young person look upon life?

    He will see how he _____.

Task 4

Directions: *After reading the following list, you are required to find the items equivalent to those given in Chinese in the list below.*

A. ——Advertisement

B. ——Advertiser

C. ——Billboard

D. ——Poster

E. ——Advertising Campaign

F. ——Advertising Copy

G. ——Advertising Agency

H. ——The Art of Advertising

I. ——Advertising War

J. ——Advertising Column

K. ——Advertising Media

L. ——Fly Sheets for Advertising

M. ——Advertising Culture

N. ——Advertising Agency Relationship

O. ——Advertisements of Health Products

P. ——Advertisements of Office Equipment

Q. ——Advertisements of Personal Articles for Daily Use

R. ——Advertisements for Non-profit Purposes

S. ——Advertisements of Books and Periodicals

T. ——Advertisements of Industrial Equipment and Business Services

Example:（C）广告牌　　　　　　（K）广告媒体

51. （　）广告艺术	（　）保健品广告
52. （　）广告大战	（　）日用品广告
53. （　）广告书刊	（　）办公用品广告
54. （　）广告文化	（　）活页传单广告
55. （　）公益广告	（　）广告稿

Task 5

Directions：*After reading the passage, you are required to complete the statements that follow the questions.*

The importance of commanding newspaper reading skills cannot be over emphasized. Without newspapers you would have to depend almost entirely on seeing and hearing the news, and although television and radio news reports also provide information, they must report the news of the day according to their selection in order to stay within a set time period.

A newspaper isn't under such strict limits and has other advantages. It can be read at your spare time, gives you a choice of articles and topics, and is available free to everyone through public libraries. Because the newspaper must meet the needs of so many people, it has many different sections.

56. What is the passage about?

_____

57. What does the author think about the newspaper reading skills?

_____

58. Why must TV and radio news reports be under strict limits?

_____

59. Where can one find newspapers according to the passage?

_____

60. Why must a newspaper have many sections?

_____

Part IV　Translation—English into Chinese　（25 minutes）

Directions：*This part is to test your ability to translate English into Chinese. Each of the four*

61. Not only I but also Jane and Mary are tired of having one meeting after another.

    A. 我、珍妮和玛丽都很疲倦,无法在一次会议后再参加一次会议。

    B. 一个会议接着一个会议,不仅我厌烦,珍妮和玛丽也都厌烦。

    C. 除我以外,珍妮和玛丽先后参加了两个会议,觉得很劳累。

    D. 不仅我,还有珍妮和玛丽有开不完的会,搞得筋疲力尽。

62. Some interviewees lose their chances simply because they fail to display self-confidence.

    A. 一些面试者失去了机会,简单地说是因为他们显得没有自信。

    B. 一些面试者因为不相信自身的能力而轻易地放弃了这次机会。

    C. 一些面试者轻易的放弃了机会,因为他们无法保持自信心。

    D. 一些面试者只是因为他们未能表现出自信心而失去机会。

63. The road department apologized for any inconvenience caused while road improvements were in process.

    A. 道路部门对道路改造期间所带来的不便表示歉意。

    B. 道路部门为修建道路可能引起的不便进行了解释。

    C. 道路部门辩解说,新近造成的麻烦是因道路正在修建。

    D. 道路部门对不断改建道路会造成的任何不便表示歉意。

64. As far as an Advertising and Sales Manager is concerned, excellent oral English is also a necessary requirement.

    A. 广告部和销售部经理都要求员工必须有良好的英语口语能力。

    B. 对广告及销售经理而言,娴熟的英语口语能力也是必要的条件。

    C. 广告部经理和销售部经理认为,熟练的英语口语能力也会是必需的。

    D. 广告部经理和销售部经理所关心的是员工也必须要有很高的英语水平。

65. China has nearly 200 million working women, constituting one-sixth of her total population. They have the right to participate in social production, therefore gaining economic independence and equal status in the society and at home.

Part V Writing (25 minutes)

Directions: *This part is to test your ability to do practical writing. You are required to finish the following writing according to the information.*

说明:请以张华的名义写一封求职信。

　　张华,22 岁,毕业于京北职业学院,主修旅游管理,各门课程都优良。已获得导游资格证书。请为她拟出一份给 W 公司的自荐信,希望能在该公司谋得导游职务。请注意书信的格式。写信的日期为 2008 年 5 月 10 日。

Words for reference:

　　职业学院 Vocational College;旅游管理 Tourism Administration;证书 Certificate

答 案 解 析

Part I   Listening Comprehension

听力原文

Section A

1. Tom, why do you take all these notes?

2. When will our summer holiday begin?

3. Will you buy this history book?

4. Excuse me, where could I find English magazines?

5. How are you going?

Section B

6. M: Did Jane have someone repair the broken bicycle?

   W: No, she did it herself.

   Q: What did Jane do?

7. W: How many classes did you have yesterday?

   M: Just one, from 8:00 to 10:00.

   Q: What does the man mean?

8. M: Going hiking is a good exercise.

   W: So is swimming.

   Q: What does the woman mean?

9. W: My wallet is lost and I am very sad.

   M: I'm sorry to hear it. Can I help you?

   Q: How does the man feel?

10. W: Did you prepare for the exam?

    M: I couldn't. I lent my notes to Jack.

    Q: What happened to the man?

Section C

Nancy walked out into the yard and took a deep **11 breath** of cool, fresh air. She was eager to begin work. This time of year, with the new growth everywhere, always made her feel that she had to help things **12 grow**. She gathered her tools and went to the patch of freshly turned earth and began to **13 dig** rows of holes. Then she carefully picked up one fragile plant and **14 placed** it in a hole. Over and over she performed this same task and then gently patted the earth around each plant. Her growling stomach and the sun high overhead told her when it was time to **15**

take a break .

答案详解

Part I Listening Comprehension

Section A

1. ［答案］B

　 ［解析］问题是"汤姆,你为什么记笔记",首先这是一个特殊疑问句,答案肯定不是 Yes 或 No 开头,故排除 A 和 D;根据问题,C 选项也不符合题意,只能是 B 选项。

2. ［答案］D

　 ［解析］问题是"暑假什么时候开始",而 A 选项给出的答案是个地点,故排除;B 选项 是个时间段,不符合题意;C 选项是过去的时间,而本题是对将来的某一时间进行提问,所以 D 选项为正确答案。

3. ［答案］D

　 ［解析］"Will you buy this history books?"是个一般疑问句,A,C 选项不是对观点的肯定 或否定,故排除;B 选项时态和意思都不对;D 选项对问句进行了肯定的回答,符合题意,所以 D 选项为正确答案。

4. ［答案］C

　 ［解析］问题是"打扰了,哪里有英语杂志"是对地点的提问,而 B 和 D 选项却是对时间 提问的回答;A 选项不符合意思;C 选项"在图书馆的三楼"符合题意,故 C 为正确答案。

5. ［答案］A

　 ［解析］"How are you going?"是我们经常听到的一句问候语,属于特殊疑问句,故不能 选择 B;C 选项的问句应为"Nice to meet you";D 选项的问句应为"How do you do";所以只有 A 选项符合题意,故正确答案为 A。

Section B

6. ［答案］B

　 ［解析］对话中男士问"简是不是让人把那辆坏的自行车修理了",女士回答"没有,她 自己修的",不难判断出 B 选项为正确答案。

7. ［答案］D

　 ［解析］本题中男士问"你昨天上了几节课",女士回答"一节课,从八点到十点",四个 选项中的信息只有 D 选项符合对话内容,其他选项不符合题意。

8. ［答案］A

　 ［解析］对话中男士说"远足是一项很好的练习",女士回答"游泳也是",很明显 A 选项 的意思符合女士的意思,所以 A 选项为正确答案。

9. ［答案］D

　 ［解析］对话中女士说"她丢了钱包感到很难过",这里面 sad 这个词很关键,问题问的是

"男士的感觉",四个选项里只有 D 选项中的 upset 和 sorry 意思相近,所以正确答案为 D。

10. [答案]D

   [解析]问题是"你准备考试了吗",男士回答"我没办法准备,我把笔记借给杰克了",故 D 选项"有个同学借了他的笔记"为正确答案。

Section C

11. breath   12. grow   13. dig   14. placed   15. take a break

Part II   Vocabulary & Structure

Section A

16. [答案]B

   [解析]答案中的四个选项都是系动词,taste 翻译为"尝起来";sound 翻译为"听起来";look 翻译为"看起来";feel 翻译为"摸起来"。根据题意可知这句话的意思是"这次他所说的听起来有道理",所以选项 B 为正确答案。

17. [答案]C

   [解析]这道题测试的是部分倒装的用法,当句子的开头出现了 seldom,hardly,never 等否定词汇,句子要部分倒装,即助动词提前。本句的意思是"自从我搬到这里来,我很少见到我的邻居有这样好的心情",是个现在完成时态的句子,所以助动词是 have,正确答案为选项 C。

18. [答案]C

   [解析]这里考查的是 need 作动词和情态动词的用法,当 need 作为动词时,本题的否定应在 need 前面加 don't,而后面和动词 go 之间应该有不定式 to,即 don't need to go;而 need 作为情态动词时,否定形式是在 need 后加 not,后面直接接动词原型 go,即 needn't go;故只有选项 C 为正确答案。

19. [答案]D

   [解析]本题的意思是"如果我们不采取一些措施,情况将会变得更糟糕",四个选项前三个不符合题意,很容易排除,但是 D 选项 unless 有很多同学翻译成"除非",这样就很难把握句子的意思,大家不妨把它看作"if …not(如果不)",这样就比较容易理解和翻译了。

20. [答案]D

   [解析]这是一道词汇辨析题,本题的意思是"据说这种药抗感冒很有效"。economic 翻译为"经济的";easy 翻译为"容易的";expensive 翻译为"昂贵的";effective 翻译为"有效的",所以根据题意应选 D。

21. [答案]C

   [解析]本题考查的是词组辨析,C 选项构成的 change one's mind 的意思是"改变主意",其他选项都不符合搭配,故正确答案为 C 选项。

22. [答案]A

   [解析]这句话的意思是"当那位老画家在巴黎待着的时候,他学会了一些法语",这

73

里考查的是分词的用法,句中的主语 the artist 和 stay 的关系是主动,现在分词表示"主动,进行",过去分词表示"被动,完成",这里应该用 stay 的现在分词 staying,故正确的答案为 A 选项。

23. [答案]B

[解析]本题的意思是"请等我一会,我马上就准备好"。by the way 翻译为"顺便问一句",right away 翻译为"马上,很快";at last 翻译为"最后";in that case 翻译为"那样的话"。故 B 选项为正确答案。

24. [答案]C

[解析]这句话的意思是"如果你在一个陌生的地方旅行,一个导游将会使你省很多时间"。这里面所缺的词是"导游",为 C 选项符合题意。

25. [答案]B

[解析]这句话的意思是"如果你不戒烟戒酒的话,她将要和你分手",这里从主句"she will…"判断出这是一个"主将从现"的句子,而不是虚拟语气,故正确答案为 B 选项。

Section B

26. [答案]to turn

[解析]这句话的意思是"当你离开的时候记得关灯",考查的知识点是"记得去做某事",即 remember to do something,故正确答案为 to turn。

27. [答案]friendly

[解析]这句话的意思是"汤姆的父母对他的女朋友很友好",本句中应填词汇在 be 动词 are 和副词 very 的后面,由此判断空白处应该用形容词"友好的",故正确答案为 friendly。

28. [答案]visit 或 should visit

[解析]这道题测试的是虚拟语气。suggest,advise,order 等表示"建议"、"请求"、"命令"的词汇,在引导宾语从句时,从句中谓语动词用"(should)+ 动词原型"。

29. [答案]farther

[解析]空白处后面是一个表示比较级的 than,所以前面应该用副词 far 的比较级,故正确答案为 farther。

30. [答案]shorten

[解析]不定式 to 的后面应该接动词原形,而所给单词 short 是形容词,要变成动词需要在单词后加 en 即 shorten。

31. [答案]began

[解析]这句话的意思是"我刚到家天就开始下雪",这里到家在前,用的是过去完成时,所以下雪就应该用过去时,故答案应为 begin 的过去式 began。

32. [答案]exciting

[解析]这句话的意思是"去外面野餐对我们来说将会是一件令人兴奋的经历","令人兴奋的"是 exciting。

33. [答案]invited

[解析]根据现在分词表示"主动,进行";过去分词表示"被动,完成",invite 与 guests

74

之间是被动关系,所以用动词的过去分词 invited。

34. [答案]repairing

[解析]need,want 后面接动词的现在分词表示被动。

35. [答案]director

[解析]本句应翻译为"我最喜欢的导演张艺谋举世闻名",这里需要的是名词"导演",即 director。

Part III   Reading Comprehension

Task 1

36. [答案]B

[解析]根据第一段第一句和第三句 "For the last hundred years the climate has been growing much warmer." 可知 B 为正确答案。

37. [答案]A

[解析]根据第一段最后两句"Secondly,rising temperatures have been causing the snow-line to retreat on mountains all over the world. In Peru,for example,it has risen as much as 2,700 feet in 60 years"本句中 retreat 和 risen 是相对应的,所以 A 选项符合题意,故为正确答案。

38. [答案]D

[解析]第二段开始提到"温度升高的结果使蔬菜种植地区发生了变化,在加拿大,农业的耕种线向北移动了 50 到 100 英里",因为温度的升高,而北部地区的温度比较低,所以适合种植,因而耕种线向北移动,符合题意的是答案 D。

39. [答案]B

[解析]整篇文章一直在谈论温度升高产生的影响,选项 A、C、D 都是其产生的结果,B 表明原因所以正确答案为选项 B。

40. [答案]B

[解析]这片文章令人信服是因为每提出一个观点都会有相应的例子来支撑,所以正确的选项为 B。

Task 2

41. [答案]C

[解析]根据文中的第二句"Some pessimists are deeply worried about the serious problems caused by the huge populations" 得知正确答案为选项 C。

42. [答案]B

[解析]文中提到悲观者的观点时,举例说"尤其是在发展中国家的大城市更为拥挤",四个选项中只有 B 选项属于发展中国家。所以正确答案为选项 B。

43. [答案]C

[解析]controversial 的意思是"有争议的",只有 C 选项意思较为接近。

44. [答案]A

[解析]"人类因素是决定大城市将来的关键因素"暗示出良好的管理很关键,符合题

意的只有选项 A。

45. ［答案］D

［解析］文中提到 London、New York，是因为一些乐观主义者提出了在一些人口多的大城市完全可以拥有有序和安全的环境。所以正确答案为 D 选项。

Task 3

46. ［答案］different situations

［解析］根据文中第二句"By intelligence we mean a way of living and behaving, especially in a new or upsetting situation. "

47. ［答案］concentrate on

［解析］根据文中 "For instance, when in a new situation, an intelligent person thinks about the situation, not about himself or what might happen to him"得出结论。

48. ［答案］how he acts

［解析］根据文中"If we want to test intelligence, we need to find out how a person acts instead of how much he knows what to do"得出答案。

49. ［答案］learn from his mistakes

［解析］根据文中"And if he cannot make things work out right, he doesn't feel ashamed that he failed; he just tries to learn from his mistakes"得出答案。

50. ［答案］fits into it

［解析］根据文中"An intelligent person, even if he is very young, has a special outlook on life, and how he fits into it"得出结论。

Task4

51. (H)(O)   52. (I)(Q)   53. (S)(P)   54. (M)(L)   55. (R)(F)

A——广告
B——顾问
C——广告牌
D——海报
E——广告活动
F——广告稿
G——广告公司
H——广告艺术
I——广告大战
J——广告专栏
K——广告媒体
L——活页传单广告
M——广告文化
N——广告公司关系
O——保健品广告
P——办公用品广告

Q——日用品广告

R——公益广告

S——广告书刊

T——工业设备和商业服务广告

Task5

56. [答案]The advantages of reading newspapers.

[解析]本题考查学生综合理解能力。通读全文,根据 a newspaper isn't under such strict limits and has other advantages 判断答案为 the advantages of reading newspapers。

57. [答案]They are very important.

[解析]从文章第一段可以找到答案。

58. [答案]Because the time (for the reports) is set.

[解析]从文章第一段最后一句话可以找到答案。

59. [答案]In public libraries.

[解析]从文章第二段第二句话后半句可以找到答案。

60. [答案]Because people have different needs.

[解析]从文章第二段最后一句话。

Part Ⅳ　Translation—English into Chinese

61. [答案]B

[解析]本句中最关键的一个词是 tired,其意思不是“劳累,疲倦”,而是“对……厌烦”。

62. [答案]D

[解析]本句最重要的是把两句话的因果关系搞清楚,D 选项因果关系最明确,所以最佳答案为 D。

63. [答案]A

[解析]apologize 翻译为“道歉”,只有 A 和 D 选项对这个词翻译正确。而 D 选项意思虽然对,但是语言不通顺,所以最佳答案是 A 选项。

64. [答案]B

[解析]本题的关键是对 as far as … is concerned 的理解,翻译为“对于……来说”。

65. [译文]中国拥有近 2 亿劳动妇女,占其人口总数的六分之一。她们有权参加社会生产,因此在社会上和家庭中享有经济独立和平等地位。

Part Ⅴ　Writing

参考答案:

May 10,2008

Dear Sir or Madam,

My name is Zhang Hua. I am 22 years old. I graduated from North Beijing Vocational Col-

77

lege. My major is Tourism Management. In college, all of my subjects are excellent and I have got the Tourist Certificate. I really like to be a tourist in your company and please give me a chance.

Sincerely Yours,
Zhang Hua

Test 6

Part I Listening Comprehension （15 minutes）

Directions: *This part is to test your listening ability. It consists of 3 sections.*

Section A

Directions: *This section is to test your ability to give proper answers to questions. The question will be spoken two times. When you hear a question, you should decide on the correct answer from the 4 choices.*

1. A. It lasted two hours.   B. It was very interesting.
     C. Yes, I am very glad.   D. No problem!

2. A. Very well. And you?   B. Thanks for everything.
     C. I'm going to see the doctor.   D. Much better. Thank you.

3. A. Sorry, I am in a hurry.   B. How could I possibly know?
     C. Ask others, will you please?   D. Sorry, I'm also a stranger here.

4. A. Sure, I will do it.   B. Why? I wouldn't.
     C. No, with pleasure.   D. Yes, many thanks.

5. A. Me too, bye-bye.   B. Surely I feel happy.
     C. I enjoy talking with you, too.   D. See you next time.

Section B

Directions: *This section is to test your ability to understand short dialogues. Both the dialogue and the question will be spoken two times. When you hear a question, you should decide on the correct answer.*

6. A. His son.
   B. His daughter.
   C. His wife.
   D. Himself.

7. A. Only blue ones fit.
   B. He likes blue than any other color.
   C. They are cheaper.
   D. They are of better quality than other shoes.

8. A. Because they are paid in cash.
   B. Because they are high-grade goods.

C. Because they are samples.

D. Because they are goods on sale.

9. A. Birthday party.   B. Graduation party.

   C. Wedding ceremony.   D. New Year party.

10. A. Mother.   B. Daughter.

   C. Father.   D. Friends.

Section C

Directions: *In this section you will hear a recorded short passage. The passage is printed on the test paper, but with some words or phrases missing. The passage will be read three times. You are required to put the missing words or phrases on the blanks.*

Manners can be quite different in different countries. In China when people _____11_____, they often ask each other "Where are you going?" or "Have you had your meal?" But in England the _____12_____ is usually about the weather. English people do not ask others about their ages and never ask how much money they _____13_____. It is rude to ask "How old are you?", especially to a woman. When someone tells you "Your English is good", you are expected to say "Thank you." If your _____14_____ is "Oh, no, my English is poor" or "Not at all", you will make the speaker _____15_____ very awkward. Try to remember the proverb: When in Rome, do as the Romans do.

Part II Vocabulary and Structure   (15 minutes)

Directions: *This part is to test your ability to use words and phrases correctly to construct meaningful and grammatically correct sentences.*

Section A

Directions: *There are 10 incomplete statements here. You are required to complete each statement by choosing the appropriate answer from the 4 choices.*

16. I really appreciate _____ to help me, but I am sure that I can manage by myself.

   A. your offering   B. you to offer

   C. that you offer   D. that you are offering

17. I'd almost given up hope of finding a house I liked, and then suddenly this one _____.

   A. turned up   B. turned out

   C. turned on   D. turned over

18. He ordered that the books _____ at once.

   A. would be sent   B. would send

   C. be sent   D. send

19. I wouldn't doubt _____ she would want to help us.

   A. whether   B. that

C. since   D. as

20. It was so deep in the night. All was quiet _____ an occasional baby cry in the neighboring building.
     A. except for   B. except
     C. but   D. beside

21. When he was elected director of the factory, he found himself _____ a serious shortage of funds.
     A. face   B. faced
     C. faced with   D. facing with

22. The book is _____ more interesting than the one I recommended to you.
     A. rather   B. very
     C. much   D. so

23. As Edison grew _____, he never lost his interest in science.
     A. elder   B. the elder
     C. older   D. the oldest

24. It's no use _____ with him. You might as well argue with a stone wall.
     A. arguing   B. in arguing
     C. of arguing   D. to argue

25. I don't know if he is _____ to come and join us.
     A. possibly   B. likely
     C. probably   D. maybe

Section B

Directions: *There are also 10 incomplete statements here. You should fill in each blank with the proper form of the word given in the brackets.*

26. The room wants _____ (clean) before National Day.

27. She asked the tailor to _____ (short) her trousers.

28. Do not judge a man by his _____ (appear)

29. _____ (luck), she survived the air crash.

30. We were all surprised at Mary's rare _____ (able) to imitate other people.

31. If you intend _____ (visit) the National Garden, please contact me soon.

32. John went to town yesterday and had his computer _____ (repair) there.

33. He has been working very hard and his schoolwork has shown much _____ (improve) since last term.

34. We've almost run out of gas, so we'd better _____ (stop) at the next gas station to fill up.

35. _____ (walk) along Fifth Avenue for a while, they decided to have dinner at Rockfeller Centre.

Part III Reading Comprehension (40 minutes)

Task 1

Directions: *After reading the following passage, you will find 5 questions or unfinished state-ments. You should make the correct choices.*

American researchers say they have found the strongest connection between *ozone*(臭氧) pollution and damage to health. Their findings show that short-term increases in ozone lead to higher death rates in cities.

Ozone is form of oxygen. The gas is produced naturally in the upper atmosphere to protect the earth against radiation from the sun. But human activities can also create ozone in the lower atmosphere. Gasses from cars and industry react with sunlight to form this ozone. Levels usually increase in the warmer months. Ozone is the main chemical in <u>smog</u>, the air pollution that is a combination of fog and smoke.

Ozone has been connected with heart and lung problems especially, and with higher rates of hospital cases. Researchers from Yale University and Johns Hopkins University did the study. Michelle Bell of Yale was the lead researcher. The Journal of the American Medical Association published the results. The researchers collected information on 95 American cities. These contain about 40 percent of the national population. The study compared death rates to ozone levels between 1987 and 2000. The research suggests that even a small increase in ozone, 10 parts per thousand million, can lead to higher death rates the following week. The study found that the average daily number of deaths rose point-six percent. And deaths among older people rose point-seven percent.

The study is one of the largest ever done of ozone and death rates. The researchers note that ozone is widespread in the United States and many other countries. The United States Environmental Protection Agency is re-examining its air pollution rules. The limit at present for ozone is 80 parts per thousand million for an eight-hour period. Limits were higher in the past. But the researchers say they found an increase in deaths even below the present levels.

36. The passage mainly tells us _____.

    A. death rates are connected with ozone levels

    B. ozone is made up of two parts

    C. lung cancers are connected with ozone levels

    D. the environment goes worse and worse in American

37. The underlined word "smog" (in Paragraph 2) mean "_____".

    A. a kind of brown smoke

    B. the main chemical in ozone

    C. smoke caused by air pollution

    D. brown unhealthy air caused by smoke from cars or factories and fog

38. According to the results of the study from Yale University and Johns Hopkins University, we

know that _____ .

A. 95 American cities contain 40% of the national population

B. children are easy to suffer from an increase in ozone

C. a small increase in ozone can cause higher death rates

D. the study placed the time between 1987 and 2000

39. According to the passage, we can infer that _____ .

A. the present ozone level in America is safe to people

B. there is no direct connection between ozone and death rates

C. the study of ozone and death rates has been done several times

D. America has a worse problem with ozone than other countries

40. Which is not true according to the passage? _____

A. American researchers' findings show that short-term increases in ozone lead to higher death rates in cities.

B. Ozone is not a form of oxygen.

C. Ozone has been connected with heart and lung problems.

D. Researchers say they found an increase in deaths even below the present levels.

Task 2

Directions: *After reading you should make the correct choices.*

She is a role model for thousands of children and teens in America. And she has proved herself to be one of the most successful figure skaters in the world. Chinese-American 21-year-old Michelle Kuan has achieved more than many people even dream of: she is a three-time US national champion, a two-time world champion, and won the 1998 Winter Olympics silver medal. And at the young age of 17, she published her autobiography(自传) *Heart of a Champion*. Yet this skating angel experienced failure at the Grand Prix· held in Ontario, Canada, earlier this month.

She missed her chance for success by failing, lost to her longtime rival(对手), Russian Irina Slutskaya. She may have lost the gold medal on that occasion, but one thing she has never lost is her confidence. "It was really just a rehearsal for the coming Winter Olympic Games. That's the stage I am setting for," Kwan said. "Knowing I have a challenger who is really good pushes me a little further and hopefully to my full potential(潜力). I want to be the best I can be."

Born in California, Michelle Kean began figure skating at the age of five. She has grown from a kid skater to an artistic skater, but her decision to be the best has never changed. "Since I was a little girl, skating has always made me feel like I am flying," Kwan said. "I love to skate and skating is in my heart, not my head." Kwan practices and works very hard to improve. She stands out for her artistry—the way she puts all the elements together to create her own style. She is able to make the story of the music come alive with emotion and meaning through her movements and expressions. "I want to be a legend(传奇人物)", she said. For years she has believed in the motto: Work hard, be yourself and have fun. She is sure this is the key to success.

Indeed, Kwan is herself. She is a successful star and she is also an ordinary girl. She is a serious bargain shopper, keeps a diary, has posters of Hollywood star Brad Pitt and observes one *superstition*(迷信)—she never takes off the gold dragon necklace her grandmother gave her for luck.

41. In Michelle Kwan's opinion, she has succeeded because _____.

    A. she has grown from a kid skater to an artistic skater.

    B. she has seldom lost her confidence.

    C. she was born with such a good gift as has brought her success

    D. she has stuck to her motto: work hard, be herself and have fun

42. The main idea of the last paragraph is that _____.

    A. Kwan is herself in her spare time

    B. Kwan's grandmother is kind to her

    C. Kwan's fond of Hollywood star Brad Pitt

    D. Kwan is a successful star but she cares about money when she is doing shopping

43. The underlined word "It" (in Paragraph 2) refers to _____.

    A. her confidence   B. her performance at the Grand Prix

    C. the Grand Prix   D. her longtime rival

44. Which of the following is Not true according to the passage? _____

    A. Kwan's figure skating has her own style.

    B. Kwan has been in figure skating for about 16 years.

    C. That Kwan has become the best figure skater known to the world.

    D. Kwan shows deep love for skating.

45. The best title for the passage might be _____.

    A. A legend   B. Michelle Kuan

    C. An ordinary girl   D. A successful pop star

Task 3

Directions: *After reading the passage, you should complete the correct answers.*

Home Healthcare Nurses

The Children's Hospital of Philadelphia and The Joseph Stokes Jr. Research Institute is proud to be an Equal Opportunity Employer.

Description

As a field RN in our expanding Home Care Department located in Philadelphia, Pennsylvania, you will be part of a progressive healthcare team that delivers nursing care to pediatric(小儿科的)patients in their homes. Perform patient assessments and family teaching. You will act as a liaison(联络人)between the patient/family and the rest of the healthcare team. Flexible schedules available.

Requirements

Two-year degree required. Three years of acute (急性的)pediatric nursing experience required. Previous home care experience a plus.

We offer competitive benefit packages: medical, vision, dental and life insurance, discounts on public transportation and employee parking, tuition assistance, continuing education classes, generous paid time off, employer contribution retirement plan and work/life benefits.

Contact Information

Company: *Children's Hospital of Philadelphia*

Contact: Jamila Kinsey RN, BSN

Phone: 215-590-3135

Fax: 215-590-2990

A Wanted Ad

Job wanted: _____46_____

Company: Children's Hospital of Philadelphia

Location of the Company: _____47_____

Education Required: two-year degree

Experienced Required: _____48_____ of acute pediatric nursing experience

Responsibilities:

1. deliver nursing care to pediatric patients in their homes

2. _____49_____

How to Contact:

Contact Person: Jamila Kinsey RN, BSN

Contact Phone Number: _____50_____

Task 4

Directions: *After reading the following list, you are required to find the items equivalent to those given in Chinese in the list below.*

A. ——intensive reading

B. ——extensive reading

C. ——check on work attendance

D. ——academic year

E. ——make-up exam

F. ——doctor

G. ——required course

H. ——examination room

I. ——syllabus

J. ——specialized course

K. ——teaching method

L. ——bachelor

M. ——postgraduate

N. ——oral examination

O. ——credit system

85

P. ——sick leave

Example：（K）教学法　　　　　（N）口试

51.（　）教学大纲	（　）研究生
52.（　）泛读	（　）必修课
53.（　）考勤	（　）专业课
54.（　）学士	（　）学年
55.（　）学分制	（　）病假

Task 5

Directions：*After reading the passage, you are required to complete the statements that follow the questions.*

CHINA—China's mainland replaced Japan as home to the world's second largest online population by the end of last year, according to a national survey released yesterday.

The mainland's online population which hit 59.1 million by the end of 2002, up nearly 30 percent from the middle of the year, is larger than Japan's latest figure of 54 million, said the China Internet Network Information Center.

The center predicted the number of net surfers in China would jump 46 percent to 86.5 million this year.

However, China still lags far behind the United States, which is home to 170 million Internet users. And China's online population is only 4.6 percent of its total population.

56. Which country has the largest online population?

_____

57. What is the online population of Japan?

_____

58. How much does China's online population take up of its total population?

_____

59. How many Internet users are there in the United States?

_____

60. What is the trend of the number of net users as predicted?

_____

Part IV　Translation—English into Chinese　（25 minutes）

Directions：*This part is to test your ability to translate English into Chinese. Each of the four sentences is followed by four choices of suggested translation. Make the best choice. Write your translation of the paragraph in the corresponding space.*

61. I wonder if I should make a reservation if I want to eat dinner here later.

　　A. 我很奇怪为什么我想如果晚点来这里用餐还需要与别人预约。

　　B. 我在想如果以后来这里用餐是否必需与别人预约？

C. 我在想如果以后来这里用餐是否必需先订位。

D. 我很奇怪为什么我想如果以后来这里用餐还需要先订位。

62. I am afraid I have little influence over her once her mind is made up on any subject.

A. 我担心一旦她改变了主意,我会受到一点影响。

B. 一旦她的头脑被任何学科所组成,我怕我会对她没影响力。

C. 一旦她能对自己的事作决定,我恐怕不能影响她了。

D. 我怕一旦她拿定主意,我就不能改变她。

63. It has been very cold lately, but it is beginning to get a bit warmer.

A. 近来天气一直很冷,但现在正开始变暖和一些。

B. 它一直都很冷酷,直到现在才开始热情起来。

C. 近来天气一直都是零下温度,但现在温度开始回升。

D. 近来天气一直都是零下温度,但现在正开始变暖和一些。

64. The scarves have a variety of designs and sell at reasonable prices.

A. 这些围巾有各种各样的设计图案,可以以合理的价格出售。

B. 这些围巾有很好的设计,所以卖了合适的价格。

C. 很多各种各样图案的围巾以合理的价格出售。

D. 围巾的花样很多,价格也很公道。

65. In some departments the coffee-break lasts a lot longer than is actually allowed. Therefore, it seems important to draw the board's attention to possible difficulties which the rapid installation of coffee-machines could bring. We need to discuss the problem with more people before taking any action.

Part V   Writing   (25 minutes)

Directions: *This part is to test your ability to do practical writing. You are required to finish the following writing according to the information.*

说明:假设你叫李红,于 2006 年 10 月 22 日将陪同代表团赴美国盐湖城访问,拟在那里逗留 4 天。请以住宿登记表的形式给 Ramada Inn 宾馆的住宿登记处发一个传真,说明你们要订四个双人房间,并于 10 月 23 日租用会议室一天。你们的付款方式为现金。

联系电话:0086-431-5689672

传真:0086-431-5689675

电子信箱的地址:lihong@ sina. com

下面是空白表格:

Reservation Form

Reservations

Ramada Inn

Salt Lake City

230 West 600 South

Salt Lake City, Utah 84101

(801)364-5200

Guest's name: _____

Check in: _____

Check out: _____

Room type and number: _____

Payment: _____

Tel. Number: _____

Fax: _____

Email address: _____

答 案 解 析

Part I   Listening Comprehension

听力原文

Section A

1. What did you think of the lecture?

2. I heard you didn't feel well. How are you now?

3. Excuse me, I am going to the city center, but I am lost.

4. Welcome to our stamp show, sir. Would you mind signing your name here?

5. Nice to have talked to you, see you.

Section B

Conversation 1

W: May I help you?

M: Yes, I'd like to buy a pair of shoes for my son. These blue ones are on sale, aren't they?

W: Yes, they are 10% off.

M: Good. I'll take them.

W: Will that be cash or charge card?

M: Cash, please. If they don't fit, I can return them, can't I?

W: No, I'm sorry. Sale items cannot be returned or exchanged.

Questions 6 to 8 are based on the conversation you have just heard.

6. For whom will the man buy the shoes?

7. For what reason does the man choose to buy the blue shoes?

8. Why can't the man return the shoes even if they don't fit?

Conversation 2

Daughter: Dad, I'm going to be 18 in two weeks, right?

Father: Yes, you are.

Daughter: May I have a birthday party?

Father: Sure you can.

Daughter: May I invite all my friends?

Father: Sure.

Daughter: Can I have my friends stay overnight?

Father: It's Ok with me, but we'll have to ask your mother.

Daughter: Thank you, Dad.

Question 9 to 10 are based on the conversation you have just heard.

9. What kind of party does the girl want to have?

10. Who has the final say in the family?

Section C

Manners can be quite different in different countries. In China when people **11 meet**, they often ask each other "Where are you going?" or "Have you had your meal?" But in England the **12 topic** is usually about the weather. English people do not ask others about their ages and never ask how much money they **13 earn**. It is rude to ask "How old are you?", especially to a woman. When someone tells you "Your English is good", you are expected to say "Thank you." If your **14 reply** is "Oh, no, my English is poor" or "Not at all", you will make the speaker **15 feel** very awkward. Try to remember the proverb: When in Rome, do as the Romans do.

答案详解

Part I Listening Comprehension

Section A

1. ［答案］B

   ［解析］"What did you think of the lecture"在此翻译成"你认为这个讲座怎么样", B 选项"It was very interesting"在此翻译为"非常有趣"。所以根据题意应选 B。

2. ［答案］D

   ［解析］"How are you"在此翻译成"（指身体）你好吗", D 选项"very well"在此翻译为"（身体）很好"。所以根据题意应选 D。

3. ［答案］D

   ［解析］"I am going to the city center, but I am lost"在此翻译成"我想去城中心，我迷路了"，这时如果知道怎么走，就应该告诉具体的路线。如果不知道，应首先表示歉意，说明理由。D 选项"I am a stranger here"的意思是我对这里不熟悉。所以根据题意应选 D。

4. ［答案］C

   ［解析］"Would you mind signing your name here"在此翻译成"在这签名你介意吗"，如

果是介意就回答"Yes,I would"不介意就回答"No,I wouldn't"。C 选项翻译成"不介意,很高兴在这签名"。所以根据题意应选 C。

5. [答案]A

[解析]"Nice to have talked to you,see you"在此翻译成"很高兴和你进行交谈,再见",A 选项意思是"我也是,再见"。所以根据题意应选 A。

Section B

6. [答案]A

[解析]"For whom will the man buy the shoes"在此翻译成"这个男子要给谁买鞋"。原文中"I'd like to buy a pair of shoes for my son"的意思是"我想给我的儿子买一双鞋"。所以根据题意应选 A。

7. [答案]C

[解析]"For what reason does the man choose to buy the blue shoes"在此翻译成"这个男子为什么选择买蓝色的鞋"。C 选项的意思是"因为打 10% 的折扣,比较便宜"。所以根据题意应该选 C。

8. [答案]D

[解析]"Why can't the man return the shoes even if they don't fit"在此翻译成"为什么即使鞋不合适,他也不能退鞋"。对话中"Sale items cannot be returned or exchanged"在此翻译成"打折的商品不退不换"。所以根据题意应该选 D。

9. [答案]A

[解析]"What kind of party does the girl want to have"在此翻译成"这个女孩要开个什么样的晚会"。对话中提到"May I have a birthday party",在此翻译成"我可以开个生日晚会吗"。所以根据题意应该选 A。

10. [答案]A

[解析]"Who has the final say in the family"在此翻译成"在家里谁说了算"。对话中爸爸说"It's Ok with me,but we'll have to ask your mother"在此翻译成"我同意但我们得问你妈妈"。可以看出妈妈在家里说了算。所以根据题意应该选 A。

Section C

11. meet   12. topic   13. earn   14. reply   15. feel

Part II   Vocabulary & Structure

Section A

16. [答案]A

[解析]appreciate 意思是"欣赏,感谢",其后需要接名词或动名词,所以 A 选项正确。

17. [答案]A

[解析]turn up 在此翻译成"出现";turn out 在此翻译成"结果是,证明是";turn on 在

此翻译成"打开";turn over 在此翻译成"翻转"。所以根据题意应该选 A。

18. ［答案］C
　　［解析］order 后接宾语从句时,宾语从句用虚拟语气"(should)＋动词原形",所以根据题意应该选 C。

19. ［答案］B
　　［解析］"doubt＋宾语从句"时,在否定句和疑问句中,doubt 后面接 that 引导的宾语从句。例如:I don't doubt that he can finish the task on time. (我相信他能按时完成任务。)在肯定句中,doubt 后面一般接 whether 或 if 引导的宾语从句。例如:I doubt whether they can swim across the river. (我怀疑他们能否游过河去。)He doubts if she will keep her word. (他不敢肯定她是否会遵守诺言。)所以正确答案为选项 B。

20. ［答案］A
　　［解析］except 在此翻译成"除了……,没有……";besides 在此翻译成"除了……还有……",but 与 except 同义;except for 在此翻译成"除了……以外",跟 except 的区别在于 except for 后面跟的词与前面提到的不是同一类别或不是同一范畴。所以正确答案为选项 A。

21. ［答案］C
　　［解析］"find oneself＋介词/现在分词/过去分词"的意思是"发现自己处于某状态;不知不觉地来到……"。be faced with 是固定短语,翻译成"面对"。所以正确答案为选项 C。

22. ［答案］C
　　［解析］very,rather,so 修饰形容词的原形,不能修饰比较级。much 可以修饰形容词的比较级。所以正确答案为 C 选项。

23. ［答案］C
　　［解析］此题考查的是形容词的比较级。old 的比较级有两种形式,older 是指年纪大、年龄大的;elder 是指辈分大的,有资格的。例:I'm two years older than she. (我比她大2岁。)My elder sister is an artist. (我年龄较大的姐姐是个艺术家)。所以正确答案为 C 选项。

24. ［答案］A
　　［解析］It is no use 后加 doing 的形式,意思是"……是没用的"。例如 It is no use crying over spilt milk. (牛奶已泼,哭也没用。)所以正确答案为 A 选项。

25. ［答案］B
　　［解析］be likely to do sth. 看来有可能做某事。所以 B 选项正确。

Section B

26. ［答案］cleaning 或 to be cleaned.
　　［解析］want 在此是"需要"的意思。当表示需要做某事时,want 后有两种形式,即 want to be done 或 want doing。

27. ［答案］shorten
　　［解析］ask sb to do sth 要某人做某事。short 是形容词,需要变成动词形式 shorten。

28. [答案]appearance

[解析]形容词性物主代词 his 修饰名词,动词 appear 在这里需要变成名词形式 appearance。

29. [答案]Luckily

[解析]副词可以放在句首修饰整句话。Luck 是形容词需要变成副词。

30. [答案]ability

[解析]be surprised at 在此的意思是"对……感到惊奇",at 是介词后接名词或代词,able 是形容词在这里需要变成名词 ability。

31. [答案]to visit

[解析]intend 后接不定式。intend to do sth 的意思是"打算做某事"。

32. [答案]repaired

[解析]have sth done 这一结构的意思是"让别人做某事"。这句话的意思是"让别人修电脑"。

33. [答案]improvement

[解析]show 后需要接名词作宾语,show much improvement 在此的意思是"表现出很大的进步"improve 是动词,在这里需要变成名词 improvement。

34. [答案]stop

[解析]had better 后加动词原形,意思是"最好做某事"。

35. [答案]Having walked

[解析]根据题意 walk 这一动作先于主句的动作发生,主句的动词用过去时态,walk 应用分词的完成式作时间状语。

Part III   Reading Comprehension

Task 1

36. [答案]A

[解析]文章第一段第一句话揭示文章的主要内容,文章主要说的是死亡率和臭氧水平的关系。可知 A 为正确答案。

37. [答案]D

[解析]第二段最后一句话 the air pollution that is a combination of fog and smoke 是对 smog 的解释。可知 D 为正确答案。

38. [答案]C

[解析]本题属细节题,从第三段的句子"The research suggests that even a small increase in ozone,10 parts per thousand million,can lead to higher death rates the following week"可知 C 选项正确。

39. [答案]C

[解析]从第四段的第一句话"The study is one of the largest ever done of ozone and death rates"可以看出,关于臭氧和死亡率关系的研究已经进行过好多次。可知 C 选项正确。

40. ［答案］B

　　［解析］从第二段的第一句话可以判断 B 是错误的。

Task 2

41. ［答案］D

　　［解析］从第三段的最后两句话"For years she has believed in the motto：Work hard，be yourself and have fun. She is sure this is the key to success"可以判断 D 选项是正确的。

42. ［答案］A

　　［解析］从最后一段所讲的是主人公在平时是什么样的。可知 A 为正确答案。

43. ［答案］B

　　［解析］it 指代的是在 the Grand Prix 的比赛中失利。可知 B 为正确答案。

44. ［答案］C

　　［解析］根据第一段的第二句话"And she has proved herself to be one of the most successful figure skaters in the world"判断出主人公是最成功的花样滑冰选手之一。可知 C 为正确答案。

45. ［答案］B

　　［解析］文章主要讲的是 Michelle Kuan。可知 B 为正确答案。

Task 3

46. home healthcare nurses　　47. Philadelphia，Pennsylvania

48. three years　　　　49. perform patient assessment　　50. 215-590-3135

Task 4

51. (I)(M)　52. (B)(G)　53. (C)(J)　54. (L)(D)　55. (O)(P)

A——精读

B——泛读

C——考勤

D——学年

E——补考

F——博士

G——必修课

H——考场

I——教学大纲

J——专业课

K——教学法

L——学士

M——研究生

N——口试

O——学分制

P——病假

Task 5

56. ［答案］The United States

[解析]文章的第一段提到中国将取代日本成为世界上第二大上网人数最多的国家。最后一段说中国仍然落在美国的后面,美国有 1 亿 7 千万网民。可以推断出美国是世界上拥有最多网民的国家。

57. [答案]54 million

[解析]依据第二段第二行提到的最新数据"日本的网民是 54 million"可知。

58. [答案]4.6%

[解析]最后一段提到了中国网民站总人口的 4.6%.

59. [答案]170 million

[解析]最后一段提到了美国有 1 亿 7 千万网民。

60. [答案]A rise

[解析]从文章中可以推断出趋势是增加的。

Part IV   Translation—English into Chinese

61. [答案]C

[解析]wonder 是"想知道"的意思,后面可以接宾语从句;make a reservation 是"订座位,订餐"。所以 C 是正确答案。

62. [答案]C

[解析]have an influence over somebody 是"对某人有影响"的意思。make up one's mind 是"决心,决定"的意思。所以 C 是正确答案。

63. [答案]A

[解析]lately 是"近来"的意思,"It is beginning to get a little warmer."是"天开始变暖"的意思。所以 A 正确。

64. [答案]A

[解析]a variety of 翻译为"各种各样的";at reasonable prices 翻译为"以合理的价格"。

65. [译文]在某些部门,休息时间比实际允许的时间延长了许多。因此,咖啡机的迅速普及极可能带来麻烦,让董事会注意到这一点似乎很重要。在我们采取行动之前我们需要与更多的人就这个问题进行讨论。

Part V   Writing

Guest's name: ___Li Hong___

Check in: ___22/10/2006___

Check out: ___25/10/2006___

Room type and number: four double rooms, one meeting-room on Oct. 23

Payment: ___in cash___

Tel. Number: ___0086-431-5689672___

Fax: ___0086-431-5689675___

Email address: ___lihong@ sina. com___

Test 7

Part I Listening Comprehension （15 minutes）

Directions: This part is to test your listening ability. It consists of 3 sections.

Section A

Directions: This section is to test your ability to give proper answers to questions. The question will be spoken two times. When you hear a question, you should decide on the correct answer from the 4 choices.

1. A. Yes, I do. But I don't like reading novels at night.

   B. I like reading novels on Sunday.

   C. No, I don't.

   D. I like watching TV in the evening.

2. A. I usually go to school at seven in the morning.

   B. I go to bed at ten every day.

   C. My mother usually goes to bed at seven in the evening.

   D. I usually get up at seven every day.

3. A. It is pink.   B. Yes, I like it.

   C. No, I like red.   D. White. But my favorite color is red.

4. A. I'm fine.   B. Don't worry.

   C. I have a bad cold.   D. Thank you.

5. A. He lives in that street.   B. Let's go.

   C. Yes, I did.   D. I'm so sorry to hear that.

Section B

Directions: This section is to test your ability to understand short dialogues. Both the dialogue and the question will be spoken two times. When you hear a question, you should decide on the correct answer.

6. A. In a fruit shop   B. In a clothing shop

   C. In a bookshop   D. In a hospital

7. A. 10：30.   B. 10：45.

   C. 10：15.   D. 10：00.

8. A. An MP4.   B. A bag.

   C. A walkman.   D. A dog.

95

9. A. A double room with bath. B. A double room without bath.

    C. A single room without bath. D. A single room with bath.

10. A. English   B. Chinese   C. French   D. Spanish

Section C

Directions: *In this section you will hear a recorded short passage. The passage is printed on the test paper, but with some words or phrases missing. The passage will be read three times. You are required to put the missing words or phrases on the blanks.*

        11   , many people like to have pets. Some buy them from the market and take them home. Pets' life is   **12**   . They eat well and have   **13**   to play with. Children like pets very much,   **14**   cats, dogs and birds. Some pets have   **15**   names like Kitty and Doggie. Do you have a pet? What do you call your pet?

Part II Vocabulary & Structure (15 minutes)

Directions: *This part is to test your ability to use words and phrases correctly to construct meaningful and grammatically correct sentences.*

Section A

Directions: *There are 10 incomplete statements here. You are required to complete each statement by choosing the appropriate answer from the 4 choices.*

16. Do you think John will call his girl friend as soon as he _____ in town?

    A. will arrive   B. arrives   C. arrived   D. had arrived

17. _____ from the top of the hill, the lake is just like a mirror.

    A. Seeing   B. Having seen   C. To see   D. Seen

18. My children are looking forward to _____ a trip to Beijing next week.

    A. make   B. be making   C. making   D. have made

19. It is important that the committee _____ about the project at once.

    A. be informed   B. will be informed   C. is informed   D. being informed

20. Something is wrong with my bike. I must have it _____.

    A. fixed   B. fix   C. to fix   D. be fixed

21. _____ is the date today?

    A. When   B. What   C. Which   D. How

22. She is flying to Shanghai _____ an important academic conference.

    A. at   B. in   C. to   D. for

23. By the end of that year Alice _____ more than a thousand foreign stamps.

    A. had collected   B. has collected

    C. had been collected   D. has been collected

24. The new coat _____ her 100 dollars.

A. took   B. cost   C. spent   D. paid

25. Encourage children to _____ some of their pocket money to buy Spring Festival presents.

A. set out   B. take off   C. put aside   D. give in

Section B

Directions: *There are also 10 incomplete statements here. You should fill in each blank with the proper form of the word given in the brackets.*

26. The roads have to be _____ (wide) so that the problems of traffic jam can be solved.

27. Mary is the _____ (bright) of the two girls.

28. The headmaster said his work was _____ (satisfy) but there was still room for improvement.

29. The teacher ordered that all the books _____ (send) at once.

30. It is high time we _____ (start) to pay attention to such mistakes.

31. Different teachers make different contributions to a student's _____ (grow)

32. _____ (fortunate), the wind dropped and the fire died down.

33. The conference was postponed because of a(n) _____ (expected) event.

34. I believe you will have trouble _____ (park) there.

35. She pretended _____ (be) asleep when her mother came into her room.

Part III Reading Comprehension (40 minutes)

Task 1

Directions: *After reading the following passage, you will find 5 questions or unfinished statements. You should make the correct choices.*

The Changjiang River is not the longest, the widest, or the most powerful river in the world. But in one sense it is the most important river, because it serves more people than any other river. In every way the Changjiang River is China's life stream.

The Changjiang River isn't just a trade river, a high way along which goods are picked up and sent. It is an agricultural river as well. A lot of irrigation(灌溉) ditches(渠) go out from it to millions of tiny garden-size farms. There men and women work endlessly with very old hand tools—planting, watering, fertilizing, weeding, harvesting, raising the family's food and raising the nation's food.

It begins somewhere high in the place north of Tibet, running down from a three-mile height. It goes for hundreds of miles, shouting loud through valleys. Only in the last 1,000 miles of its 3,900-mile journey does the Changjiang River become the sunny and cheerful river.

36. The Changjiang River is _____.

A. not only a trade river but also an agricultural river

B. just an agricultural river

C. not the widest river in the world, but it is the longest one

D. a very famous river mainly because it runs hundreds of miles

37. The starting spot of the Changjiang River may be _____.

A. somewhere in the eastern part of China

B. somewhere in the northern part of China

C. somewhere in the place north of Tibet

D. somewhere in the place north to Tibet

38. How long is the Changjiang River? _____

A. Three thousand, nine hundred miles.

B. One thousand miles.

C. Hundreds of miles.

D. Three miles.

39. The upper part of the Changjiang River _____.

A. flows through wide plains

B. rushes down from high places

C. is mild and peaceful

D. is more valuable to China than the lower part

40. From this article we have learned that _____.

A. the Changjiang River is the most powerful river in the world

B. the Changjiang area provides a lot of food for many people in China

C. two thirds of the Changjiang River is sunny and cheerful

D. the Changjiang River is mainly a trade river

Task 2

Directions: *After reading you should make the correct choices.*

Computer programmer David Jones earns £ 35,000 a year designing new computer games, yet he cannot find a bank prepared to let him have a cheque card(支票卡). Instead, he has been told to wait another two years, until he is 18.

The 16-year-old works for a small firm in Liverpool, where the problem of most young people of his age is finding a job. David's firm releases two new games for the home computer market each month.

But David's biggest headache is what to do with his money. Despite his salary, earned by inventing new programs, with bonus payments and profit-sharing, he cannot drive a car, buy a house, or obtain credit cards.

He lives with his parents in Liverpool. His company has to pay £ 150 a month in taxi fares to get him the five miles to work and back every day because David cannot drive.

David got his job with the Liverpool-based company four months ago, a year after leaving school and working for a time in a computer shop. "I got the job because the people who run the firm knew I had already written some programs," he said.

"I suppose £ 35,000 sounds a lot but I hope it will come to more than that this year." He spends some of his money on records and clothes, and gives his mother £ 20 a week. But most of his spare time is spent working.

"Unfortunately, computing was not part of our studies at school," he said. "But I had been studying it in books and magazines for four years in my spare time. I knew what I wanted to do and never considered staying on at school. Most people in this business are fairly young, anyway. "

David added: "I would like to earn a million and I suppose early retirement is a possibility. You never know when the market might disappear. "

41. David has a greatest problem. That is _____ .

    A. to deal with his money

    B. to invent computer games

    C. to obtain a credit card

    D. to learn to drive

42. David is different from other young people of his age because _____ .

    A. he does not go out much

    B. he is unemployed

    C. he earns an extremely high salary

    D. he lives at home with his parents

43. Why was he employed by the firm? _____

    A. Because he had worked in a computer shop.

    B. Because he had learned to use computers at school.

    C. Because he had worked very hard.

    D. Because he had written some computer programs.

44. He left school because _____

    A. it's no use staying at school for his work with computers.

    B. he did not like school.

    C. he was afraid of getting too old to start computing.

    D. he wanted to earn a lot of money.

45. David thinks he might retire early because _____ .

    A. people have to be young to write computer programs

    B. he wants to stop working when he is a millionaire

    C. he thinks his firm might go bankrupt

    D. he thinks computer games might not always sell so well

Task 3

Directions: *After reading the passage, you should complete the correct answers.*

        In the 20th decennial U. S. census, taken in 1980, the resident population in the United States numbered 226,547,346. About 188. 3 million (83. 2%) were classified as white, 26. 5 million (11. 7%) as black, 11. 7 million (5. 1%) as members of other races.

The history of the United States is really the story of various immigrants groups working together to build a unique nation. During the 1500s, French and Spanish explorers visited the New World. But the first Europeans who came to stay were mostly the English. In 1790, when the first U. S. census was taken, the white population of the 13 original states totaled slightly more than 3 million. About 75 percent of these first Americans were of British ancestry; the rest were German, Dutch, French, Swiss, and Spanish. The English gave the new nation its language, its laws and its philosophy of government.

The composition of the American population:

Census of 1980: the number of the United States is __46__.

About __47__ percent were classified as white.

The history of the United States:

__48__ were mostly the first Europeans who came to stay.

The total white population in 1790 numbered about __49__.

The language, laws, and philosophy of government of the U. S. come from __50__.

Task 4

Directions: *After reading the following list, you are required to find the items equivalent to those given in Chinese in the list below.*

A. ——Provisional Programme

B. ——Arrival of directors and staff

C. ——Arrival of guests

D. ——Anniversary folders

E. ——Cocktail

F. ——Hostess of Ceremony

G. ——Opening address

H. ——Slides presentation

I. ——Buffet supper

J. ——Toastmaster

K. ——Closing address

L. ——Registration

Example: (L)报到　　　　　　　　　　(A)暂定计划

51. ( )董事和职员到会	( )闭幕词
52. ( )庆典活动主持人	( )祝酒词
53. ( )鸡尾酒招待	( )自助晚餐
54. ( )庆典文件夹	( )放幻灯片
55. ( )来宾到会	( )开幕词

Task 5

Directions: *After reading the passage, you are required to complete the statements that follow the questions.*

This autumn term, spring term, or academic year program offers advanced students an opportunity to improve their spoken and written Chinese, and to be familiar with a range of people and organizations that are helping to shape China's relationship with the United States and the world. All students who take intermediate or advanced Chinese language may make a choice to participate in the Professional Development Program that includes guest lectures by Chinese and foreign professionals on areas such as politics, foreign affairs, economics, trade, media, art, and culture. This program is supplemented (补充) by field trips and short journeys in and around Beijing.

Housing and meals: Students live in the foreign student dormitories and take meals in the dormitory dining hall.

Requirements: Two years of college-level Chinese and one Chinese studies course; graduate students accepted.

Program Fee: 1998 Autumn Term: $6,995; 1999 Spring Term: $6,995. Fees include tuition, housing and all meals, cultural activities, local journeys and field trips, insurance, and the International Student Identity Card.

56. Who can take part in the academic year program?

    _____ students.

57. What areas will the Professional Development Program involve?

    Politics, _____, economics, trade, media, art, and culture.

58. Where will the foreign students take meals when they are in China?

    In _____.

59. Besides academic activities, what else will the foreign students do in this program?

    They will take field tips and _____ in and around Beijing.

60. How many requirements are there for one who wants to be accepted to the program?

    _____.

Part IV Translation—English into Chinese (25 minutes)

Directions: *This part is to test your ability to translate English into Chinese. Each of the four sentences is followed by four choices of suggested translation. Make the best choice. Write your translation of the paragraph in the corresponding space.*

61. The president said in the telephone that he would not attend the meeting himself, but his secretary would come instead.

    A. 院长打来电话说,他不能亲自来参加会议了,但他让秘书代替他参加。

    B. 院长在电话里说,他不能来参加会议了,但他将让秘书代他来参加。

    C. 院长用电话形式通知他的秘书参加他不愿意参加的会议。

    D. 院长通过电话说,让他的秘书代替参加他不能出席的会议。

62. It is commonly believed that the more complicated animals developed from the simpler ones.

    A. 人们认为,复杂的动物是由比较简单的动物发展而来的。

B. 人们普遍认为,较高级的动物是由比较低级的动物进化而来的。

C. 人们一般认为,动物都是从简单到复杂转变而来的。

D. 它被相信,动物的变化都是从麻烦到简单。

63. A busy shopping center is usually also a good location for a restaurant.

   A. 忙碌的购物中心常常也是饭店好生意的来源。

   B. 忙碌的购物中心经常也有一家地理位置好的饭店。

   C. 繁忙的购物中心常常也是就餐的好地方。

   D. 繁忙的购物中心通常也是建造饭店的好地方。

64. Jefferson obtained the first-hand information needed in his research work through making on-the-spot observation.

   A. 杰弗逊通过现场勘查,获得了研究工作所需要的第一手资料。

   B. 杰弗逊借助于实地观察,获得了科研工作所需要的第一手资料。

   C. 杰弗逊通过对某一点的观察得到需要的第一手资料。

   D. 杰弗逊用实践观察获得了科研工作的第一手资料。

65. As evidence that the Earth's atmosphere is warming continues to accumulate, scientists are making slow progress toward an answer to the big question raised by the evidence: How much of the warming is due to human activity and how much to natural causes?

Part Ⅴ   Writing   (25 minutes)

Directions: *This part is to test your ability to do practical writing. You are required to finish the following writing according to the information.*

说明:黄东,男,未婚,身体健康,1966 年 5 月 16 日出生。1981 年 9 月至 1984 年 7 月,在济南第十六中学学习。1984 年 9 月至 1988 年 7 月在中国人民大学获得商业管理学士学位。英语水平:阅读中级,口语流利。1998 年 8 月至 2000 年 8 月,在济南制药厂行政部门任主管,负责管理员工二十名,制定、掌管部门各方面运作并拟定工作日程。2000 年至今,在济南市外商投资企业行政与服务中心任副主管,负责指导投资与贸易活动,引用投资计划和潜在合伙伙伴、安排学习、考察并组织商务会谈活动。欲求一份青岛合资企业的总经理工作。如有要求可提供证明。

地址:山东济南黄河路 54 号

电话:0531-4567891

_____

_____

_____

Tele：0531-4567891

Objective

To work as a general manager in a joint venture enterprise in Qingdao.

_____

10/2000-present Vice Director of Jinan Administration and Service Center for Enterprises with Foreign Investment. Responsible for providing guidance for investment and trading activities, introducing investment projects and potential partners, arranging study and inspection tours, and organizing business talks.

8/1998-8/2000 Supervisor of Administrative Department of Jinan Pharmaceutical General Factory. Responsibilities included supervision of twenty staff members, planning and directing all phases of departmental operations, and preparing work schedules.

Education

_____Bachelor of Business Administration at People's University of China (Beijing)

_____Jinan No. 16 High School

Foreign Language

English: Intermediate in reading and _____

Personal Data

_____: May 16,1966

Sex: _____

_____: Excellent

Marital Status: _____

References

_____

答 案 解 析

Part I Listening Comprehension

听力原文

Section A

1. Do you like reading novels at night?

2. When do you usually go to school in the morning?

3. What color are your new trousers?

4. You look so pale. What's the matter with you?

5. His grandfather passed away yesterday, don't you know?

Section B

6. M: What can I do for you?

W: I'd like to buy a shirt.

Q: Where did the conversation take place?

7. M: Hurry, Mary. We will be late for the train.

   W: The train starts at 11:05. We still have 50 minutes to get there.

   Q: What's the time now?

8. M: I have an MP4, a walkman, and a new bag. Which will you choose for a birthday gift?

   W: May I have a dog as my gift?

   Q: What does the girl want?

9. W: Good morning. China Hotel Reception. Can I help you?

   M: Good morning. My name is Tom Smith. I'd like to book a double room without bath for three days.

   Q: What kind of room does Tom Smith want?

10. M: Can you speak any foreign languages?

    W: Yes, I can speak Chinese, French, and Spanish.

    Q: What kind of language did not mention in the dialogue?

Section C

__11 Nowadays__, many people like to have pets. Some buy them from the market and take them home. Pets' life is __12 comfortable__. They eat well and have __13 toys__ to play with. Children like pets very much, __14 especially__ cats, dogs and birds. Some pets have __15 sweet__ names like Kitty and Doggie. Do you have a pet? What do you call your pet?

答案详解

Part I   Listening Comprehension

Section A

1. [答案]C

   [解析]这是一般疑问句,所以首先以 yes、no 来回答,故排除 B、D。选项 A 后面的 don't 和前面的 yes 互相矛盾。所以选 C。

2. [答案]A

   [解析]when 是用来问时间的,根据 go to school 这一关键词可判断答案 A 正确。

3. [答案]D

   [解析]用 what 来提问,不用 yes、no 来回答,故排除 B、C。关键词 trousers 为复数,所以排除 A。

4. [答案]C

   [解析]问题是"你看起来脸色不好。你怎么了"。I'm fine 翻译为"我很好";don't worry 翻译为"别担心";I have a bad cold 翻译为"我得了重感冒";thank you 翻译为"谢谢"。所以应选 C。

5. [答案]D

   [解析]问题是"他祖父去世了,你不知道吗"。选项 D"听到这事,我很难过"这是一种英语口语习惯表达,听到别人不幸的事情要表示同情和难过。

Section B

6. [答案]B

[解析]问题是"对话发生在哪儿"选项 A 翻译为"水果店";选项 B 翻译为"服装店";选项 C 翻译为"书店";选项 D 翻译为"在医院"。从听力材料中我们知道女士要买一件衬衣,所以应该在衣服店。答案 B。

7. [答案]C

[解析]问题是"现在几点"。火车开的时间是 11:05,我们还有 50 分钟到那儿,所以现在是 10:15。选项 C 为正确答案。

8. [答案]D

[解析]问题是"女孩想要什么",听力材料中说"一只狗"。所以选 D。

9. [答案]B

[解析]对话中说道 double room,先排除选项 C 和 D。因为选项 B "a double room without bath"和对话中的内容"I'd like to book a double room without bath"相一致,所以选 B。

10. [答案]A

[解析]对话中说"我能说中文、法语和西班牙语",问题是"哪种语言选项中没有提到"。选项 A 翻译为"英语"符合问题,所以选 A。

Section C

11. Nowadays   12. comfortable   13. toys   14. especially   15. sweet

Part II   Vocabulary & Structure

Section A

16. [答案]B

[解析]在 as soon as 引导的时间状语从句中,主句用一般将来时,从句用一般现在时表示将来。所以选 B。

17. [答案]D

[解析]逻辑主语 the lake 与动词 see 是被动关系,所以用过去分词。

18. [答案]C

[解析]look forward to 中 to 是介词,后边跟动名词。

19. [答案]A

[解析]"It is important…"结构要求从句用虚拟语气,即"should + 动词原形"的结构,should 可以省略。根据句意 committee 与 inform 之间是被动关系,所以用 should be informed。

20. [答案]A

[解析]句中 it 代替 my bike,my bike 和 fix(修理)之间是被动关系,用过去分词。也

可理解为使役动词的用法,即 have something done 使某事被做。所以选 A。

21. [答案]B

[解析]本题翻译为"今天几号"。属固定句型用法。

22. [答案]D

[解析]for 介词,表示目的。但在中文翻译时可以翻译成动词用法"参加"。

23. [答案]A

[解析]"by the end of..."状语要求动词用完成时态。that year 表示过去,所以用过去完成时态。

24. [答案]B

[解析]take 句型:It + takes/took + someone + some time + to do something;cost 应该是"物"作主语,句型是:Something cost somebody some money;spend 句型:someone spend some money + on something;someone spend some time + doing;pay 句型:to pay someone money;to pay money for something.

25. [答案]C

[解析]set out 翻译为"出发,动身;开始做某事";take off 翻译为"脱下,起飞";put aside 翻译为"储存";give in 翻译为"屈服。"根据句意选择 C。

Section B

26. [答案]widened

[解析]句子里"路"作主语,与 wide 之间是被动关系,所以应填入动词的过去分词,而 wide 的动词形式是 widen,过去分词形式是 widened。

27. [答案]brighter

[解析]两者作比较,用比较级形式 brighter。

28. [答案]satisfying

[解析]当分词作表语时,现在分词说明事物;过去分词说明人。题中工作作主语,所以用现在分词形式。

29. [答案]be sent

[解析]order 的宾语从句要求用虚拟语气"should + 动词原形",should 可以省略。all the book 与 send 之间是被动关系,所以用被动语态。

30. [答案]started

[解析]"It is high time..."从句中要求用过去式。虚拟语气中的特殊句式。

31. [答案]growth

[解析]名词性物主代词后用名词形式。

32. [答案]Fortunately

[解析]副词作状语修饰全句。

33. [答案]unexpected

[解析]分词作定语时,过去分词表示被动、已经做过的事;现在分词表示主动、正在做的事。本句谓语用的是过去时,所以用过去分词作定语。根据意思要求用否定形式。

34. [答案]parking

[解析]本题考核句子结构"have trouble（in）doing"翻译为"做某事有麻烦"。介词 in 往往省略，所以用 parking。

35. ［答案］to be

[解析]本题考查词汇用法。pretend 后面要求跟不定式，asleep 是形容词，所以用 to be。

Part III Reading Comprehension

Task 1

36. ［答案］A

[解析]第二段中提出"The Changjiang River isn't just a trade river...","It is an agricultural river..."从中可知答案应该选 A。

37. ［答案］C

[解析]从最后一段中"It begins somewhere high in the place north of Tibet..."（它起源于西藏北部高原。）可得知答案。

38. ［答案］A

[解析]从最后一段中可以知道长江长度是 3,900 英里。

39. ［答案］B

[解析]从最后一段可以得出答案。

40. ［答案］B

[解析]从第一段最后一句"长江是中国的生命河"可以得出答案。

Task 2

41. ［答案］A

[解析]从第三段第一句话"令他最头疼的问题是如何处理他的钱"可得出答案。

42. ［答案］C

[解析]从第一段第一句话"计算机程序员大卫·琼斯设计新程序，每年可以挣 35000 英镑"；第二段第一句话"这个 16 岁的青年人在利物浦的一家小公司工作，在那里，许多跟他同龄的年轻人很难找到一个合适的工作。可得出答案。

43. ［答案］D

[解析]从第五段最后一句"我获得这个工作是因为经营这家公司的人看过我设计的程序"可得出答案。

44. ［答案］A

[解析]从倒数第二段第一句"不幸的是，学校里不学习计算机"；倒数第二句"我知道自己要做什么（前文提到从事电脑工作），因此离开了学校"可得出答案。

45. ［答案］D

[解析]从最后一段"我可能会先挣 100 万，然后早点退休。你不知道什么时候这个市场（指计算机程序设计）会消失"可得出答案。

Task 3

46. ［答案］226,547,346

[解析]从第一段第一句"20 世纪的美国人口(根据 1980 年的人口普查)数量是 226,547,346"可得出答案。

47. [答案]83.2

[解析]从第一段第二句"大约 188,300,000 人(占 83.2%)为白人"可得出答案。题目括号后已经有 percent(百分之……)一词,因此不能填人口数量。

48. [答案]The English

[解析]从第二段第三句"但是最先来美国定居的很可能是英国人"可得出答案。

49. [答案]3 million/3,000,000

[解析]从第二段第四句"1790 年,美国做了第一次人口普查,整个美国 13 个州中白人人口略微高于三百万"可得出答案。

50. [答案]The English

[解析]从最后一句"英国人给这个新国家带来了语言、法律和统治体系"可得出答案。

Task 4

51. (B)(K)   52. (F)(J)   53. (E)(I)   54. (D)(H)   55. (C)(G)

A——暂定计划

B——董事和职员到会

C——来宾到会

D——庆典文件夹

E——鸡尾酒招待

F——庆典活动主持人

G——开幕词

H——放幻灯片

I——自助晚餐

J——祝酒词

K——闭幕词

L——报到

Task 5

56. [答案]The advanced

[解析]从第一段第一句"学术年(包括春季班和秋季班)给高级水平的学生提供了提高汉语说和写的锻炼机会"可得出答案。

57. [答案]foreign affairs

[解析]从第一段第二句"在本次的专业发展项目中,高级汉语学习的学生都可以选择参加中外专家的讲座,讲座涉及以下领域:政治、外事、经济、贸易、媒体、艺术以及文化"可得出答案。

58. [答案]the dormitory dining hall

[解析]从第二段"学生们住在留学生公寓,在学生食堂吃饭"可得出答案。

59. [答案]short journeys

[解析]从第一段最后一句"本项目还包括实地考察旅行和北京及周边地区的短途旅

行"可得出答案。

60. [答案]2（requirements）

[解析]从倒数第二段得知提出了两个要求。

Part IV Translation—English into Chinese

61. [答案]A

[解析]C的翻译意思根本不对；B和D基本意思能表达出来，但是很别扭。A最符合汉语习惯。平时应该注意带有instead的句子的翻译。

62. [答案]B

[解析]It is believed...通常被翻译为"人们认为…"

63. [答案]D

[解析]主要是对location这个词的理解，它在这儿是"地址"的意思，the location for a restaurant翻译为"建造饭店"。

64. [答案]A

[解析]on-the-spot翻译为"现场的"。

65. [译文]地球大气层正在转暖，这种迹象日益明显，这向人们提出了一个重大问题，科学家们对这一问题也逐步给出了答案即：地球变暖在多大程度上应归咎于人类的活动，又在多大程度上是自然原因引起的？

Part V Writing

Huang Dong

Huanghe Street, Jinan

Shandong Province, China

Tele：0531-4567891

Objective

To work as a general manager in a joint venture enterprise in Qingdao.

Experience

10/2000-present Vice Director of Jinan Administration and Service Center for Enterprises with Foreign Investment. Responsible for Providing guidance for investment and trading activities, introducing investment projects and potential partners, arranging study and inspection tours, and organizing business talks.

8/1998-8/2000 Supervisor of Administrative Department of Jinan Pharmaceutical General Factory. Responsibilities included supervision of twenty staff members, planning and directing all phases of departmental operations, and preparing work schedules.

Education

9/1984-7/1988 Bachelor of Business Administration at People's University of China (Beijing)

9/1981-7/1984 Jinan No. 16 High School

Foreign Language

English: Intermediate in reading and fluent in speaking

Personal Data

Date of birth/ Born: May 16,1966

Sex: Male

Health: Excellent

Marital Status: Single

References

References are available upon request

Test 8

（2006 年 12 月高等学校英语应用能力考试真题试卷）

Part I Listening Comprehension （15 minutes）

Directions：*This part is to test your listening ability. It consists of 3 sections.*

Section A

Directions：*This section is to test your ability to give proper answers to questions. There are 5 recorded questions in it. After each question, there is a pause. The questions will be spoken two times. When you hear a question, you should decide on the correct answer from the 4 choices marked A), B), C) and D) given in your test paper. Then you should mark the corresponding letter on the Answer Sheet with a single line through the centre.*

Example：*You will hear*：

You will read：A) I'm not sure.

B) You're right.

C) Yes, certainly.

D) That's interesting.

From the question we learn that the speaker is asking the listener to leave a message. Therefore, **C**）**Yes, certainly** *is the correct answer. You should mark C*）*on the Answer Sheet. Now the test will begin.*

1. A. No, you can't.   B. How are you?
   C. Where is she?   D. Who is calling, please?
2. A. That's all right.   B. It's possible.
   C. No way.   D. My pleasure.
3. A. Yes, of course.   B. You are welcome.
   C. Is it true?   D. No, thanks.
4. A. Well, how?   B. Well, who?
   C. Yes, When?   D. Yes, What?
5. A. Quiet well.   B. Not likely.
   C. I'm afraid I can't.   D. Never mind.

Section B

Directions: *This section is to test your ability to understand short dialogues. There are 5 recorded dialogues in it. After each dialogue, there is a recorded question. Both The dialogues and questions will be spoken two times. When you hear a question, you should decide on the correct answer from the 4 choices marked A), B), C) and D) given in your test paper. Then you should mark the corresponding letter on the Answer Sheet with a single line through the centre.*

6. A. Children's food.   B. Holiday food.
   C. Chinese food.   D. Western food.

7. A. In a bookstore.   B. In a theater.
   C. At a bank.   D. At the customs.

8. A. The woman is calling Jack.   B. There is a visitor at the door.
   C. The door is open.   D. The telephone is ringing.

9. A. To finish her work.   B. To attend a meeting.
   C. To meet somebody.   D. To get an important paper.

10. A. To look after the man.   B. To have a check-up.
    C. To visit a patient.   D. To get some medicine.

Section C

Directions: *In this section you will hear a recorded short passage. The passage is printed in the test paper, but with some words or phrases missing. The passage will be read three times. During the second reading, you are required to put the missing words or phrases that you hear on the Answer Sheet in order of the numbered blanks. The third reading is for you to check your writing. Now the passage will begin.*

Scientists have discovered that tea is good for us. It tastes good and it is refreshing. In recent _____11_____ studies, tea has been found to help prevent heart attacks and cancer.

One study suggests that both black and green tea help _____12_____ the heart. In the study, tea drinkers had a 44 percent _____13_____ death rate after heart attacks than non-drinkers. Other studies have shown that tea, like fruit and vegetables, helps fight against chemicals that may __ _____14_____ the development of certain cancers.

Many people really like tea. Next to plain water, it's the world's most _____15_____ drink.

Part II   Vocabulary & Structure   (15 minutes)

Directions: *This part is to test your ability to use words and phrases correctly to construct meaningful and grammatically correct sentences. It consists of 2 sections.*

Section A

Directions: *There are 10 incomplete statements here. You are required to complete each statement by choosing the appropriate answer from the 4 choices marked A), B), C) and D). You should mark the corresponding letter on the Answer Sheet with a single line through the centre.*

16. It is the general manager who makes the _____ decisions in business.
    A. beginning
    B. finishing
    C. first
    D. final

17. Never _____ such a good boss before I came to this company.
    A. do I meet
    B. had I meet
    C. I met
    D. I had met

18. If the medicine should _____ call this number immediately.
    A. break down
    B. set out
    C. put on
    D. go up

19. The manager showed the new employee _____ to find the supplies.
    A. what
    B. where
    C. that
    D. which

20. Look at the clock! It's time _____ work.
    A. we started
    B. we'll start
    C. we're starting
    D. we have started

21. The sales department was required to _____ a plan in three weeks.
    A. turn up
    B. get up
    C. come up with
    D. put up with

22. Price is not the only thing customers consider before _____ what to buy.
    A. deciding
    B. decided
    C. to decide
    D. having decided

23. All the traveling _____ are paid by the company if you travel on business.
    A. charges
    B. money
    C. prices
    D. expenses

24. Sorry, we can't _____ you the job because you don't have any work experience.
    A. make
    B. send
    C. offer
    D. prepare

25. This article is well written because special attention _____ to the choice of words and style of writing.
    A. had been paid
    B. has been paid
    C. will be paid
    D. will have been paid

Section B

Directions: *There are also 10 incomplete statements here. You should fill in each blank with the*

113

proper form of the word given in the brackets. Write the word or words in the corresponding space on the Answer Sheet.

26. It is a fact that traditional meals are (healthy) _____ than fast food.

27. Nurses should treat the sick and wounded with great (kind) _____.

28. All visitors to the lab (expect) _____ to take off their shoes before they enter.

29. (personal) _____, I think he is a nice partner, though you may not agree.

30. They talked to him for hours, (try) _____ to persuade him to change his mind.

31. His effort to improve the sales of this product have been very (help) _____.

32. When we arrived, there was a smell of cooking (come) _____ from the kitchen.

33. We have to find new ways to (short) _____ the process of production.

34. By this time next year, my family (live) _____ in this small town for 20 years.

35. Jane, as well as some of her classmates, (work) _____ in the Quality Control Department now.

Part III   Reading Comprehension   (40 minutes)

Directions: *This part is to test your reading ability. There are 5 tasks for you to fulfill. You should read the reading materials carefully and do the tasks as you are instructed.*

Task 1

Directions: *After reading the following passage, you will find 5 questions or unfinished statements, numbered 36 through 40. For each question or statement there are 4 choices marked A), B), C), or D). You should make the correct choice and mark the corresponding letter on the Answer Sheet with a single line through the centre.*

People who work night shifts are constantly fighting against an "internal clock" in their bodies. Quite often the clock tells them to sleep when their job requires them to remains fully awake. It's no wonder that more accidents happen during night shifts than at any other time. Light therapy with a bright light box can help night-shift workers adjust their internal clock. However, many doctors recommend careful planning to help improve sleep patterns. For example, night-shift workers often find it difficult to sleep in the morning when they got off work because the body's natural rhythm fights back, no matter how tired they are. Some experts recommend that night-shift workers schedule two smaller sleep periods—one in the morning after work, and another longer one in the afternoon, closer to when the body would naturally need to sleep. It's also helpful to ask friends and family to cooperate by avoiding visits and phone calls during the times when you are sleeping.

36. Night-shift workers are those who _____.

   A. have to rely on their internal clock

   B. need to re-adjust their clock

   C. fall asleep late at night

   D. have to work at night

114

37. In order to remain fully awake at work, people working night shifts should _____.

 A. have longer sleep periods after work

 B. make the light darker than usual

 C. try to re-set their "internal clock"

 D. pay more attention to their work

38. Many doctors think it is helpful for night-shift workers _____.

 A. to sleep with a bright light on

 B. to plan sleep patterns carefully

 C. to avoid being disturbed at work

 D. to sleep for a long time after work

39. Night-shift workers often find it difficult to sleep in the morning because _____.

 A. their internal clock will not allow them to

 B. they are often disturbed by morning visits

 C. they are not trying hard enough to do so

 D. they are too tired to go to sleep well

40. According to the passage, some doctors recommend that night-shift workers should _____.

 A. have frequent visits and phone calls

 B. improve their family relationship

 C. have two smaller sleep periods

 D. rely mainly on light therapy

Task 2

Directions: *This task is the same as Task 1. The 5 questions or unfinished statements are numbered 41 through 45.*

A few ways Greyhound can make your next trip even easier

Tickets By Mail. Avoid lining up together, by purchasing your tickets in advance, and having them delivered right to your mailbox. Just call Greyhound at least ten days before your departure (1-800-231-2222).

Prepaid tickets. It's easy to purchase a ticket for a friend or friend member no matter how far away they may be. Just call or go to your nearest Greyhound terminal and ask for details on how to buy a prepaid ticket.

Ticketing Requirement. Greyhound now requires that all tickets have travel dates fixed at the time of purchase. Children under two years age travel free with an adult who has a ticket.

If your destination is to Canada or Mexico. Passengers traveling to Canada or Mexico must have the proper travel documents. U. S. , Canadian or Mexican citizens should have a birth certificate, passport or naturalization (入籍) paper. If you are not a citizen of the U. S. , Canada or Mexico, a passport is required. In certain cases a visa may be required as well. These documents will be necessary and may be checked at, or before, boarding a bus departing for Canada or Mexico.

41. From the passage, we can learn that "Greyhound" is probably the name of _____.

A. an airline   B. a hotel   C. a website   D. a bus company

42. Why should people call Greyhound for tickets in advance? _____

    A. To avoid waiting in lines at the booking office.

    B. To hand in necessary traveling documents.

    C. To get tickets from the nearest terminal.

    D. To fix the traveling destination in time.

43. What can we learn about the Greyhound tickets? _____

    A. They are not available for traveling outside the U. S.

    B. Travelers should buy their tickets in person.

    C. Babies can not travel free with their parents.

    D. They have the exact travel date on them.

44. When people are traveling to Canada or Mexico, a passport is a must for _____.

    A. American citizens   B. Japanese citizens

    C. Mexicans citizens   D. Canadians citizens

45. This passage mainly offers information about _____.

    A. how to prepare documents for traveling with Greyhound

    B. how to purchase a Greyhound ticket and travel with it

    C. how to make your trip with Greyhound interesting

    D. how to travel from the U. S. to Canada and Mexico

Task 3

Directions: *The following is a letter of complaint. After reading it, you should complete the information by filling in the blanks marked 46 through 50 in not more than 3 words in the table below.*

December 10th, 2006

Dear Sirs,

I know that your company has a reputation for quality products and fairness toward its customers. Therefore, I'm writing to ask for a replacement for a lawn mower.

I bought the mower about half a year ago at the Watching Discount Center. Watching, Nebraska. I'm enclosing a copy of a receipt for the mower.

A month later I bought the lawn mower, the engine failed, and it was repaired under warranty. So far, I have had the engine repaired four times.

Now the engine has broken down again.

I have already spent more than $300 on repairs, and I am beginning to seriously question the quality of your mowers.

I am requesting that you replace this mower with a new one.

I hope that you will live up to your reputation of the good customer service that has made your business successful.

Faithfully,

Rod Green

116

Letter of Complaint

Purpose of the letter: requesting a ___46___ for a lawn mower

Time of purchase: about ___47___ ago

Trouble with the machine: ___48___

Times of repairs so far: ___49___

Money spent on repairs: more than ___50___

Task 4

Directions: *The following is a list of terms of modern business management. After reading it, you are required to find the items equivalent to those given in Chinese in the table below. Then you should put the corresponding letters in the brackets on the Answer Sheet, numbered 51 through 55.*

A. ——employee turnover

B. ——life-long employment

C. ——role conflict

D. ——profit sharing

E. ——scientific management

F. ——comparable worth

G. ——flexible working hours

H. ——social support

I. ——survey feedback

J. ——core competence

K. ——public relations

L. ——group culture

M. ——wage and salary surveys

N. ——honesty testing

O. ——human resource planning

Example: (I) 调查反馈　　(A) 人员流动

51. (　　) 测谎　　　　　(　　) 工薪调查
52. (　　) 社会支持　　　(　　) 终身雇用制
53. (　　) 团队文化　　　(　　) 公共关系
54. (　　) 利润分享　　　(　　) 人力资源策划
55. (　　) 科学管理　　　(　　) 弹性工作时间

Task 5

Directions: the following is a letter applying for a job. *After reading it, you are requited to complete the statements that follow the questions (No. 56 through No. 60). You should write your answers in not more than 3 words on the Answer Sheet correspondingly.*

Dear Sirs,

For the past 8 years I have been a statistician in the Research Unit of Baron & Smallwood Ltd. I am now looking for a change of employment which would broaden my experience. A large and well-known organization such as yours might be able to use my services.

I am 31 years old and in excellent health. I majored in advertising at London University and I am particularly interested in work involving statistics.

Although I have had no experience in market research, I am familiar with the methods used for recording buying habits and trend. I hope that you will invite me for an interview. I could then give you further information.

I am looking forward to hearing from you soon.

Yours faithfully,

Mike Smith

56. What's Mike Smith's present job?

He's working as a _____.

57. What was Mike Smith's major at London University?

_____.

58. What kind of work does he like to do?

Working involving _____

59. In what area does he lack experience?

He has no experience in _____.

60. What's the purpose of the writer in sending this letter?

To be invited for _____.

Part IV   Translation—English to Chinese   (15 minutes)

Directions: *This part, numbered 61 through 65, is to test your ability to translate English into Chinese. Each of the four sentences (No. 61 through No. 64) is followed by four choices marked A), B), C) and D). Make the best choice and write the corresponding letter on the Composition/Translation Sheet. Write your translation of the paragraph (No. 65) in the corresponding space of the Composition/Translation Sheet.*

61. For safely, all passengers are required to review this card and follow these instructions when needed.

A. 为了安全,请各位乘客反复阅读本卡片,务必按照各项规定执行。

B. 为了保险起见,请各位乘客务必阅读本卡片,并参照相关内容认真执行。

C. 为了保险起见,要求所有乘客在需要时都能看到这张卡片及以下这些内容。

D. 为了安全,要求所有乘客仔细阅读本卡片各项内容,必要时照其执行。

62. Peter misunderstood the instructions his boss gave him and mailed the wrong documents to the supplier.

A. 彼得按照老板给他的指示把单据误寄给了供货商。

B. 彼得误解了老板对他的指示,向供货商发错了单据。

C. 彼得对老板的指示还没理解就把错误的单据交给了供货商。

D. 彼得没来得及听取老板的指示就给供货商寄去了错误的单据。

63. People now have more leisure time, which is the reason why the demand for services has increased so rapidly.

A. 如今人们有更多的时间去娱乐,从而影响了劳务资源的快速上升。

B. 如今希望有实践娱乐的人越来越多,这是因为服务质量在迅速提高了。

C. 如今人们有了更多的闲暇时间,因而对各种服务的需求增长得如此快。

D. 如今人们有了更多的空闲时间,这就是要求迅速提高服务质量的原因。

64. Passengers going to the airport by arranged buses must take the bus at the time and place as shown below.

A. 搭乘专车前往机场的旅客,务必在下列制定的时间和地点乘车。

B. 乘公共汽车去机场的旅客必须乘这路车,时间和地点安排如下。

C. 经安排搭乘汽车去机场的旅客,应按指定的时间和地点上车。

D. 机场即将为旅客安排汽车,请注意下车制指定的上车时间和地点。

65. I'm writing to confirm our telephone conversation of Thursday, the 7th, about our visit to your company. Next Monday, December 11, will be fine for us and we hope that it will suit you, too. My secretary, Miss Mary Brown, and Sales Manager, Mr. Zhang Ming, will be coming in the morning. It's unfortunate that I will not by able to go with them.

Thanks again for giving us this opportunity to visit with you.

Part V Writing （25 minutes）

Directions：*This part is to test your ability to do practical writing. You are required to complete a Visitor's Message according to the instructions given in Chinese. Remember to write it on the corresponding space of the Answer Sheet.*

假定你是假日酒店的前台工作人员 Linda。根据以下内容填写来访客人留言表。

内容:

1. 来访客人:李华,男,PKK 公司总公司助理;联系电话:65734363

2. 来访时间:12 月 20 日上午 10 点

3. 被访客人:Mr. John Smith ,住假日酒店 422 房间

4. 事由:李华来酒店与 Mr. John Smith 商谈工作,Mr. John Smith 外出。

5. 留言:李华约 Mr. John Smith 明天去 PKK 公司洽谈业务。李华明天上午9:00 驾车来酒店接他;下午安排 Mr. John Smith 参观公司新建成的一条生产线。

Words for reference：

驾车接人   to pick somebody up

生产线   assembly line

总经理助理 Assistant to General Manager

```
Holiday Inn
Visitor's Message
MR. /MS. (1) Mr. John Smith          Room No.  (2)
While you were out
Mr. /Ms.   (3)
Of    (4)              telephone (5) 65734363
☐ Telephone              ☑ Came to see you
☐ Will call again        ☐ Will come again
☐ Asked you to call back
Message :
(6)_____
_____
_____
_____
_____
Clerk  (7) Linda    Date (8)              time (9)
```

注意:请将要求填写在表格中的内容按以下顺序填入答题卡中的 Writing 部分并注明所填内容的顺序号! 即:

(1) Mr. John Smith   (2)_____   (3)_____   (4)_____   (5) 65734363
(6)_____
(7) Linda   (8)_____   (9)_____

答 案 解 析

Part Ⅰ   Listening Comprehension

听力原文

Section A

1. Can I speak to Susan?

2. I'm terribly sorry that I'm very late.

3. Thank you very much for your help.

4. Shall we meet again to discuss further?

5. How does the new product sell in the market?

Section B

6. M: I wonder if you have a special menu for children.

W: I'm sorry, but we don't have one.

Q: What kind of food does the man ask for?

7. M: What can I do for you?

W: I'd like to open a saving account here.

Q: Where does the conversation most likely take place?

8. M: Someone is knocking at the door.

W: I think it's Jack again.

Q: What can we learn from the conversation?

9. M: Why are you in such a hurry?

W: I lost an important paper in the office.

Q: Why is the woman going back to the office?

10. M: What's wrong with you?

W: Nothing wrong. I just come for a medical check-up.

Q: What does the woman want to do in the hospital?

Section C

Scientists have discovered that tea is good for us. It tastes good and it is refreshing. In recent **11 medical** studies, tea has been found to help prevent heart attacks and cancer.

One study suggests that both black and green tea help **12 protect** the heart. In the study, tea drinkers had a 44 percent **13 lower** death rate after heart attacks than non-drinkers. Other studies have shown that tea, like fruit and vegetables, helps fight against chemicals that may **14 lead to** the development of certain cancers.

Many people really like tea. Next to plain water, it's the world's most **15 popular** drink.

答案详解

Part I   Listening Comprehension

Section A

1. ［答案］D

［解析］本题考查的是打电话用语内容。来电话找苏珊,接电话者会问对方是谁。

2. ［答案］A

［解析］本题考查的是日常用语。"对不起,我迟到了"。回答时应该是"没关系"。

3. ［答案］B

［解析］题目中说"谢谢你的帮助",回答应该是"不用谢"或"不客气"。本题 B 符合题意。

4. ［答案］C

［解析］本题考查的是表建议的句型。"我们是否再找个机会谈论一下这个问题",回答应该是"好的,什么时候"。所以 C 符合题意。

5. ［答案］A

[解析]本题考查的是商务实用英语。"我们的新产品在市场上卖的怎么样"。根据选项 A 的意思"很不错";B"不可能";C"我恐怕不能";D"从不介意"。所以 A 是正确答案。

Section B

6. ［答案］A

[解析]本题关键是听清男士的问句和问题的意思。男士问"这里有为孩子准备的特殊菜单吗";问题是"这个男士要买哪类食物"。所以选项 A"儿童食品"符合题意。

7. ［答案］C

[解析]本题考查的是对对话发生地点的判断。关键是对"open a saving's account"开个账户"的理解,经过推断 C 为正确答案。

8. ［答案］B

[解析]本题考查学生对细节题的推断。关键是听清"knocking at the door(有人在敲门)",据此可以推断出门口有人。答案应该是 B。

9. ［答案］D

[解析]对话中问句是"女士为什么回办公室了"。女士回答说:"自己的一份重要文件落在办公室了"。根据这一问一答我们可以推断答案应该是 D。

10. ［答案］B

[解析]问题是"女士在医院做什么"。解题关键 medical check-up 翻译为"体检"的意思。所以正确答案为 B。

Section C

11. medical　　12. protect　　13. lower　　14. lead to　　15. popular

Part II　Vocabulary & Structure

Section A

16. ［答案］D

[解析]本题考查的是词义和句义的辨析。beginning 翻译为"开始的";finishing 翻译为"结束的";first 翻译为"首先的";final 翻译为"最后的"。根据句意"在企业,是由总经理作最后的决定"故选 D。

17. ［答案］B

[解析]本题考查的是语法"倒装句"。否定意义的副词放在句首时,句子主谓要部分倒装。从句用的是过去时,主句也应该是过去时。所以答案为 B。

18. ［答案］A

[解析]词义辨析题。break down 翻译为"坏了";set out 翻译为"出发";put on 翻译为"穿上";go up 翻译为"上升"。根据句意,只能选 A。

19. ［答案］B

[解析]本题考查的是语法题。what 和 which 在不定式短语中作宾语;that 不和不定式连用;where 在不定式短语中作状语;本题中不定式 to find 已有宾语 supplies,所以答案是 B。

20. [答案]A

[解析]虚拟语气题。"It's high time. . ."后面的句子用一般过去时。

21. [答案]C

[解析]考查词义辨析。turn up 翻译为"出现";get up 翻译为"起来";come up with 翻译为"拿出,提出";put up 翻译为"忍受,忍耐"。根据句意,只能选 C。

22. [答案]A

[解析]本题中,可以把 before 看作是介词,deciding 动名词作介词宾语;也可以将 before 看作是连词,在分词短语中,分词意义上的主语与主句的主语不同时被称为独立主格结构。本题中主句主语是 price,分词 deciding 意义上的主语是 customers 。所以正确答案应该是 A。

23. [答案]D

[解析]本题考查的是词义辨析。charge 翻译为"价钱";money 翻译为"钱";price 翻译为"价格";expense 翻译为"费用"。根据句子意思,答案应该是 D。

24. [答案]C

[解析]词义辨析。make 翻译为"制造";send 翻译为"发送";offer 翻译为"提供";prepare 翻译为"准备"。offer sb. a job 译为"给某人提供一份工作"。根据句意答案应为 C。

25. [答案]B

[解析]考查时态。根据主句意思"这篇文章写得很好",说明文章已经写完。主句用一般现在时,从句应该用现在完成时,表示过去发生的动作对现在产生的结果。所以选 B。

Section B

26. [答案]healthier

[解析]比较连词 than 前用形容词比较级作表语。

27. [答案]kindness

[解析]great 是形容词,应该修饰名词。所以用名词 kindness。

28. [答案]are expected

[解析]主语 visitors 和动词 expect 之间是动宾关系,所以用被动语态。

29. [答案]Personally

[解析]副词修饰全句。

30. [答案]trying

[解析]主语 they 和 try 之间是逻辑上的主谓关系,因此用现在分词作状语。

31. [答案]helpful

[解析]主系表结构,形容词作表语。

32. [答案]coming

[解析]smell 和 come 之间是逻辑上的主谓关系,所以用现在分词。

33. ［答案］shorten

　　［解析］不定时后面接动词原形。所以用 short 的动词形式 shorten。

34. ［答案］will have lived/ will have been living

　　［解析］时间 next year 要求用将来时; by the time 要求用完成时, 所以用 live 的将来完成时。

35. ［答案］is working

　　［解析］主语后面有 as well as 短语时, 谓语动词仍和前一个主语保持一致。根据时间状语, 填入 is working。

Part III　Reading Comprehension

Task 1

36. ［答案］D

　　［解析］根据文章内容, night shift workers 指的是"上夜班的人", 所以选 D。

37. ［答案］C

　　［解析］从文章第一、第二句得知: 生物钟对上夜班的人影响很大。要保证清醒, 应注意调整自己的生物钟。

38. ［答案］B

　　［解析］文中第五句话, 医生建议他们仔细规划睡眠方式。

39. ［答案］A

　　［解析］从文中第六句推出: 上晚班的人早上很难入睡是因为身体自然规律的影响。

40. ［答案］C

　　［解析］从文章倒数第二句话的关键词 two smaller periods 可得出答案。

Task 2

41. ［答案］D

　　［解析］从文章内容可以推断出 Greyhound 是一家巴士公司。

42. ［答案］A

　　［解析］从第一段可以找到答案。

43. ［答案］D

　　［解析］从第三段可以推出答案。

44. ［答案］B

　　［解析］从文章倒数第二句话可以找到答案。

45. ［答案］B

　　［解析］文章前三部分讲的是有关 Greyhound 公司的购票规则, 第四部分讲的是旅游常识, 所以答案 B 是正确的。

Task 3

46. ［答案］replacement

　　［解析］答案在文章倒数第二段。

47. ［答案］half a year

[解析]答案在文章第二段。

48. ［答案］engine failure ∕ engine failed

　　［解析］根据第三和第四段说的是"发动机坏了几次。"可得出答案。

49. ［答案］four

　　［解析］答案在第三段第二句话。

50. ［答案］$ 300

　　［解析］答案在倒数第三段。

Task 4

51.（N）（M）　　52.（H）（B）　　53.（L）（K）　　54.（D）（O）　　55.（E）（G）

A——人员流动

B——终身雇佣制

C——角色冲突

D——利润分享

E——科学管理

F——可比价值

G——弹性工作时间

H——社会支持

I——调查反馈

J——核心竞争力

K——公共关系

L——团队文化

M——工薪调查

N——测谎

O——人力资源策划

Task 5

56. ［答案］statistician

　　［解析］答案在文章第一句话。

57. ［答案］Advertising

　　［解析］答案在第二段第二句话。

58. ［答案］statistics

　　［解析］答案在第二段第二句后半句话。

59. ［答案］market research

　　［解析］答案在第三段第一句话。

60. ［答案］an interview

　　［解析］答案在第三段第二句话。

Part IV　Translation—English into Chinese

61. ［答案］D

[解析]关键"for safety"翻译为:"为了安全";"review"翻译为:"仔细阅读"。

62. [答案]B

[解析]"and"连接两个并列谓语动词"misunderstand"和"mail";"misunderstand"翻译为"误解","mail"译为"邮寄发送"。

63. [答案]C

[解析]本句考查的是非限定性定语从句内容,which 引导的句子修饰前面的整个句子;"leisure time"指的是"闲暇时间"。

64. [答案]A

[解析]本句主句是"Passengers···must take the bus···"其中"going to···buses"作后置定语修饰"passengers";"at the time and place ···"为时间和地点状语。

65. [译文]

我写此信确认一下我们7日(星期四)在电话中所谈的事情。即关于赴贵公司参观的事。我们认为下周一(12月11日)很合适,希望这个时间对贵公司也合适。我的秘书玛丽布朗和销售部经理张明先生于当日上午到达贵公司。很遗憾,此次我不能和他们一起前往。再次感谢您给我们参观贵公司的机会。

Part V Writing

Holiday Inn

Visitor's Message

MR. /MS. (1) Mr. John Smith   Room No. (2) 422

While you were out

Mr. /Ms. (3) Li Hua

Of (4) PKK Company   telephone (5) 65734363

☐Telephoned   ☑Came to see you

☐Will call again   ☐Will come again

☐Asked you to call back

Message：

(6) Li Hua wants to make an appointment with Mr. John Smith to discuss something about the business at PKK Company, Li Hua will pick up Mr. John Smith at the Hotel a 9:00 tomorrow morning. In the afternoon, Mr. John Smith will be invited to visit a new assembly line of PKK Company.

Clerk (7) Linda   Date (8) December 20th   Time (9) 10:00

Test 9

Part I Listening Comprehension (15 minutes)

Directions: *This part is to test your listening ability. It consists of 3 sections.*

Section A

Directions: *This section is to test your ability to give proper answers to questions. The question will be spoken two times. When you hear a question, you should decide on the correct answer from the 4 choices.*

1. A. Sorry, but Jennifer is not here.
   B. He's a manager.
   C. Yes, speaking.
   D. No, you can't.
2. A. I don't like English.
   B. Once a week.
   C. 5 years.
   D. In 1998.
3. A. Sorry, I don't know.
   B. The market is next to it.
   C. I go to the bookshop every week.
   D. There are many books in the bookshop.
4. A. At the school gate.
   B. How about tomorrow morning?
   C. It's 2 p. m. now.
   D. See you at school.
5. A. It's exciting and interesting.
   B. I feel cold.
   C. I like reading books.
   D. I saw it yesterday.

Section B

Directions: *This section is to test your ability to understand short dialogues. Both the dialogue and the question will be spoken two times. When you hear a question, you should* *decide on the correct answer.*

6. A. Yes, she will.

   B. No, she won't, because she has to do her homework.

   C. She doesn't want to help him.

   D. She is free now.

7. A. Employer and employee.

   B. Interviewer and interviewee.

   C. Teacher and student.

   D. seller/Shop assistant and customer.

8. A. Jack.

   B. Tommy.

   C. Nick.

   D. The speaker.

9. A. Because life is less expensive in the city.

   B. Because jobs are easier to find in the city.

   C. Because her job is in the city.

   D. Because living in the suburbs is expensive.

10. A. By telephone.

    B. By email.

    C. Both A and B.

    D. None of the above.

Section C

Directions: *In this section you will hear a recorded short passage. The passage is printed on the test paper, but with some words or phrases missing. The passage will be read three times. You are required to put the missing words or phrases on the blanks.*

There are some great differences between a traditional family and a modern one. The first important difference is in the __11__. In the past, the husband was the only one who worked outside the home. And it was the husband who usually made decisions about __12__. But now the husband is not the only one who may do so. The __13__ is in the woman's role. In the past, a woman worked until she had children. But now she works outside the home even when she has children. __14__, she is busier. The final difference is in the role of the children. In the past, children were mostly __15__ by their mother. But now children have to get up early and get ready for school themselves and some of them may even have to make breakfast themselves.

Part II Vocabulary & Structure (15 minutes)

Directions: *This part is to test your ability to use words and phrases correctly to construct mean-*

ingful and grammatically correct sentences.

Section A

Directions: *There are 10 incomplete statements here. You are required to complete each statement by choosing the appropriate answer from the 4 choices.*

16. When you _____ back to Beijing next month, let me know the exact date.
    A. will come   B. had come   C. be coming   D. come
17. I _____ an old friend on the way home yesterday.
    A. meet   B. met   C. have met   D. had met
18. The weather _____ fine for many days this month.
    A. is   B. has been   C. had been   D. was
19. Since last century, his family _____ teachers.
    A. are   B. are being   C. have been   D. were being
20. The old man repented that he _____ idle when young.
    A. has been   B. having been   C. had been   D. have been
21. If I _____ you, I would go to the party with her.
    A. am   B. were   C. had been   D. be
22. If it had not rained so hard yesterday, we _____ to Tianjin.
    A. should have gone   B. should go   C. go   D. went
23. If he _____ to the gate last night, I would have given him the letter.
    A. would come   B. comes   C. had come   D. come
24. Much of what he says _____ not true.
    A. does   B. do   C. is   D. are
25. Bread and butter _____ what he needs for breakfast.
    A. is   B. are   C. being   D. was

Section B

Directions: *There are also 10 incomplete statements here. You should fill in each blank with the proper form of the word given in the brackets.*

26. Have they made any(inquire) _____ after me?
27. Many foreign words and phrases have (rich) _____ the English language.
28. His (perform) _____ in the sports meet was not good.
29. They are busy with preparing for the evening (gather) _____.
30. It is not (reason) _____ for children to ask their parents for too many things.
31. You can judge his feeling from his (face) _____ expressions.
32. He left the house without my (aware) _____.
33. In the relationship with others, you will notice some (annoy) _____ habits.
34. (obvious) _____, he hasn't realized the mistake he made.
35. If you had been more (care) _____, you wouldn't have made so many mistakes.

Part III　Reading Comprehension　(40 minutes)

Task 1

Directions: *After reading the following passage, you will find 5 questions or unfinished statements. You should make the correct choices.*

A special laboratory at the University of Chicago is busy only at night. It is a dream laboratory where researchers are at work studying dreamers. Their findings have proved that everyone dreams from three to seven times a night, although in normal life a person may remember none or only one of his dreams.

While the subjects—usually students—sleep, special machines record their brain waves and eye movements as well as the body movements that signal (信号显示) the end of a dream. Surprisingly, all subjects sleep soundly. Observers report that a person usually fidgets (烦躁不安) before a dream. Once the dream has started, his body relaxes and his eyes become more active, as if the curtain had gone up on a show. As soon as the machine shows that the dream is over, a buzzer (电铃声) wakens the sleeper. He sits up, records his dream, and goes back to sleep perhaps to dream some more.

Researchers have found that if the dreamer is awoken immediately after his dream, he can usually recall (回忆) the entire dream. If he is allowed to sleep even five more minutes his memory of the dream will have disappeared.

36. According to the passage, researchers at the University of Chicago are studying _____.

　　A. the reason of dreams

　　B. the meaning of dreams

　　C. what happens in dreams

　　D. dreamers while they dream

37. The result of their research shows that _____.

　　A. dreams are easily remembered

　　B. dreams are likely to be frightening

　　C. everyone dreams every night

　　D. persons dream only one dream a night

38. The researchers were surprised to find that _____.

　　A. people sleep soundly while they dream

　　B. dream memories are often incomplete

　　C. sleepers fidget while dreaming

　　D. dreamers can record their own dreams

39. We can infer from the story that in the dream laboratory, _____.

　　A. dreams are recorded about five minutes after the end of each dream

　　B. if the dreamer is awoken immediately after his dream, he can usually recall the entire dream.

C. it is found that what happens during the day often affects what one dreams

D. dreams' contents are analyzed according to the brain waves recorded

40. A person would be most likely to remember the dream that _____.

    A. was of most interest to him

    B. happened immediately after he went to sleep

    C. happened just before he woke up

    D. was much frightening

Task 2

Directions: *After reading the passage, you should make the correct answers.*

Many teenagers feel that the most important people in their lives are their friends. They believe that their family members don't know them as their friends do. In large families, it is quite often for brothers and sisters to fight with each other and then they can only go to their friends for some ideas.

It is very important for teenagers to have one good friend or a group of friends. Even when they are not with themselves on the phone. This communication (交际) is very important in children's growth, because friends can discuss something. These things are difficult to say to their family members.

However, parents often try to choose friends for their children. Some parents may even stop their children from meeting some of their best friends. Have you ever thought of the following questions: Who chooses your friends? Do you choose your friends or do your friends choose you? Have you got a friend your parents don't like? Your answers are welcome.

41. Many teenagers think that _____ can understand them better.

    A. friends   B. brothers   C. sisters   D. parents

42. _____ is very important to teenagers.

    A. To make friends

    B. Communication

    C. To stop meeting friends

    D. To discuss with their friends

43. When teenagers have something difficult to say to their parents, they usually _____.

    A. stay alone at home

    B. fight with their parents

    C. discuss it with their friends

    D. go to their brothers and sisters for help

44. The sentence "Your answers are welcome" means _____.

    A. you are welcome to discuss the questions with us

    B. we've got no idea, so your answers are welcome

    C. your answers are always right

    D. you can give us all the right answers

45. Which of the following is the writer's attitude? _____

A. Parents should choose friends for their children.

B. Children should choose anything they like.

C. Parents should understand their children better.

D. Teenagers should only go to their friends for help.

Task 3

Directions: *After reading the passage, you should complete the answer in the form.*

Each year, thousands of Chinese middle school students go to study in foreign countries. Recent research shows among 428 middle school students in Shanghai, nearly half of them would like to study abroad.

"Chinese children are eager to go abroad to get a wider view, less academic (学业) competition or even family honor," said Chen Yi, a Chinese writer who has lived in the US for 16 years. "But life in foreign countries can be hard for young people."

"We have to face the culture shock and language problems," said Hong Guang, a Chinese student in London.

However, these are not always the most difficult things to overcome (克服). To most children, controlling themselves when studying alone in a foreign country is a big challenge.

Zhang Jia, a 16-year-old student from Shanghai, entered high school in Melbourne, Australia last October. To his surprise, his teachers there seldom pushed students to study. And usually there wasn't much homework.

Some of his friends spent their whole year's money in the first two months of the new term. "Studying abroad at a young age can help students learn foreign languages quickly and broaden their minds, but students and parents should know about the challenges." Chen said.

What does the research tell us?	_____46_____.
Chinese students expect to go abroad to get	a wide view, less academic competition or _____47_____.
To study alone in a foreign country, students have to	both face the culture shock and language problems and _____48_____.
Students in Australia have more free time	because there is _____49_____.
What's the article mainly about?	_____50_____.

46. _____

47. _____

48. _____

49. _____

50. _____

Task 4

Directions: *After reading the following list, you are required to find the items equivalent to those* *given in Chinese in the list below.*

A. —— Keep right/left

B. —— No passing

C. —— Reduce your speed / Slow

D. —— Road closed ahead

E. —— No cycling

F. —— Lost and found

G. —— One way

H. —— No photos

I. —— For use only in case of fire

J. —— Hands off

K. —— Luggage depository

L. —— Do not enter

Example:（G）单行道　　　　（C）减速行驶

51.（　）请勿拍照	（　）禁止骑车
52.（　）请勿入内	（　）火警时专用
53.（　）请勿用手摸	（　）失物招领处
54.（　）行李存放处	（　）禁止通行
55.（　）靠右/左通行	（　）前方道路关闭

Task 5

Directions: *After reading the passage, you are required to complete the statements that follow the questions.*

Guided Tours of United Nations Headquarters include an explanation of the aims, structure and activities of the United Nations. Tours leave approximately every 20 minutes seven days a week, from 9:00 a.m. until 4:45 p.m. Fees charged are used to cover the expense of the Visitors' Service operation. Children under 5 years of age are not admitted on tours.

Official Meetings of United Nations bodies are open to the public. Tickets are distributed free of charge at the Information Desk in the Lobby of the General Assembly （联合国大会大厅） building on a first-come, first-served basis. Meetings are rarely held on Saturdays and Sundays. Meetings may be scheduled or cancelled on short notice: tickets for specific meeting cannot be guaranteed.

United Nations Films are offered to visitors Monday through Friday, free of charge, subject to the availability of a conference room.

The Delegates' Dining Room is open for luncheon （工作午餐） Monday through Friday. For reservations and details, inquire at the Information Desk.

The Public Hall is located one level below the General Assembly Lobby. Guided tours stop here. Public telephones, water fountains （饮水处） and rest rooms as well as other facilities are in this area.

56. Who is the above information intended for?

_____.

57. What kind of visitors will not be received?

_____.

58. When should visitors come if they want to observe meeting?

_____.

59. Why films are sometimes not offered on weekdays?

_____.

60. Which part of the building should a visitor go to if he wants to make a phone call?

_____.

Part V Translation—English into Chinese (25 minutes)

Directions: *This part is to test your ability to translate English into Chinese. Each of the four sentences is followed by four choices of suggested translation. Make the best choice. Write your translation of the paragraph in the corresponding space.*

61. Distance learners usually depend on written materials.
   A. 远程教育的学生通常依赖文字材料。
   B. 远程教育的学生通常依赖手写材料。
   C. 远距离学者通常依靠手写材料。
   D. 远距离的学习者经常依靠文字材料。

62. Really? An MP3 player for 10 dollars is a great bargain. Is it real though?
   A. 真的吗？一个 MP3 卖 10 美元是个很棒的交易。但它是正品吗？
   B. 真的吗？一个 MP3 卖 10 美元是个很棒的讨价还价。但它是正品吗？
   C. 现实吗？一个 MP3 玩家卖 10 美元是个很棒的交易。但它是正品吗？
   D. 真的吗？一个 MP3 卖 10 美元是个很棒的交易。但它是真的吗？

63. The most exciting thing for him was that he finally found two tinned fruits in what seemed to him to be a servants bedroom.
   A. 最激动的是他在他的那间看起来像仆人的房间里找到了两听水果
   B. 让他感到最激动的是他终于在他的那间看起来像仆人的卧室里发现了两听水果
   C. 最激动的是那个他最后在他的那间看起来像服务员的卧室里找到了两听水果罐头
   D. 让他感到最激动的是他终于在他的那间看起来像仆人的房间里找到了两听水果罐头。

64. Television is one of the means by which these feelings are created and conveyed.
   A. 电视是制造和传播这种感觉的媒介之一。
   B. 电视是制造和传播这种情绪的媒介之一。
   C. 电视是制造和传播这种情绪的意思之一。
   D. 电视是创造和传递这种感情的媒介之一。

65. In the early fifties, only eight or nine out of a hundred young men changed their jobs within

the first three years with a company. Since most jobs take only a year and a half to master, in order to continue learning, they have to make a job change. They have worked for a few years as technical specialists and quickly moved into higher management positions.

Part V Writing (25 minutes)

Directions: *This part is to test your ability to do practical writing. You are required to finish the following writing according to the information.*

国际文化交流中心将组织一次由各国学生参加的"和平友谊"夏令营活动,要求报名者提交英文个人简历。假设你是王姗,请根据下列信息写一篇个人简历。

姓名:王姗　　　　　性别:女
年龄:16 岁　　　　　学校:北京阳光中学
其他:爱好音乐、摄影;善于与人交流,乐于助人;热爱自然,热爱和平。
参加夏令营的目的:结交朋友,了解外国文化。
注意:
1. 词数不少于 60 词。
2. 可根据内容要点适当增加细节,以使行文连贯。

答 案 解 析

Part I Listening Comprehension

听力原文

Section A

1. Hello, this is Jennifer. Could I speak to Mr. Lee?

2. How long have you been learning English?

3. Excuse me, could you tell me how can I go to the bookshop?

4. When shall we meet?

5. How do you like this movie?

Section B

6. M: Monica, could you help me with my paper?

   W: I'd like to, but I have too much homework to do.

   Q: Will Monica help the man with his paper?

7. W: I like this blue dress. How much is it?

   M: It's 80 yuan. You can try it on.

   Q: What's the relationship between the two speakers?

8. W: Tommy, you have more CDs than Jack, right?

M: Yes, but Nick has much more CDs than me.

Q: Who has the most CDs?

9. M: Have you decided where you're going to live when you get married?

W: I'd like to live in the city near my work place, but my fiancè wants to live in the sub-urbs to save on money.

Q: Why does the woman want to live in the city?

10. M: Do you often write letters to your friends?

W: Seldom. But I often call them and send emails to them.

Q: How does the woman often communicate with her friends?

Section C

There are some great differences between a traditional family and a modern one. The first important difference is in the **11 man's role** . In the past, the husband was the only one who worked outside the home. And it was the husband who usually made decisions about **12 spending money**. But now the husband is not the only one who may do so. The **13 second difference** is in the woman's role. In the past, a woman worked until she had children. But now she works outside the home even when she has children. **14 Therefore**, she is busier. The final difference is in the role of the children. In the past, children were mostly **15 taken care of** by their mother. But now children have to get up early and get ready for school themselves and some of them may even have to make breakfast themselves.

答案详解

Part I Listening Comprehension

Section A

1. [答案]C

[解析]问题是"你好,我是 Jennifer,我能和 Mr. Lee 说话吗"。首先这是一个打电话找人的场景,既然打电话的人是 Jennifer,答案肯定不是 A;根据问题,B 选项也不符合题意;而 D 选项是否定的答案,不符合一般的礼貌习俗,只能是 C 选项:"我就是,请讲"。

2. [答案]C

[解析]问题是"你学英语有多长时间了",所以回答应该是一个时间段,而不是时间点,而 D 选项给出的答案是个时间点,故排除;B 选项是个时间的频率,也不符合题意;A 选项说的是不喜欢英语,而本题是对时间段进行提问,所以 A 不符合题意。故选 C。

3. [答案]A

[解析]"Could you tell me how can I go to the bookshop?"是个问路的情景题,C 和 D 选项不符合题意,故排除;B 选项说的是市场就在它旁边,而问题问的是"书店怎么走",所以 B 不恰当;A 选项回答是不知道怎么走,所以 A 选项为正确答案。

4. [答案]B

[解析]"When shall we meet?"(我们什么时候碰面?)是对时间的提问,而 A 和 D 选项

却是对地点提问的答案;C 选项说的是现在是下午 2 点,不符合意思;B 选项"明天上午怎么样"符合题意,故为正确答案。

5. [答案]A

[解析]"How do you like this movie?"问的是"你觉得这部电影怎么样",B 和 C 讲的与电影无关,故排除;D 选项回答的是时间,也不符合题意。A 选项的意思是"很精彩很有意思"符合题意,故为正确答案。

Section B

6. [答案]B

[解析]对话中问题是"你能帮我写论文吗",回答"我很想帮你,可是我有很多作业要做",不难判断出 B 选项为正确答案。

7. [答案]D

[解析]本题中女士问"这件蓝衬衣多少钱",回答"80 元,你可以试穿一下",四个选项中的信息只有 D 选项符合对话内容,其他选项不符合题意。

8. [答案]C

[解析]对话中女士问"汤米,你的 CD 比杰克的多,对吧",汤米的回答是"是的,但是尼克的 CD 比我的还多"。很明显 C 选项的意思符合问题"谁的 CD 最多",所以 C 选项为正确答案。

9. [答案]C

[解析]对话中男士问"你决定婚后去哪居住了吗",女士回答说她想住在城市,上班近,而她的未婚夫想住在郊区可以省钱。而问题问的是"这位女士为什么想住在城市",所以正确答案为 C。

10. [答案]C

[解析]题中问道"你经常给朋友写信吗",女士回答道:"很少,但是我经常给他们打电话和发电子邮件",故 C 选项为正确答案。

Section C

11. man's role　　12. spending money　　13. second difference　　14. Therefore　　15. taken care of

Part II Vocabulary & Structure

Section A

16. [答案]D

[解析]本句中的 when 引导的不是特殊疑问句,而是表示时间的状语,所以排除 A 和 B 选项,而句子中暗含的是将来时态,在时间状语中,从句用一般现在时表示将来,所以 D 选项用动词的一般现在时是正确的。

17. [答案]B

[解析]这道题测试的是动词的时态,当句子中出现了 yesterday 这个表示昨天的词时,句子要用过去时,所以正确答案为选项 B。

18. [答案]B

[解析]句子中出现了 for many days this month 一个表示持续的时间段,表示动作过去发生并一直持续到现在,所以句子是现在完成时。而且主语是第三人称单数,故只有选项 B 为正确答案。

19. [答案]C

[解析]本句话翻译为"自从上个世纪开始,他的家里人就一直从事教师行业",动作从过去发生,一直持续到现在,所以本句是现在完成时,只有 C 选项是现在完成时的用法,故选 C。

20. [答案]C

[解析]本题考查的是间接引语中的时态,主句是过去时,所以从句中也应该是过去的时态,而从句中是完成时,所以应该是过去完成时,故 C 选项为正确答案。

21. [答案]B

[解析]这是一道虚拟语气题,本题的意思是"如果我是你,我会和她一起参加聚会的",在表示与现在相反的虚拟语气中,不管主语是第几人称,be 动词都用 were,故 B 选项为正确答案。

22. [答案]A

[解析]这是一道虚拟语气题,从句是过去完成时,所以本句表示与过去相反的假设,主句应该用"should/would/could/might + have done",故正确答案为 A 选项。

23. [答案]C

[解析]这是一道虚拟语气题,主句是 would have given,表示与过去相反,所以从句中要用过去完成时,本句意思是"如果他昨晚去了大门口,我就已经把信交给他的",但实际上他没去。C 选项为正确答案。

24. [答案]C

[解析]这句话的意思是"他说的话大多不是真的",本句的主语是不可数的,动词要用单数,故排除 B 和 D,而本句是主系表结构,A 选项不是系动词,所以 C 选项是正确的。

25. [答案]A

[解析]本句的主语是 bread and butter,在英美国家,黄油和面包经常是一起吃的,被作为一种食品,故后面 be 动词要用单数,因为本句时态是一般现在时,故正确答案为 A 选项。

Section B

26. [答案]inquiry

[解析]本句是一个动宾短语"make any …",any 是不定代词,后面接名词,故要把 inquire 变成名词,故正确答案为 inquiry。

27. [答案]enriched

[解析]本句翻译为"很多外来词汇和短语丰富了英语",本句缺少动词,应该把 rich

变成动词,再变成过去分词,故正确答案为 enriched。

28. ［答案］performance

［解析］his 后面要接名词,所以 perform 要变成名词形式,即 performance。

29. ［答案］gathering

［解析］空白处前面是"the evening…",有定冠词 the,所以后面应该用名词,故正确答案为 gathering。

30. ［答案］reasonable

［解析］本句中的句型是"it is ＋ *adj.* ＋ to do sth",it is 的后面应该接形容词,而所给单词 reason 是名词,要变成形容词 reasonable。

31. ［答案］facial

［解析］形容词性物主代词与名词之间要用形容词形式。所以 face 要变成形容词形式,即 facial。

32. ［答案］awareness

［解析］my 后面要接名词,所以 aware 要变成名词 awareness。

33. ［答案］annoying

［解析］根据前后的词 some…habits,判断这里应该用一个形容词来修饰 habits,所以用 annoying。

34. ［答案］Obviously

［解析］此处用来修饰整个句子,应该用 obvious 的副词形式即 obviously,句首单词首字母大写,应为 Obviously。

35. ［答案］careful

［解析］本句翻译为"如果你更仔细点,你就不会犯这么多错误。"这里面 had been more 后面应该接形容词表示比较级,所以要用 careful。

Part III   Reading Comprehension

Task 1

36. ［答案］D

［解析］根据文中第一段第二句"It is a dream laboratory where researchers are at work studying dreamers."可知 D 为正确答案。

37. ［答案］C

［解析］根据第一段第三句 "Their findings have proved that everyone dreams from three to seven times a night"得知,C 选项符合题意,故为正确答案。

38. ［答案］A

［解析］根据第二段第二句"Surprisingly, all subjects sleep soundly"符合题意的是答案 A。

39. ［答案］B

［解析］根据第三段第一句"...if the dreamer is awoken immediately after his dream, he can usually recall（回忆）the entire dream"故选 B。

40. [答案]C

[解析]根据第三段第二句"If he is allowed to sleep even five more minutes his memory of the dream will have disappeared." 所以正确选项为C。

Task 2

41. [答案]A

[解析]根据文中的第一段得知,父母和兄弟姐妹都不如朋友重要,正确答案为选项A。

42. [答案]A

[解析]从文中第二段第一句"It is very important for teenagers to have one good friend or a group of friends."得知,四个选项中只有A选项正确。

43. [答案]C

[解析]从第二段第三句中"... because friends can discuss something"得知,只有C选项意思正确。

44. [答案]A

[解析]根据上下文得知,符合题意的只有选项A。

45. [答案]C

[解析]根据文章内容得知作者希望父母能理解孩子,所以C选项恰当。

Task 3

46. [答案]Many middle school students want to study abroad

[解析]根据文中第一段第二句"Recent research shows among 428 middle school students in Shanghai, nearly half of them would like to study abroad."得出答案。

47. [答案]family honor

[解析]根据文中第二段第一句中"to go abroad to get a wider view, less academic (学业) competition or even family honor"得出结论。

48. [答案]control themselves / manage their time and money

[解析]根据文中第四段第二句"To most children, controlling themselves when studying alone in a foreign country is a big challenge."得出答案。

49. [答案]not much homework

[解析]根据文中第五段第三句"And usually there wasn't much homework"可得知答案。

50. [答案]The problem of young students studying abroad

[解析]根据文章大意得出结论。

Task 4

51. (H)(E)　　　52. (L)(I)　　　53. (J)(F)　　　54. (K)(B)　　　55. (A)(D)

A——靠右/左通行

B——禁止通行

C——减速行驶

D——前方道路关闭

E——禁止骑车

140

F——失物招领处

G——单行道

H——请勿拍照

I——火警时专用

J——请勿用手摸

K——行李存放处

L——请勿入内

Task5

56. ［答案］Tourists to the United Nations.

［解析］从文章第一段第一句话可以找到答案。

57. ［答案］Children under 5 years of age.

［解析］从文章第一段最后一句话可以找到答案。

58. ［答案］Monday through Friday.

［解析］从文章第三段第一句话可以找到答案。

59. ［答案］Because the conference room are not available.

［解析］文章中第三段中的词组 subject to 翻译为"以某事物为条件,取决于某事物"。根据全句的含义,会议室有时候是不能提供的。所以答案为 Because the conference room are not available。

60. ［答案］The Public Hall.

［解析］答案在文章最后一段最后一句话。

Part IV   Translation—English into Chinese

61. ［答案］A

［解析］本句中最关键的词是 Distance learners,其意思是"远程教育的学生"。

62. ［答案］A

［解析］本句最重要的是把后半句的意思搞清楚,A 选项翻译最恰当,所以最佳答案为 A。

63. ［答案］D

［解析］two tinned fruits 的意思是"两听水果罐头",servants 意思是"仆人",只有 D 选项翻译正确了这两个词,所以最佳答案是 D 选项。

64. ［答案］B

［解析］照字面翻译为"电视是一种手段或者媒介,通过这个手段前面讲的情绪,被制造出来和表达出来"。如果这样翻译的话,就不能够通顺地表达意思。此时通常把英文的被动语态翻译成中文的主动语态。

65. ［译文］

在五十年代初期,有百分之八九的年轻人在一家公司工作三年后往往会跳槽。由于大多数工作只需花一年多就可以掌握,为了继续学习,他们就会调换工作。作为技术专家,他们在工作了几年之后会更快地跳到更高的管理岗位。

Part V   Writing

参考答案:

Dear Sir/Madam,

    I'm Wang Shan, a girl of sixteen, presently attending Beijing Yangguang Middle School. I like music, especially classical music. I'm also interested in photography because it allows me to record the beautiful moments in my life. I've made many friends with the same hobbies. In fact, I like meeting new people and enjoy talking with them. Believing we all need help from each other, I appreciate friends'help, and I'm willing to help anyone in need. I love life; I love Mother Nature; and I love peace. I hate any form of violence. I would like to join the Peace & Friendship Summer Camp since it would be a great opportunity to make friends with young people from different countries and learn about their cultures.

Sincerely Yours,

Wang Shan

Test 10

Part I   Listening Comprehension   (15 minutes)

Directions: *This part is to test your listening ability. It consists of 3 sections.*

Section A

Directions: *This section is to test your ability to give proper answers to questions. The question will be spoken two times. When you hear a question, you should decide on the correct answer from the 4 choices.*

1. A. It's very far from here.　　　　　B. I come from other country.

   C. Sorry, I'm new here.　　　　　　D. I work in a bank.

2. A. It's him.　　　　　　　　　　　B. Yes, it is.

   C. It's mine.　　　　　　　　　　D. It's my.

3. A. I'm reading the book.　　　　　　B. Thank you very much.

   C. I think it is very interesting.　　D. I think so.

4. A. Since yesterday.　　　　　　　　B. Two weeks ago.

   C. Yes, it's a long way to China.　　D. Three weeks.

5. A. No, you can't.　　　　　　　　　B. I am kind-hearted.

   C. You're right.　　　　　　　　　D. Go ahead.

Section B

Directions: *This section is to test your ability to understand short dialogues. Both the dialogue and the question will be spoken two times. When you hear a question, you should decide on the correct answer.*

6. A. She loves to come along.

   B. She feels it a pity not to be able to join them.

   C. She doesn't like a party.

   D. She spent a nice day in that way before.

7. A. Jill.　　　　　B. Lucy.　　　　　C. Jane.　　　　　D. John.

8. A. In a bank.　　B. In a restaurant.　　C. In a grocery shop.　D. In a radio studio.

9. A. Two turns.　　B. Four turns.　　　C. One turn.　　　D. Three turns.

10.A. It's 6:15.　　B. It's 6:05.　　　C. It's 5:35.　　　D. It's 5:45.

Section C

Directions: *In this section you will hear a recorded short passage. The passage is printed on the* *test paper*, *but with some words or phrases missing. The passage will be read three times. You are required to put the missing words or phrases on the blanks.*

John R. Wilmoth, a demographer (人口统计学家) at the University of California, Berkeley, has ____11____ a wealth of ____12____ on humankind's increasing longevity (寿命) over the past two centuries. And this week in *Science*(美国《科学》杂志), he has some good news：The maximum ____13____ age we can reach too is on the rise. This finding contradicts the common scientific belief that life span has a biological upper ____14____ of 120 years or so. "Whether 115 or 120 years, it is a legend created by ____15____ who are quoting each other," Wilmoth says.

Part II Vocabulary & Structure   (15minutes)

Directions：*This part is to test your ability to use words and phrases correctly to construct meaningful and grammatically correct sentences.*

Section A

Directions：*There are 10 incomplete statements here. You are required to complete each statement by choosing the appropriate answer from the 4 choices.*

16. Tom says this is the _____ decision he has ever made in his career life.
    A. bad   B. badly   C. worse   D. worst

17. The flower needs _____.
    A. to water   B. watered   C. watering   D. being watered

18. It was Tom _____ was absent from class yesterday.
    A. which   B. /   C. that   D. he

19. The project is worth _____ again.
    A. discussed   B. discussing   C. to discuss   D. discuss

20. —How about visiting Summer Palace this weekend?
    —That _____ good, but I have a lot of work to do.
    A. sounds   B. smells   C. appears   D. looks

21. Jane can't speak France, _____ write it.
    A. and she can't   B. or can she   C. nor can she   D. or can't she

22. She found _____ rather difficult to cooperate with Jane.
    A. it is   B. that   C. he is   D. it

23. I _____ at six o'clock, but now I get up very late.
    A. used to getting   B. used to get
    C. am used to getting   D. am used to get

24. Will she participate _____ the Coming Job fair?
    A. with   B. in   C. on   D. at

25. They will be _____ if you don't go to their wedding.

A. offended   B. protected   C. objected   D. defended

Section B

Directions: *There are also 10 incomplete statements here. You should fill in each blank with the proper form of the word given in the brackets.*

26. He has been looking forward to (play) _____ with the best football player in the world.
27. He avoided (look) _____ into my eyes when he told lies.
28. The scene in my hometown is really (attract) _____.
29. My sister got (marry) _____ when I was sixteen.
30. The scientist's (explain) _____ is clear enough.
31. Some of my colleagues spent a lot of time in (learn) _____ Japanese.
32. With the (develop) _____ of economy, more people lead a better life.
33. I asked him not (say) _____ anything about the plan we made last week.
34. It is his parents' wish that he (enter) _____ Peking University.
35. Every day, Tom is the (early) _____ pupil to get to school.

Part III Reading Comprehension (40 minutes)

Task 1

Directions: *After reading the following passage, you will find 5 questions or unfinished statements. You should make the correct choices.*

When you want to go shopping, you should decide first how much money you can pay for new clothes. Think about the kind of clothes you really need. Then look for those clothes on sale, that is to say, you can buy some new clothes at a lower price.

There are labels inside all new clothes. The labels tell you how to take care of your clothes. The label for a shirt may tell you to wash it in warm water. A sweater label may tell you to wash it in cold water. The label on a coat may say "Dry Clean Only". Washing may ru-in this coat. If you do as the directions say on the label, you can keep your clothes looking their best. Many clothes today must be dry cleaned. Dry cleaning is expensive. When you buy new clothes, you should look at them carefully to make sure if they need to be dry cleaned. You will save money if you buy clothes that can wash easily.

If you buy some well made clothes, you can save money because they can last longer. They look good even after they have been washed many times. Sometimes some clothes cost more money, but it does not mean that they are always better made, or they always fit better. In other words, some less expensive clothes look and fit better than more expensive clothes.

36. If you want to save money, what clothes can you buy? _____
    A. Clothes which are well made.   B. Clothes which can be washed easily.
    C. Clothes which can be clean dried only.   D. Both A and B.
37. According to this passage, what is the function of labels? _____

145

A. They tell us how much the clothes are.

B. They tell us how to wash the clothes.

C. They tell us how to repair the clothes.

D. They tell us what color the clothes are.

38. When you buy some new clothes, what should you think of first? _____

A. The kind of the clothes you really need.

B. Looking for the clothes on sales.

C. Finding the newest clothes.

D. How much money you can pay for the new clothes.

39. What can you learn from the passage? _____

A. Cheaper clothes can sometimes fit you better.

B. You cannot buy some new clothes at a lower price.

C. Expensive clothes are always well made.

D. When you buy new clothes, you'd better choose the clothes that need to be dry cleaned.

40. Which is the following statement is right? _____

A. Expensive clothes are always well-made.

B. Expensive clothes always fit better than cheap clothes.

C. If you do as the directions say on the label, you can keep your clothes looking their best.

D. Some well made clothes can't look good after they have been washed many times.

Task 2

Directions: *After reading you should make the correct choices.*

People travel a lot with Heaven Air because they know they will get what they want.

They want to go quickly and safely across the land, across the sea or right across the world, and they know Heaven Air will take them where they want to go whenever they want to go. Heaven Air flies all the newest and fastest planes to more towns and cities of the world than any other airlines.

Do you want to go to Paris, Washington, Tokyo? Heaven Air will take you there, at all times of the day or night, right through the week. But Heaven Air flies not only to the biggest cities; we also fly three or four times a week to towns and cities in the very center of Asia, Africa and South America.

People fly with Heaven Air because they know they will leave on time and arrive on time. They know that they will receive the best food and watch the best films.

Heaven Air is second to none.

41. What is Heaven air? _____

A. The name of a plane.

B. The name of an airline.

C. The name of a travel agency.

D. The name of an advertising program.

42. Travelling with Heaven Air is _____.

A. comfortable and cheap

B. expensive but pleasant

C. exciting but rare

D. quick and safe

43. Heaven Air can take you to Tokyo _____.

A. on weekends only

B. just on weekdays

C. any time in a week

D. three or four times a week

44. Most flights of Heaven Air go to _____.

A. small towns

B. big cities

C. both big and small cities

D. the very center of Africa

45. According to the advertisement, Heaven Air believes it is _____.

A. the second best in the world

B. the second biggest in the world

C. the biggest in the world

D. the best in the world

Task 3

Directions: *After reading the passage, you should complete the correct answers.*

Sleep

Sleep is part of a person's daily activity cycle. There are several different stages of sleep, and they too occur in cycles. If you are an average sleeper, your sleep cycle is as follows. When you first drift off into slumber, your eyes will roll about a bit, your temperature will drop slightly, your muscles will relax, and your breathing will slow and become quite regular. Your brain waves slow and become quite regular. That is stage 1 sleep. For the next half hour or so, as you relax more and more, you will drift down through stage 2 and stage 3 sleep. The lower your stage of sleep, the slower your brain waves will be. Then about 40 to 69 minutes after you lose consciousness you will have reached the deepest sleep of all. Your brain will show the large slow waves that are known as the delta rhythm. This is stage 4 sleep.

You do not remain at this deep fourth stage all night long, but instead about 80 minutes after you fall into slumber, your brain activity level will increase again slightly. The delta rhythm will disappear, to be replaced by the activity pattern of brain waves. Your eyes will begin to dart around under your closed eyelids as if you were looking at something occurring in front of you. This period of rapid eye movement lasts for some 8 to 15 minutes and is called REM sleep. It is during REM sleep period, your body will soon relax again, your breathing will slip gently back from stage 1 to stage 4 sleep.

Sleep is part of a person's daily activity cycle. There are ___46___ different stages of sleep, and they too occur in cycles. At the first stage, your ___47___ drift off into slumber, your eyes will roll about a bit, your muscles will relax. As you ___48___ more and more, you will drift down through stage 2 and stage 3 sleep. After you lose ___49___ you will have reached the deepest sleep of all. That is the ___50___ step.

Task 4

Directions: *After reading the following list, you are required to find the items equivalent to those given in Chinese in the list below.*

A. —— speech pathologist

B. —— traffic police

C. —— cost accounting

D. —— information analysis

E. —— continued story

F. —— bluetooth

G. —— amusement park

H. —— development engineer

I. —— traffic regulation

J. —— school psychologist

K. —— electrical engineer

L. —— ski jump

M. —— electric work

N. —— the silk road

O. —— telecommunications

P. —— locker

Example:（O）电信服务　　　　　　　　　　（P）保管业务

51.（　）跳高滑雪	（　）成本会计
52.（　）游乐园	（　）丝绸之路
53.（　）交通规则	（　）蓝牙技术
54.（　）信息分析	（　）开发工程师
55.（　）语言心理学家	（　）心理咨询教师

Task 5

Directions: *After reading the passage, you are required to complete the statements that follow the questions.*

Dear sir,

I am writing to confirm the loss of my credit card(信用卡). I telephoned your office earlier today.

The details of my card are as follows. It is an Apex Silver card in the name of Paul R. Wilmoth. The credit card number is 5421 7612 2597 8413. I have had an Apex card since 1990. This card is valid(有效的)from August 1990 to August 2000.

I lost the card yesterday at about 8:30 in the evening. The only case I used the card yesterday was to buy three dictionaries at the Tony's Bookstore in Yingbin Street. By accident, I left the card at the shop. When I realized what I had done, I telephoned the shop, but the shop assistant there could not find the card.

Could you please cancel my card immediately and make the necessary arrangements to issue a replacement card to me? I can be contacted at the telephone number of 89661534.

Thank you for your assistance.

Yours faithfully,
Paul R. Wilmoth

56. Why did the man call the office?
    Because he _____.

57. What's the name of the card?
    _____.

58. When is the card invalid?
    In _____.

59. Where did the man lose his card?
    At _____ in Yingbin Street.

60. What did the man ask the company to do about the lost card?
    He asked the company to _____ the card immediately.

Part IV Translation—English into Chinese (25 minutes)

Directions: *This part is to test your ability to translate English into Chinese. Each of the four sentences is followed by four choices of suggested translation. Make the best choice. Write your translation of the paragraph in the corresponding space.*

61. Children under 12 are not allowed to enter before 2 pm unless accompanied by an adult.
    A. 低于 12 岁的小孩下午两点前不许入内,只有成年人可以完成。
    B. 12 岁以下的小孩在下午两点前可以入内, 除非有一个成年人作伴。
    C. 如果有一个成年人完成, 低于 12 人下午两点钟可以入内。
    D. 如果没有成人陪同,下午两点前任何 12 岁以下的小孩不许入内。

62. Whatever he did, he did very well.
    A. 凡是他做的事情,都很好。
    B. 凡是他做的事,他都做得很好。

C. 他能把他能做的任何事情做好。

D. 凡是他能做的事,他都好好做。

63. Whenever circumstances permitted, they would come and lend us a hand.

A. 只要情况允许,他们总是会来帮助我们。

B. 无论什么环境,只要他们愿意,他们就会来并且借给我们一只帮助之手。

C. 无论何时,只要环境许可,他们都将来并且借给我们一只帮助的手。

D. 无论何时环境被许可,他们都会来助我们一臂之力。

64. Will you need an experienced manager assistant for company next summer?

A. 下年夏季你是否有经验为您公司设一名经理?

B. 你的公司下一个夏季想找一名有经验的清洁工吗?

C. 来年夏季你的公司是否招收有经验的助理?

D. 不知您的公司明年夏天是否需要一名有经验的经理助理?

65. What would you do if you failed? Many people may choose to give up. However, the best way to success is to keep your direction and stick to your goal. It is just like a lamp, guiding you in darkness and helping you overcome obstacles on your way. Otherwise, you will easily get lost or hesitate to go ahead. Direction means objective. You can get nowhere without an objective in life.

Part V   Writing   (25 minutes)

Directions: *This part is to test your ability to do practical writing. You are required to finish the following writing according to the information.*

说明:根据下列信息,写一张失物招领布告。

失物招领

一位夫人三月六日下午在超市内捡到钱包一个,交至本室。失主请带身份证前来认领,特此布告。

Words for reference:超市 supermarket　　钱包 purse

答 案 解 析

Part I   Listening Comprehension

听力原文

Section A

1. Could you please tell me the way to the nearest China Bank?

2. Is this bag yours or Tom's?

3. What do you think of the book?

4. How long will you be away from China?

5. Do you mind if I use the pen on the desk?

Section B

6. M: We're going to have a party this Saturday evening. Would you like to join us?

   W: What a good way to spend a nice day.

   Q: What does the woman mean?

7. W: Lucy is taller than Jane in our class.

   M: I think so, but Lucy isn't as tall as Jill.

   Q: Who is the tallest?

8. M: Can I help you?

   W: Yes. I want two kilos of eggs.

   Q: Where does the conversation most probably take place?

9. M: Could you tell me where the nearest post office is?

   W: Go straight until you come to the traffic light. Turn right there and go about 200 meters and there you can't miss it.

   Q: How many turns will the man take before he gets to the post office?

10. W: Excuse me. Do you have the time?

    M: It's a quarter to six by my watch. But my watch is 10 minutes slow.

    Q: What's the correct time?

Section C

John R. Wilmoth, a demographer（人口统计学家）at the University of California, Berkeley, has **11 collected** a wealth of **12 data** on humankind's increasing longevity（寿命）over the past two centuries. And this week in *Science*（美国《科学》杂志）, he has some good news: The maximum **13 average** age we can reach to is on the rise. This finding contradicts the common scientific belief that life span has a biological upper **14 limit** of 120 years or so. "Whether 115 or 120 years, it is a legend created by **15 scientists** who are quoting each other," Wilmoth says.

答案详解

Part I   Listening Comprehension

Section A

1. ［答案］C

   ［解析］问题为"您能告诉我到最近的中国银行怎么走吗"。选项"I'm new here."翻译为"对不起,我也是初来乍到",根据题意应选 C。

2. ［答案］C

   ［解析］问题为选择疑问句,翻译为"这是你的包还是汤姆的"。A 选项翻译为"是他的";B 选项翻译为"是的";C 选项翻译为"是我的";D 选项句子出现语法错误。根

据形容词性物主代词"my"不能单独使用,应在其后加上名词。根据题意应选 C。

3. [答案]C

[解析]题干中 think of 翻译为"认为"。问题译为"你认为这本书怎么样"。选项 A 翻译为"我正在读一本书";选项 C interesting 翻译为"有趣";选项 D"I think so"翻译为"我也这样认为"。根据题意应选 C。

4. [答案]D

[解析]How long 翻译为"多久或是多长时间",问题翻译为"你将离开中国多长时间"。"Since yesterday"翻译为"自从昨天";"Two weeks ago"翻译为"两个星期前";"far from..."翻译为"到……很远";"Two weeks"翻译为"两个星期的时间"。根据题意应选 D。

5. [答案]D

[解析]题干翻译为"您是否介意我用一下桌子上的笔"。选项 A 翻译为"不,你不能",对应的问句应该用 can 来提问。kind-hearted 翻译为"热心肠的";"Go ahead."翻译为"请用吧"。根据题意选 D。

Section B

6. [答案]A

[解析]本题中,男士问女士:"我们周六晚上要举办个聚会,你想参加吗?"女士回答说:"这是多么好的一个方式来度过美好的一天啊。"问题翻译为"这位女士的话是什么意思"。选项 A 翻译为"她想去参加";选项 B 翻译为"她感到不能去参加很遗憾";选项 C 翻译为"她不喜欢这个聚会";选项 D 翻译为"她过去曾这样度过美好一天"。根据题意应选 A。

7. [答案]A

[解析]在本题中,女士说:"Lucy 比 Jane 高。"男士说:"我也这样认为,但是 Lucy 没有 Jill 高。""as...as..."翻译为"和……一样"。问题为"谁最高",根据题意应选 A。

8. [答案]C

[解析]在本题中,女士问:"Can I help you" 可以作为服务业的行业用语,翻译为"我能帮您做点什么"。bank 翻译为"银行";restaurant 翻译为"饭店";grocery shop 翻译"杂货店";two kilos eggs 翻译为"两公斤鸡蛋"。根据题意应选 C。

9. [答案]C

[解析]在本题中,turn 翻译为"转弯",总共出现了一次。根据题意应选 C。

10. [答案]C

[解析]本题中"Do you have the time"翻译为"你知道几点了吗";"It's a quarter to six by my watch. But my watch is 10 minutes slow"翻译为"我的表显示是 5:45。但是我的表慢十分钟"。问题中 correct 翻译为"正确的"。
根据题意应选 C。

Section C

11. collected   12. data   13. average   14. limit   15. scientists

Part II Vocabulary & Structure

Section A

16. ［答案］D

［解析］这道题测试的是形容词及其最高级的用法。题干中 decision 翻译为"决定",是名词。因此在其前面应该用形容词来修饰。又因为画线前有 the,所以要使用形容词最高级。bad 翻译为"坏的"是形容词。badly 是副词。worse 翻译为"更糟糕的",是比较级。worst 翻译为"最坏的;最糟糕的。"是最高级。根据题意应选 D。

17. ［答案］C

［解析］这道题测试的是 need 的用法。need,require...等词在表示"需要……",并且物作主语时,要用动名词的形式表示被动的含义。本句的意思是"花需要浇水了"。正确答案应选 C。

18. ［答案］C

［解析］这道题测试的是强调句式。强调句式的结构是:It is/was + 强调的部分 + that/who(人) + 其他部分。本题的意思是"昨天迟到的是汤姆"。正确答案应是 C。

19. ［答案］B

［解析］这道题测试的是形容词 worth 的搭配关系。be worth + n./doing sth. 翻译为"值得做某事"。正确答案应选 B。

20. ［答案］A

［解析］这道题测试的是系动词的用法。sound 翻译为"听起来";smell 翻译为"闻起来";appear 翻译为"看起来";look 翻译为"看起来"。本题的问题翻译为"这周我们去颐和园怎么样"回答翻译为"听起来不错。但是我有好多事情要做"。根据题意应选 A。

21. ［答案］C

［解析］这道题测试的是"not(neither)...nor..."的句式,翻译为"既不……也不……"并且 nor 后边的部分要倒装,助动词提到主语前。本句的意思是"简既不会说法语,也不会写法语。"根据题意应选 C。

22. ［答案］D

［解析］这道题测试的是复合宾语。复合宾语第一部分有时是一个从句、不定式或动名词,这时通常要用 it 代替它,把动名词、不定式或从句放到句子后边。本题翻译为"她发现和简合作很困难"。因此正确答案应选 D。

23. ［答案］B

［解析］这道题测试的是和 use 相关的搭配用法。used to do 翻译为"过去常常做(而现在不);be used to doing 翻译为"习惯于做某事";be used to do 翻译为"被用于做……"。本题的意思是"我过去常常六点钟起床。但是现在起床很晚"。因此正确答案应选 B。

24. ［答案］B

［解析］这道题测试的是词语搭配。participate in 翻译为"参与"。正确答案应

153

为 B。

25. ［答案］A

［解析］这道题测试的是词汇。offend 翻译为"冒犯"；protect 翻译为"保护"；object 翻译为"反对"；defend 翻译为"防卫"。根据句意应选 A。

Section B

26. ［答案］playing

［解析］look forward to 翻译为"期盼着做某事"；其中 to 为介词，因此后边要接名词或动名词。

27. ［答案］looking

［解析］本题测试固定搭配。avoid doing sth 翻译为"避免做某事"。

28. ［答案］attractive

［解析］attract（吸引）为动词，需变成形容词作 be 的表语，与前面的 be 一起构成系表结构。

29. ［答案］married

［解析］marry（结婚）为动词。需变成形容词作 get 系动词的表语。

30. ［答案］explanation

［解析］explain（解释）为动词。本句 The scientist's 为所有格形式，后边应加名词构成本句完整的主语部分，因此需把动词改为名词。

31. ［答案］learning

［解析］spend sometime（in）doing sth（花费时间做某事）为固定用法。

32. ［答案］development

［解析］由于本句缺少主语中心词，因此把动词 develop 变为名词，翻译为"随着经济的发展"。

33. ［答案］to say

［解析］本题考查动词固定用法。ask sb not to do sth 翻译为"不让某人做某事"。

34. ［答案］（should）enter

［解析］本题考查虚拟语气。wish（期望），后边的从句用（should）do 的形式。

35. ［答案］earliest

［解析］early（早的），是形容词。the 是形容词最高级的标志，因此应改为最高级的形式。本题翻译为"每天，汤姆都是最早到学校的学生"。

Part III Reading Comprehension

Task 1

36. ［答案］D

［解析］根据文中第二段最后一句"You will save money if you buy clothes that can wash easily."和第三段第一句"If you buy some well made clothes, you can save money because they can last longer"可知。

154

37. ［答案］B

［解析］根据文中第二段"The labels tell you how to take care of your clothes. The label for a shirt may tell you to wash it in warm water. A sweater label may tell you to wash it in cold water. The label on a coat may say "Dry Clean Only""可知。

38. ［答案］D

［解析］根据文中第一段"When you want to go shopping, you should decide first how much money you can pay for new clothes"可知。

39. ［答案］A

［解析］根据文中第三段"Sometimes some clothes cost more money, but it does not mean that they are always better made, or they always fit better. In other words, some less expensive clothes look and fit better than more expensive clothes"可知。

40. ［答案］C

［解析］根据文中第三段可知。

Task 2

41. ［答案］B

［解析］根据文中第一段"Heaven Air flies all the newest and fastest planes to more towns and cited of the world than any other airlines."可知。airline 翻译为"航空公司"。

42. ［答案］D

［解析］根据文中第一段"They want to go quickly and safely across the land, across the sea or right across the world, and they know Heaven Air will take them where they want to go whenever they want to go"可知。

43. ［答案］C

［解析］根据文中第三段"Do you want to go to Paris, Washington, Tokyo? Heaven Air will take you there, at all times of the day or night, right through the week"可知。

44. ［答案］B

［解析］根据文中第三段"Heaven Air will take you there, at all times of the day or night, right through the week. But Heaven Air flies not only to the biggest cities"可知。

45. ［答案］D

［解析］根据文中最后一段"Heaven Air is second to none"可知。

Task 3

46. ［答案］four

［解析］根据文中第二段"You do not remain at this deep fourth stages all night long"可知。

47. ［答案］fist

［解析］根据文中第一段"When your fist drift off into slumber..."可知。

48. ［答案］relax

［解析］根据文中第一段"... as you relax more and more, you will drift down through stage 2 and stage 3 sleep"可知。

49. ［答案］consciousness

[解析]根据文中第一段"Then about 40 to 69 minutes after you lose consciousness you will have reached the deepest sleep of all"可知。

50. [答案]fourth

[解析]根据文中第一段"Then about 40 to 69 minutes after you lose consciousness you will have reached the deepest sleep of all. Your brain will show the large slow waves that are known as the delta rhythm. This is stage 4 sleep"可知。

Task 4

51. (L)(C)　52. (G)(N)　53. (I)(F)　54. (D)(H)　55. (A)(J)

A——语言心理学家

B——交警

C——成本会计

D——信息分析

E——续集

F——蓝牙技术

G——游乐园

H——开发工程师

I——交通规则

J——心理咨询教师

K——电子工程师

L——跳高滑雪

M——电子相关工作

N——丝绸之路

O——电信服务

P——保管业务

Task 5

56. [答案]lost credit card

[解析]根据文中第一段第一二句"I am writing to confirm the loss of my credit card. I telephoned your office earlier today"可知。

57. [答案]Apex Silver card

[解析]根据文中第二段第二句"It is an Apex Silver card in the name of Paul R. Wilmoth"可知。

58. [答案]September 2000

[解析]根据第二段最后一句"This card is valid from August 1990 to August 2000"可知。

59. [答案]Tony's Bookstore

[解析]根据文中第三段第二三句"The only case I used the card yesterday was to buy three dictionaries at the Tony's Bookstore in Yingbin Street. By accident, I left the card at the shop."可知。

60. [答案]cancel

156

[解析]根据文中第四段第一句"Could you please cancel my card immediately and make the necessary arrangements to issue a replacement card to me"可知。

Part IV   Translation—English into Chinese

61. ［答案］D

   ［解析］重点考查 accompany,翻译为"陪伴;unless 翻译为"除非……"。

62. ［答案］B

   ［解析］重点考查 whatever he did,翻译为"凡是他做过的事情"。

63. ［答案］A

   ［解析］重点考查 lend us a hand 翻译为"帮忙";permit 翻译为"允许"。

64. ［答案］D

   ［解析］被考查点 experienced 翻译为"有经验的";manager assistant 翻译为"经理助理"。

65. [译文]如果失败了你会怎么做? 很多人可能会选择放弃。然而,要想成功,最好的方法就是坚持你的方向和目标。在通往成功的路上,你必须坚持你的方向。它就像一盏灯,在黑暗中为你指路,帮助你度过难关。否则,你很容易就会迷失方向或犹豫不前。方向意味着目标。人生如果没有目标,将一事无成。

Part V   Writing

参考答案

Lost and Found

   A lady has picked a purse in the supermarket on March 6th, and turned it over to our office. The owner of the purse may come to claim it with his or her identification card.

Lost and Found Office

Test 11

Part I Listening Comprehension   (15 minutes)

Directions: This part is to test your listening ability. It consists of 3 sections.

Section A

Directions: This section is to test your ability to give proper answers to questions. The question will be spoken two times. When you hear a question, you should decide on the correct answer from the 4 choices.

1. A. It doesn't matter.　　B. Yes, it is.　　C. No, it isn't.　　D. So am I.

2. A. But the food was not very good.　　B. My pleasure.
   C. Never mind.　　D. It's something small.

3. A. In the morning.　　B. Very well.
   C. In the library.　　D. By taking a course.

4. A. One hundred dollars.　　B. It's next to the station.
   C. Sorry, I have no money.　　D. Sorry, I don't know the way.

5. A. That's great.　　B. That's all right.
   C. Here you are.　　D. It doesn't matter.

Section B

Directions: This section is to test your ability to understand short dialogues. Both the dialogue and the question will be spoken two times. When you hear a question, you should decide on the correct answer.

6. A. Going shopping.　　B. Giving directions.
   C. Buying vegetable.　　D. Introducing himself.

7. A. Worried and frightened.　　B. Quite unhappy.
   C. Very relaxed.　　D. Angry with the professor.

8. A. They are having breakfast.　　B. They are eating some fruit.
   C. They are preparing hot soup.　　D. They are drinking cold milk.

9. A. She does not have to make a decision right away.
   B. He wants to help her make a decision.
   C. He will not make a decision for her.
   D. He does not know whether to help her.

10. A. He wants to save it.　　B. He has a toothache.
    C. He doesn't like it.　　D. He has trouble eating anything.

158

Section C

Directions: *In this section you will hear a recorded short passage. The passage is printed on the test paper, but with some words or phrases missing. The passage will be read three times. You are required to put the missing words or phrases on the blanks.*

A lift is wonderful. It's also ___11___ for us. Think about a tall building. Maybe it has twenty floors, maybe it has ___12___ or more. Who can walk all these stairs every day? So if we use a lift to go up and down, it will be easier for us to live in a tall building. We can have tall buildings because we have lifts. Sometimes a worker ___13___ in the lift. He or she runs it up and down. In ___14___ lifts there is no worker. The people walk in. They know what floor they want to go. They push a ___15___ and the lift goes to that floor. It's very fast and easy.

Part II   Vocabulary & Structure   (15 minutes)

Directions: *This part is to test your ability to use words and phrases correctly to construct meaningful and grammatically correct sentences.*

Section A

Directions: *There are 10 incomplete statements here. You are required to complete each statement by choosing the appropriate answer from the 4 choices.*

16. It is _____ of you to go into the dark room only by yourself at midnight.
    A. efficient   B. proud   C. bold   D. greedy
17. People used to think that the surface of the moon was smooth, _____?
    A. don't they   B. wasn't it   C. didn't they   D. usedn't they
18. I hope they _____ this tall building up by the time I come back next year.
    A. are to build   B. will build   C. have built   D. will have built
19. My teacher speaks to me _____ she were my mother.
    A. even though   B. if   C. even if   D. as if
20. The star was named _____ the scientist who found it.
    A. after   B. with   C. by   D. from
21. Where could my son _____ the key? I couldn't find anywhere.
    A. put   B. have put   C. has put   D. had put
22. I would rather you _____ them to those who appreciate them as presents.
    A. give   B. gave   C. will give   D. have given
23. I think nobody wants to have their new car _____.
    A. repair   B. repairing   C. to repair   D. repaired
24. He was asked to _____ the pencil for the little boy.
    A. sharp   B. sharped   C. sharping   D. sharpen
25. The Olympic Games, _____ in 776 B. C. , has become the most important sports event

159

in the world.

    A. first playing   B. to be first played C. first played   D. to be first playing

Section B

Directions: *There are also 10 incomplete statements here. You should fill in each blank with the proper form of the word given in the brackets.*

26. _____ (not finish) today's lessons, I have no time to watch TV.

27. Of the two kinds of ball games, I'd prefer basketball _____ (well).

28. We have gained a large _____ (grow) of light industry during these years.

29. There are (differ) _____ between the two similar pictures.

30. Jane is the only girl who _____ (keep) short hair in our class now.

31. He will come to see his girlfriend as soon as he (be) _____ free.

32. Don't forget (lock) _____ the door when you leave.

33. I suggested that he (get) _____ all the things ready a week later.

34. He is _____ (tall) of the two boys.

35. Nothing can (do) _____ unless the teacher gives us enough instructions.

Part III   Reading Comprehension   (40 minutes)

Task 1

Directions: *After reading the following passage, you will find 5 questions or unfinished statements. You should make the correct choices.*

    Many people in the world live in big cities, which are often dirty and difficult places to live in. So, some cities will get bigger. They will also get higher, and lower, because people will begin to live under the ground as well as in tall buildings. Scientists also say that men can begin to live in cities under the sea, when there is not enough space on the land. Of course, these new cities will be very expensive, and difficult to build, but they are not impossible. Already, some countries are building places to live under the ground so their people can go there if there is a new war. There are underground cities in Switzerland and China, built by the government to help some of the people live after a great war.

    But will the people change if they live under the ground for a long time? For example, some fish go blind if they live in the dark for a long time. People will not go blind, because there will be light underground, but they may change in some way. Scientists say that people who live in cities today are losing their senses of smell, touch and taste. They can't smell the dirty air, they can't taste the chemicals in their food. These senses are not as strong as before, when people lived in the country and grew their own food. The city has changed that. What will the underground city change us?

36. People will live under the ground because _____.

    A. it's neither hot nor cold there

B. they'll be afraid of the war

C. there'll be less space on the ground

D. they'll make their life comfortable

37. The passage tells us _____.

A. some new cities have been built under the ground

B. it'll be difficult to build the new cities under the ground

C. people will spend much money building new cities under the ground

D. both B and C

38. Some countries try to build some palaces under the ground so that people will be able to live there _____.

A. when summer comes

B. when a war breaks out

C. because they think it'll be safer for them

D. when they're fed up with the life on the land

39. People will lose some senses under the ground because _____.

A. the world are polluted

B. it's dark there

C. they can't see the far-away things

D. they can't grow their own food in the sun

40. In the author's opinion, the cities have changed people's senses except _____.

A. the sense of smell

B. the sense of taste

C. the sense of sight

D. both A and B

Task 2

Directions: *After reading you should make the correct choices.*

The age-old riddle of why many women live longer than men has been solved. It's their pumping power, British researchers have found.

On average, women live five years longer than men and women over the age of 60 are now the fastest-growing section of the British population. The average male heart becomes weaker with age, and by the age of 70 its power to pump blood around the body could have decreased by up to a quarter of its youthful strength.

David Goldspink, Professor of Cell and Molecular Sports Science at Liverpool John Moores University, said yesterday that women's longevity is linked to the strength of their hearts. Unlike men, they pump just as strongly at 70 as they do at 20.

"We have found that the power of the male heart falls by 20 – 25 percent between 18 and 70 years of age," Professor Goldspink said. "In stark contrast, over the same period there was no age-related decline in the power of the female heart, meaning that the heart of a healthy 70-

year-old woman could perform almost as well as a 20-year-old's."

The dramatic difference between the sexes might explain why women live longer. The good news is that men of any age can improve the health of their hearts simply by taking more regular exercise.

41. Why do women live longer than men? _____
    A. Because women's pumping power is better.
    B. Because women live five years longer than men.
    C. Because male's heart is weaker than female's.
    D. Because the power of women's hearts decrease.

42. Male's heart power to pump blood around the body could have decreased by _____ of its youthful strength.
    A. 1/2   B. 1/3   C. 1/4   D. 1/5

43. Women's longevity is because of _____.
    A. the blood around the body
    B. the strength of their hearts
    C. the ages
    D. the health

44. A 70-year-old woman's heart's pumping power is _____ a 20-year-old woman.
    A. weaker than
    B. stronger than
    C. almost the same as
    D. different from

45. The title of this passage can be _____.
    A. Women's Hearts
    B. Why Women Live Longer Than Men
    C. People's Hearts Pumping Power
    D. How Can Women Live Longer Than Men

Task 3

Directions: *After reading the passage, you should complete the correct answers.*

How do successful people think? What drives them? Interviews and investigations indicate that there are several keys to success that successful people share.

First of all, successful people never blame someone or something outside of themselves for their failure to go ahead. They realize that their future lies in their own hands. They understand that they cannot control things in life, such as nature, the past and other people. But in the meantime, they are well aware that they can control their own thoughts and actions. They take responsibility for their life and regard this as one of the most empowering things they can do.

Perhaps what most separates successful people from others is that they live life "on purpose". They are doing what they believe they are put here to do. In their opinion, having a purpose in their life is the most important element that enables them to become fully functioning people. They hold that when they live their life on purpose, their main concern is to do the job right. They love what they do and it shows. People want to do business with them because of their commitment. To live their life on purpose, successful people find a cause they believe in and create a business around it. Besides, they never easily give up. Once they have set up goals in their life, they're willing to do whatever it takes to achieve their goals. Top achievers always bear in mind that they don't have forever.

Rather than seeing it negative or depressing, they use the knowledge to support themselves and go after what they want energetically and passionately.

How Does a Successful People Succeed?

This passage mainly tells us the thoughts of __46__.

Successful people can realize that their future lies __47__.

Successful people never __48__ someone or something outside themselves for their failure. They take responsibility for their life.

Living life __49__ is the most important element to enable them to become successful.

Successful people use __50__ to support themselves.

Task 4

Directions: *After reading the following list, you are required to find the items equivalent to those given in Chinese in the list below.*

A. —— vocational guidance

B. —— occupational disease

C. —— work permit

D. —— work contract

E. —— work shop

F. —— serial production

G. —— shift work

H. —— teamwork work

I. —— piecework work

J. —— timework work

K. —— seasonal work

L. —— to be paid by the hour

M. —— labor management

N. —— labor market

O. —— department of labor

P. —— employment exchange

Q. —— handcrafts

R. —— full employment

Example：(L) 按小时付酬　　　　　(H) 联合工作

51.（　）职业病	（　）劳务合同
52.（　）车间	（　）工作许可证
53.（　）全日制工作	（　）劳务市场
54.（　）计时工作	（　）职业指导
55.（　）职业介绍所	（　）换班工作

Task 5

Directions：*After reading the passage, you are required to complete the statements that follow the questions.*

Name：Liu Fei

Date of Birth：July 23, 1965 Hangzhou, P. R. C.

Sex：Male

Marital Status：Unmarried

Education：

1973—1979 Yu Ying School, 79 West Zhongshan Rd, Nanjing

1979—1985 No. 9 High School, 160 Shanxi Rd, Nanjing

1985—1989 Nanjing University, majoring in International Trading, and completing requirements for the Bachelor of Arts, degree to be granted June 20, 1989

Hobbies：making friends, listening to music, reading, swimming

Employment Record：May, 1989. A part-time job in the Engineering Technology Trading Corporation, responsible for operation and typing.

Sept. 1989— present. Assistant Manager in Dong Xing-Trade Company, in charge of international trading fair.

Reference：Wang Zhanjun, General Manager in Dong Xing Company.

56. When was Mr. Liu born?

　　_____.

57. Is he married?

　　_____.

58. From which university did he graduate?

He graduated from _____.

59. What's his position now?

_____ in Dong Xing Trade Company.

60. With whom you can consult if you want to know more about Mr. Liu?

His _____, Mr. Wang Zhanjun.

Part IV　Translation—English into Chinese　（25 minutes）

Directions：*This part is to test your ability to translate English into Chinese. Each of the four*

61. The most urgent problem that still remains unsolved, however, is how to stop water from wasting.

   A. 然而,仍然没有得到解决的最紧迫的问题是怎样阻止水的浪费。

   B. 但是,最紧迫的还没有得到解决的问题是怎样阻止水的浪费。

   C. 然而,仍然没有得到解决的最紧迫的问题是怎么停止水的浪费。

   D. 最紧迫的问题还没有解决,但是,又怎么能停止水的浪费。

62. No sooner had he got home than it began to rain heavily.

   A. 他刚到家就开始下大雨了。

   B. 他还没到家,就开始下大雨了。

   C. 他在下大雨前,就到家了。

   D. 他到家前,就开始下大雨了。

63. She was alone in the strange place, but she was not lost.

   A. 她孤零零地留在陌生的地方,但她心里并没有发慌。

   B. 她独自一个人在陌生的地方,但她并没有迷路。

   C. 只有她一个人在陌生的地方,但是她并没有发慌。

   D. 只有她一个人在陌生的地方,但她并没有丢失。

64. It was very kind of her to do the cleaning-up, but she didn't have to do it.

   A. 如果她把这些东西都打扫了就太好了,但是她没打扫。

   B. 她真好,把这些东西都打扫了,但是她原本没有必要打扫。

   C. 如果她把这些东西都打扫了就太好了,但是她不是必须要打扫。

   D. 她真好,把这些东西都打扫了,但是已经没有必要了。

65. Many people—and their employers—have found that telecommuting(远程办公) is a wonderful way to work. Telecommuters can follow their own schedules. They work in their homes comfortably, where they can also look after their children or elderly parents. They save time and money by not traveling to work. And their employers save many things too, because they need fewer offices and furniture. Studies show that telecommuters change jobs less often.

Part V   Writing   (25 minutes)

Directions: *This part is to test your ability to do practical writing. You are required to finish the following writing according to the information.*

说明:请按照中文提供的信息,将下述内容填入英文表格。

郁秀公园欢迎您!

公园开放时间为 3 月到 10 月,每周 7 天,从上午 10 点至下午 6 点。成人票价 10 美元,儿童 5 美元,也可以花 20 美元买家庭票!每周六、周日有动物表演。表演从下午三点开始,持续两个小时。星期一至星期五上午 8:00—10:00 有免费巴士从市区开往公园,节假日和周末全天都有免费巴士从市区开往公园。可以在网上预订门票,也可以打电话订票。演出开始前半小时可以买到半价票。

Welcome to Yu Xiu Park

Opening months: From _____ to _____

Opening days in a week: _____

Opening hours: From _____

Time of Animal Show: _____

Show starts: _____

Show lasts: _____

Ticket price: Adults $ _____ ; Children $ _____ ;

Family Ticket $ _____

Additional information:

    1. Bus service

    _____

    2. Booking information

    _____

答案解析

Part I Listening Comprehension

听力原文

Section A

1. I am quite interested in playing table-tennis. What about you?

2. Thank you for your invitation, Mrs. White.

3. How did you learn Korean?

4. How much is the air-ticket to New York, please?

5. Pass me the bottle of water, please.

Section B

6. M: Can you tell me where I can buy some carrots?

    W: Yes. Go down this street and you will see a vegetable shop on your left.

    Q: What's the man doing?

7. W: Weren't you nervous when you had the oral exam?

    M: I'd say I was shaking all over.

    Q: How did the man feel when he had the oral exam?

8. W: Would you like some bread?

    M: No, thank you. I'm not used to eating bread in the morning.

Q: What are the two speakers doing now?

9. W: I don't know what I should do next.

M: There's not much time left, so you'd better make your own decision.

Q: What does the man mean?

10. W: Why don't you eat your nuts, Sam? Don't you like nuts?

M: Yes, I do. But I have some trouble with my tooth recently.

Q: Why doesn't Sam eat his nuts?

Section C

A lift is wonderful. It's also **11 important** for us. Think about a tall building. Maybe it has twenty floors, maybe it has **12 fifty** or more. Who can walk all these stairs every day? So if we use a lift to go up and down, it will be easier for us to live in a tall building. We can have tall buildings because we have lifts. Sometimes a worker **13 stands** in the lift. He or she runs it up and down. In **14 modern** lifts there is no worker. The people walk in. They know what floor they want to go. They push a **15 button** and the lift goes to that floor. It's very fast and easy.

答案详解

Part I Listening Comprehension

Section A

1. [答案]D 询问兴趣爱好题

[解析]题目"I am quite interested in playing table-tennis. What about you"翻译为"我对打网球非常感兴趣。你呢",意在询问对方"你对打网球感兴趣吗"。A 选项"It doesn't matter"翻译为"没关系",B 选项"Yes, it is"翻译为"是的",C 选项"No, it isn't"翻译为"不,不是"。因此只有 D 选项"So do I"(我也是)符合题意。

2. [答案]B 礼貌用语题

[解析]题目"Thank you for your invitation, Mrs. White"是在表达谢意:"谢谢您的邀请,怀特夫人。"回答别人的感谢的话时,应该用 B 选项"my pleasure(乐意效劳)回答,C 选项"Never mind"翻译为"没关系",一般用于回答"对不起"。A 选项"But the food was not very good"翻译为"但是这些食物不太好",D 选项"It's something small"翻译为"有点小"。

3. [答案]D 询问方式题

[解析]题目"How did you learn Korean"翻译为"你是怎样学习韩语的",是在问对方学习韩语的方式。A 选项"In the morning"翻译为"在早晨",B 选项"Very well"翻译为"很好",C 选项"In the library"翻译为"在图书馆",D 选项"By taking a course"翻译为"通过上课",因此 D 选项符合题意。

4. [答案]A 询问价格题

[解析]题目"How much is the air-ticket to New York, please"翻译为"请问到纽约的飞机票多少钱"。B 选项"It's next to the station"翻译为"在车站隔壁",C 选项"Sorry, I have no money"翻译为"对不起,我没有钱",D 选项"Sorry, I don't know the way"翻译为"对不起,我不认识路",均不用来回答价格,因此只有 A 选项 "One hundred dollars(一百美元)"符合题意。

5. [答案]C 回答请求题

[解析]题目"Pass me the bottle of water, please"翻译为"请递给我一瓶水",是在向对方提出请求。A 选项"That's great"翻译为"太棒了",B 选项"That's all right"翻译为"没什么",D 选项"It doesn't matter"翻译为"没关系"。因此只有 C 选项"Here you are(给你)"符合题意。

Section B

6. [答案]A 推断题

[解析]由对话中男士说:"Can you tell me where I can buy some carrots?(你能告诉我在哪里能买到胡萝卜吗?)"可以推断出,那位男士是要去买东西,而不是正在买。题目问"那位男士在干什么"。B 选项"Giving directions"翻译为"指路",C 选项"Buying vegetable"翻译为"正在买蔬菜",D 选项为"介绍自己"。所以选项 A"Going shopping(去买东西)"符合题意。

7. [答案]A 判断题

[解析]对话中女士问:"Weren't you nervous when you had the oral exam?(难道你在参加口语考试时不紧张吗?)"男士回答:"I'd say I was shaking all over。(我得说我一直都在颤抖)"。由此可以判断,这位男士在参加口语考试时的感觉是害怕的。B 选项"Quite unhappy"翻译为"非常不高兴",C 选项"Very relaxed"翻译为"非常放松",D 选项"Angry with the professor"翻译为"生教授的气",所以选项 A"Worried and frightened。(担心又害怕。)"符合题意。

8. [答案]A 推断题

[解析]由对话中女士问男士:"Would you like some bread?(来点面包怎么样?)"男士回答:"No, thank you. I'm not used to eating bread in the morning(不,谢谢。我早晨不习惯吃面包。)"可以推断出两人正在吃早餐。B 选项"They are eating some fruit"翻译为"他们正在吃水果",C 选项"They are preparing hot soup"翻译为"他们正在准备热汤",D 选项"They are drinking cold milk"翻译为"他们正在喝冷牛奶",因此只有 A 选项"They are having breakfast"翻译为"他们正在吃早餐",符合题意。

9. [答案]C 推断题

[解析]对话中女士说:"I don't know what should I do next(我不知道下面该做什么。)"男士回答:"There's no much time left, so you'd better make your own decision。(剩下的时间不多了,你最好自己拿主意。)"由此可以推断,这位男士的意思是他不会替这位女士做决定。A 选项"She does not have to make a decision right away"翻译为"她不必立刻做决定",B 选项"He wants to help her make a decision"翻译为"他要帮她做决定",D 选项"He does not know whether to help her"翻译为"他不知道是否要帮助她",故选项 C"He will not make a decision for her。(他不会为她做决定。)"符合题意。

10. ［答案］B 判断题

［解析］由对话中女士问男士："Why don't you eat your nuts, Sam? Don't you like nuts? (山姆,你为什么不吃坚果呢? 你不喜欢吗?)"男士回答："Yes, I do. But I have some trouble with my tooth recently.(不,我喜欢。但是最近我的牙齿出了点问题。)"所以我们可以判断,山姆不吃坚果的原因是他的牙齿不舒服。A 选项"He wants to save it"翻译为"他要省着吃",C 选项"He doesn't like it"翻译为"他不喜欢",D 选项"He has trouble eating anything"翻译为"他吃任何东西都不舒服",故选项 B"He has a tooth-ache.(他牙疼。)"符合题意。

Section C

11. important 12. fifty 13. stands 14. modern 15. button

Part Ⅱ Vocabulary & Structure

Section A

16. ［答案］C

［解析］efficient 翻译为"有效率的,有效的";proud 翻译为"骄傲的";bold 翻译为"大胆的";greedy 翻译为"贪婪的"。因此只有 C 选项符合题意。

17. ［答案］C

［解析］used to do 翻译为"过去常常……",时态为一般过去时,因此对动词 used 的反意疑问部分应用一般过去时 didn't,而不是 usedn't.

18. ［答案］D

［解析］by the time...翻译为"到……时候为止",是完成时的时间状语,又因为题中的时间到 next year 为止,因此这句话的时态为将来完成时,应用 will have done 的表达模式。故只有选项 D 符合题意。

19. ［答案］D

［解析］even though 翻译为"尽管";if 翻译为"如果,是否";even if 翻译为"即使,虽然",as if 翻译为"好像,仿佛"。因此只有 D 选项符合题意。

20. ［答案］A

［解析］name after...翻译为"以……命名",其他选项中的介词均不能与 name 构成短语。故选项 A 为正确答案。

21. ［答案］B

［解析］由本句句意可以推断出该句为完成时态,又因为 could 后须跟动词原形,故选项 B"have put"符合题意。

22. ［答案］B

［解析］本题考查的是虚拟语气。would rather 翻译为"宁愿",后面跟从句时,从句中的动词用一般过去时表示对将来或现在发生的动作的虚拟。

23. ［答案］D

［解析］不定式在感官动词和使役动词后面作宾语补足语时,应省略 to。have 在此翻

译为"使……",属于使役动词的范畴。have sb. do 翻译为"使某人做某事"。但当后面的动词与主语之间是被动关系时,即变成"have sth. done",翻译为"使某事被做"。

24. ［答案］D

　　［解析］根据句意和动词不定式 ask sb. to do sth. 可知,空白处应填动词,sharp 翻译为"尖锐的",是形容词性,它的动词形式为 sharpen,因此选项 D 为正确答案。

25. ［答案］C

　　［解析］根据句意,第一次奥运会是过去已经举行的,而且"奥林匹克运动会"与"举行"之间是被动关系。不定式 to do 作状语用于动作还未发生;现在分词 doing 作状语用于动作与主体之间是主动关系;过去分词 done 作状语用于动作与主体之间是被动关系。因此 C 选项符合题意。

Section B

26. ［答案］Not having finished

　　［解析］由题意可知,该句为现在完成时态。本句中主语为 I,与动词短语"finish today's lessons(完成今天的家庭作业)"为主动关系,现在分词作状语可以表示主语与动作之间的主动联系。故正确答案为 Not having finished。

27. ［答案］better

　　［解析］prefer 翻译为"更喜欢",后面连接形容词或副词时,须跟形容词或副词的比较级。故该题的正确答案应为 better。

28. ［答案］growth

　　［解析］根据句意,句中空白处前为形容词 large,因此可以判断该空白处须填名词。动词 grow 的名词形式为 growth。

29. ［答案］differences

　　［解析］there be 句型可表示"某地有某物",根据题意,该空白处应填名词"不同之处"。动词 differ 的名词形式为 difference,属可数名词。由于空白处前为表示复数的 be 动词 are,因此该题正确答案为 differences。

30. ［答案］keeps

　　［解析］根据题意可知珍妮留短发是现在状态,因此应用 keep 的一般现在形式。由于珍妮属于第三人称单数,故填 keeps。

31. ［答案］is

　　［解析］在条件状语从句和某些时间状语从句中,如果主句为一般将来时态,那么从句则用一般现在时表示将来。在该题中,主句为 He will come to see his girlfriend,主句动词 will come 为一般将来时,所以从句的动词 be 应用一般现在时表示单数的 is。

32. ［答案］to lock

　　［解析］本题考查 forget 的用法。forget 翻译为"忘记",后面可跟动词的两种形式。跟带 to 的不定式 to do,表示忘记的动作其实还没有做;跟动名词 doing 可以表示忘记的动作事实上已经做了。根据题意,"锁门"的动作其实还没做,所以应填 to lock。

33. ［答案］get/should get

　　［解析］一些表达命令、建议、要求的动词,例如 require,request, ask, order, demand,

suggest, command, advice, decide 等,在引导宾语从句时,从句中的动词一般用 should do 形式表示虚拟,其中 should 可省略。

34. ［答案］the taller
［解析］在比较级的用法中,如果比较的范围是"of ＋两者"的情况,那么形容词或副词在变比较级时,应在比较级前加 the。

35. ［答案］be done
［解析］根据题意,主语 nothing 和谓语动词 do 构成了被动关系。因此,此处应填情态动词的被动语态,即 can be done。

Part Ⅲ Reading Comprehension

Task 1

36. ［答案］C
［解析］从第一段的第四句话"Scientists also say that men can begin to live in cities under the sea, when there is not enough space on the land.(科学家们说,当陆地上的空间不够时,人们可能会开始在海下的地下城市生活。)可知人们将会在地下生活的原因是陆地的生活空间不够。因此 C 选项符合题意。

37. ［答案］D
［解析］由原文第一段的第五句话"Of course, these new cities will be very expensive, and difficult to build, but they are not impossible.(当然,这些新城市的建成会很贵,也很不容易,但并非不可能。)可以推断出,这篇文章告诉了我们建立地下城市会花很多钱并且非常难。故 D 为正确答案。

38. ［答案］B
［解析］由第一段的这句话"Already, some countries are building places to live under the ground so their people can go there if there is a new war"可知,一些国家建了地下城市后,人们就可以在战争爆发的时候去地下居住。因此 B 选项符合题意。

39. ［答案］D
［解析］由原文第二段中的"Scientists say that people who live in cities today are losing their senses of smell, touch and taste. They can't smell the dirty air, they can't taste the chemicals in their food. These senses are not as strong as before, when people lived in the country and grew their own food"可以推断出,人们各种感觉下降是因为不能在正常的光照下种植农作物,所以 D 选项符合题意。

40. ［答案］C
［解析］从第二段的"Scientists say that people who live in cities today are losing their senses of smell, touch and taste"可以看出,城市生活唯独没有改变人们的视觉。因此 C 选项符合题意。

Task 2

41. ［答案］A
［解析］由文中第一段的第二句话"The age-old riddle of why many women live longer

171

than men has been solved. It's their pumping power"可以总结出男性和女性的寿命差异与心脏的活力有关,同时根据第二段的数据对比可知,女性比男性的寿命长是因为女性的心脏活力好于男性。因此 A 选项符合题意。

42. [答案]C

[解析]由文中第二段的最后一句话"The average male heart becomes weaker with age, and by the age of 70 its power to pump blood around the body could have decreased by up to a quarter of its youthful strength"可知,男性心脏的力量在 70 岁时比年轻时降低 a quarter,即"四分之一"。因此 C 选项为正确答案。

43. [答案]B

[解析]文章第三段"... said yesterday that women's longevity is linked to the strength of their hearts"告诉我们,女性的寿命长跟她们的心脏力量有关系。所以 B 为正确答案。

44. [答案]C

[解析]文中这句话"... meaning that the heart of a healthy 70-year-old woman could perform almost as well as a 20-year-old's"告诉我们,一名健康的 70 岁女性的心脏力量与一名 20 岁女性的心脏力量是一样的。所以 C 选项符合题意。

45. [答案]B

[解析]通过阅读全文可以看出,文章讲述的是女性比男性寿命长的原因,故本文最合适的题目应该是 B"为什么女性比男性寿命长"。

Task 3

46. [答案]successful people

[解析]从本文第一句话"How do successful people think"以及下文的主要内容可以看出,本文主要讲的是成功人士的想法。所以正确答案应为 successful people。

47. [答案]in their own hands

[解析]由本文第二段的第二句话"They realize that their future lies in their own hands"可知,成功的人意识到了他们的未来掌握在自己手中。因此正确答案为 in their own hands。

48. [答案]blame

[解析]文章第二段第一句话"First of all, successful people never blame someone or something outside of themselves for their failure to go ahead"告诉我们,成功的人在经历失败的时候从来不埋怨别人。所以正确答案为 blame。

49. [答案]on purpose

[解析]由文章第三段的第二句话"In their opinion, having a purpose in their life is the most important element that enables them to become fully functioning people"可知,有目的地生活是促使成功的人获得成功的一个基本原因。因此该题正确答案为 on purpose。

50. [答案]knowledge

[解析]文章最后一句话"... they use the knowledge to support themselves and go after what they want energetically and passionately"告诉我们,成功的人用知识来支撑自己。因此 knowledge 为正确答案。

Task 4

51. (B)(D)　52. (E)(C)　53. (R)(N)　54. (J)(A)　55. (P)(G)

A——职业指导

B——职业病

C——工作许可证

D——劳务合同

E——车间

F——组装线工作

G——换班工作

H——联合工作

I——计件工作

J——计时工作

K——季节工作

L——按小时付酬

M——职业介绍经纪人

N——劳务市场

O——劳工部

P——职业介绍所

Q——手艺

R——全日制工作

Task 5

56. ［答案］On July 23, 1965

　　［解析］由文中 Date of Birth 可知,答案应为 On July 23, 1965。

57. ［答案］No, he isn't

　　［解析］由文中"Marital Status(婚姻状况)",可知他是未婚的。

58. ［答案］Nanjing University

　　［解析］从文中 Education 中的"1985—1989 Nanjing University",可得出该答案。

59. ［答案］Assistant Manager

　　［解析］文中"Sept. 1989—present. Assistant Manager in Dong Xing-Trade Company"告诉我们,他现在的职位是 Assistant Manager。

60. ［答案］General Manager

　　［解析］由文中"Reference：Wang Zhanjun, General Manager in Dong Xing Company"可知,GeneralManager 为正确答案。

Part Ⅳ　Translation—English into Chinese

61. ［答案］A

　　［解析］翻译此句需要注意两个问题:一是 however 应翻译为"然而",二是 stop...from...应译为"阻止"。

62. ［答案］A

［解析］翻译本句时,关键要注意 no sooner...than 应译为"刚……就……"。

63. ［答案］A

［解析］翻译此句的关键在于,lost 在此处译为"慌张"更合适,而不能译为"丢失"。

64. ［答案］B

［解析］翻译此句应把握好本句的时态为一般过去时,说明"打扫"这件事她已经做了,另外 have to 译为"必须,不得不",而不是"有必要"的意思。

65. ［译文］许多人及其老板们发现远程办公是一种非常棒的工作方式。远程办公者可自主安排自己的时间。在家里办公舒适又能照顾子女或父母。由于不用出门,既省时间又省金钱。他们的老板也一样节省了办公室和办公家具。研究表明,远程办公者换工作的通常较少。

［解析］翻译这段话时应注意一些长句子的翻译,例如,非限定性定语从句等。在本文中出现了一个定语从句,"They work in their homes comfortably, where they can also look after their children or elderly parents"。此句中连接副词 where 引导定语从句修饰 home,翻译为"在家里既办公舒适又能照顾子女或父母"。

Part V　Writing

【参考范文】

Welcome to Yu Xiu Park

Opening months：From March to October

Opening days in a week：Seven days a week/Every day

Opening hours：From 10：00 a. m. to 6：00 p. m.

Time of Animal Show：Saturday and Sunday

Show starts：3：00 p. m.

Show lasts：Two hours

Ticket price：Adults ＄10；Children ＄5；Family Ticket ＄20

Additional information：

1. BUS service

Free buses to the park from downtown from 8：00 a. m. to 10：00 a. m. during weekdays and available throughout the day during weekends and holidays.

2. Booking information

Tickets can be booked online or by phone. (Some) tickets may be available at half price half an hour before the show starts.

Test 12

Part I　Listening Comprehension　(15 minutes)

Directions: *This part is to test your listening ability. It consists of 3 sections.*

Section A

Directions: *This section is to test your ability to give proper answers to questions. The question will be spoken two times. When you hear a question, you should decide on the correct answer from the 4 choices.*

1. A. Yes, I came to Qingdao from Beijing.　　C. It is possible to travel by bus and by plane.
   B. I like both bus and plane.　　　　　　　D. I flew there.

2. A. Yes, I do.　　　　　　　C. Once a week.
   B. I like it very much.　　　D. I don't know.

3. A. Yes, she is.　　　　　　C. No, she isn't.
   B. No, she didn't.　　　　　D. Yes, she does.

4. A. It was a waste of time.　　C. No, I didn't.
   B. Yes, I did.　　　　　　　　D. It lasts two hours.

5. A. It's six o'clock.　　　C. The traffic was terrible.
   B. It is not my fault.　　D. The bus was on time.

Section B

Directions: *This section is to test your ability to understand short dialogues. Both the dialogue and the question will be spoken two times. When you hear a question, you should decide on the correct answer.*

6. A. It is easy.　　C. It is boring.
   B. It is hard.　　D. It is interesting.

7. A. At six.　　　C. An hour earlier.
   B. At seven.　　D. At five.

8. A. 4 dollars.　　C. 12 dollars.
   B. 7.5 dollars.　　D. 8 dollars.

9. A. At a book store.　　C. In a library.
   B. In a classroom.　　D. In a reading room.

10. A. It is not very good.　　C. It's not as good as his other novels.
    B. It's excellent.　　　　　D. There is room for improvement.

Section C

Directions: *In this section you will hear a recorded short passage. The passage is printed on the test paper, but with some words or phrases missing. The passage will be read three times. You are required to put the missing words or phrases on the blanks.*

I work in a small, high-class restaurant. I've been there since ___11___ I was lucky to ___12___ because they'd had a boy before. They didn't ___13___ for a girl and it was a big ___14___ for them to ___15___ me. It's harder for a girl to be accepted because men are better able to cope physically.

Part II Vocabulary & Structure (15 minutes)

Directions: *This part is to test your ability to use words and phrases correctly to construct meaningful and grammatically correct sentences.*

Section A

Directions: *There are 10 incomplete statements here. You are required to complete each statement by choosing the appropriate answer from the 4 choices.*

16. The climate in London doesn't _____ with me; therefore, I've decided to move to China.

    A. suit   B. apply   C. fit   D. agree

17. The twins were dressed _____ in red T-shirt so I couldn't tell which was which.

    A. like   B. likely   C. alike   D. liking

18. She didn't have the _____ to walk any further.

    A. quality   B. strength   C. experience   D. attitude

19. They decided to teach Tom a good _____.

    A. thing   B. task   C. lesson   D. class

20. It was Japan _____ launched the war against China.

    A. that   B. when   C. whom   D. which

21. People won't go out after dark because they are afraid of _____.

    A. attacking   B. being attacked   C. having been attacked D. attacked

22. The word _____ that a new model of cell phones would soon come onto the market.

    A. communicated B. issued   C. spoke   D. spread

23. He likes reading books, and he bought _____ novels.

    A. many too far   B. too far many   C. far too many   D. far too much

24. It's high time we _____ something to stop road accidents.

    A. did   B. are doing   C. will do   D. do

25. I've never seen the boy _____ next to the woman.

    A. sits   B. sitting   C. sat   D. to sit

Section B

Directions: *There are also 10 incomplete statements here. You should fill in each blank with the proper form of the word given in the brackets.*

26. When he called her on the phone, she pretended (not know) _____ him.

27. By this time, there were quite a few people (stand) _____ in line.

28. The prices here are not _____ (reason). They are too expensive.

29. The couple sent out wedding (invite) _____ to their friends.

30. By the end of next month, we _____ (learn) two thousand English words.

31. She told a very (live) _____ story about his life in America.

32. The teacher should raise his voice in order to make himself (hear) _____.

33. The little boy happily looks forward to (meet) _____ the movie star at the party.

34. The woman is (fortune) _____ in having an ideal husband.

35. He talked as if he (do) _____ all the work himself, but in fact I did most of it.

Part III Reading Comprehension (40 minutes)

Task 1

Directions: *After reading the following passage, you will find 5 questions or unfinished statements. You should make the correct choices.*

Do you find getting up in the morning so difficult that it's painful? This might be called laziness, but Dr. Kleitman has a new explanation. He has proved that everyone has a daily energy cycle.

During the hours when you labor through your work, you may say that you're "hot". That's true. The time of day when you feel most energetic is when your cycle of body temperature is at its peak. For some people the peak comes before noon. For others it comes in the afternoon or evening. No one has discovered why this is so, but it leads to such familiar saying as: "Get up, John! You're late for work again!" The possible explanation to the trouble is that John is at his temperature-and-energy peak in the evening. Much family quarrelling end when husbands and wives realize what these energy cycles mean, and which cycle each member of the family has.

You can't change your energy cycle, but you can learn to make your life fit it better. Habit can help, Dr. Kleitman believes. If your energy is low in the morning but you have an important job to do early in the day, rise before your usual hour. This won't change your cycle, but you'll work better at your low point.

Get off to slow start which saves your energy. When you get up, sit on the edge of the bed a minute before putting your feet on the floor. Avoid the troublesome search for clean clothes by laying them out the night before. Whenever possible, do routine work in the afternoon and save tasks requiring more energy or concentration for your sharper hours.

177

36. According to the new findings of Dr. Kleitman, if a person finds getting up early is difficult, most probably _____.

    A. he is a lazy person

    B. he refuses to follow his own energy cycle

    C. he is not sure when his energy is low

    D. he is at his energy peak in the afternoon or evening

37. Which of the following may lead to family quarrels according to the passage? _____

    A. Unawareness of energy cycles.

    B. A change in a family member's energy cycle.

    C. Familiar saying.

    D. Attempts to control the energy of other family members.

38. If one wants to work more efficiently at his low point in the morning, he should _____

    A. change his energy cycle

    B. overcome his laziness

    C. get up earlier than usual

    D. go to bed earlier

39. You are advised to act slowly when you rise in the morning because it will _____

    A. help to keep your energy for the day's work

    B. help you to control your mood early in the day

    C. enable you to concentrate on your routine work

    D. keep your energy cycle under control all day

40. Which of the following statements is NOT true? _____

    A. Getting off to work with a minimum effort helps save one's energy.

    B. Dr. Kleitman explains why people reach their peak at different hours of day.

    C. Habit helps one adapt to his own energy cycle.

    D. Children have energy cycles, too.

Task 2

Directions: *After reading you should make the correct choices.*

We were late as usual. My husband had insisted on watering the flowers in the garden by himself, and when he discovered that he couldn't manage, he asked me for help at the last moment. So now we had an hour to get to the airport. Luckily, there were not many cars or buses on the road and we were able to get there just in time. We checked in and went straight to a big hall to wait for flight to be called. We waited and waited, but no announcement was made. We asked for information and the girl there told us that the plane hadn't even arrived yet. In the end, there was another announcement telling us that passengers waiting for Flight LJ108 could get a free meal voucher(凭单) and that the plane hadn't left Spain for technical problems. We thought that meant that it wasn't safe for the plane to fly. We waited again for a long time until late evening when we were asked to report again. This time we were given vouchers to spend the night in a nearby hotel.

The next morning after a bad night because of all the planes taking off and landing, we were reported back to the airport. Guess what had happened while we were asleep! Our plane had arrived and taken off again. All the other passengers had been forgotten. You can imagine how we felt!

41. The plane the writer and her husband would take _____.

    A. came from Spain   B. passed by Spain

    C. was going to Spain   D. had gone to Spain

42. The plane was delayed _____.

    A. by the bad weather   B. by the passengers

    C. because of many cars on road   D. because something was wrong with the machine

43. They were in a big hall, waiting for _____.

    A. the girl to give them information   B. their flight to be announced

    C. the free meal voucher   D. other passengers to arrive

44. The passengers were given a free meal because _____.

    A. they arrived at the airport early   B. they hadn't had a meal yet

    C. they had no money with them   D. their plane was delayed

45. The plane took off again _____.

    A. as soon as it had arrived   B. after all the passengers were woken up

    C. while the passengers were sleeping D. early the next morning

Task 3

Directions: *After reading the passage, you should complete the correct answers.*

There's the emperor of northern India, Shah Jehan, also called the King of the World. In 1612, Shah Jehan married Mumtaz Mahal. Madly in love, they had 14 children over the next 20 years. But then sadness came. As Mumtaz was about to give birth to child number 14, she said she had heard her unborn baby cry out. It was a sign of death. And as Mumtaz lay dying, she asked Jehan to build a lasting memorial(纪念物) to celebrate their love.

When the heartbroken Jehan appeared eight days after his wife's death, his people were shocked to see that his coal-black hair had turned snow-white.

Putting away his sadness, Jehan ordered his wife's dying wish carried out. More than 20,000 workers labored nearly 22 years to complete the construction. In 1653, Jehan placed Mumtaz's remains in the center under the building.

And then, son number five, Aurangzeb, murdered his brothers and took over the power from his aging father. Jehan lived the rest of his days—eight years, to be exact —imprisoned not far from the Taj Mahal. Jehan was only allowed to climb onto the top of his prison to see the time-less treasure from a distance. But never again would he be allowed to visit it—until he was buried next to his wife.

Today 25,000 people visit the Taj Mahal each day. Though the reason for building the tower was a strange, sad story, those who see its breath-taking beauty are reminded of the happiness that inspired(激发……的灵感)its construction.

46. The Taj Mahal was first built as _____.

47. Mumtaz thought _____ was a sign of death.

48. People were shocked to see that Jehan's coal-black hair had _____ after his wife's death.

49. _____ took over the power from Jehan.

50. We learn from the text that Mumtaz probably died in _____(which year).

Task 4

Directions: *After reading the following list, you are required to find the items equivalent to those given in Chinese in the list below.*

A. —— tap

B. —— lavatory

C. —— wash-conditioner

D. —— perfume

E. —— nail-clipper

F. —— slippers

G. —— street index

H. —— bathing towel

I. —— double bedroom

J. —— barber's shop

K. —— desk lamp

L. —— quilt

M. —— bed sheet

N. —— switch

Example：(G) 街名索引   (J)理发店

51. ( ) 指甲刀	( )拖鞋
52. ( ) 开关	( )双人间
53. ( ) 水龙头	( )台灯
54. ( ) 床单	( )厕所
55. ( ) 被子	( )香水

Task 5

Directions: *After reading the passage, you are required to complete the statements that follow the questions.*

· Course：Intercultural Communication

· LECTURER ：John Smith

· CLASS MEETS ON TUESDAYS AND THURSDAYS

· TIME：from 3：15 to 4：50

· CLASSROOM：Room 505（ first half)

- Room 405 (last two months)
- TEXTBOOK: Beyond Language
- OFFICE HOUR: 1:00 to 2:00 on Wednesdays
- Grading is determined by your performance on a midterm and final test, periodic quizzes, a research project, and classroom participation

56. What's the content of the course?
   _____

57. When should you take the course?
   On _____ and _____

58. How long will the course take?
   _____

59. Which book should you bring when you take the course?
   _____

60. If you want to take the course, when should you sign up?
   _____

Part IV   Translation—English into Chinese   (25 minutes)

Directions: *This part is to test your ability to translate English into Chinese. Each of the four sentences is followed by four choices of suggested translation. Make the best choice. Write your translation of the paragraph in the corresponding space.*

61. The containers were generally used for food, wine and water, and they often placed in the graves with the dead.
   A. 这容器一般来说是为了放食物、红酒和水,而且也可以存放死人的尸体。
   B. 这容器通常用来装食物、酒和水,而且还常与死人一起葬在坟墓里。
   C. 这容器通常装好了食物、酒和水,然后埋葬在坟墓里。
   D. 这容器一般来说是用来装食物、酒和水,有时候也可以存放尸体。

62. All passengers except American citizens must complete this form.
   A. 除了美国公民以外,所有的乘客都得填此卡。
   B. 所有的乘客都得填此卡,美国公民也不例外。
   C. 除了住在美国大城市的人员以外,所有的乘客都得填此卡。
   D. 所有住在美国乡村的公民都必须填写此卡。

63. It will save you much time when you go through the Customs.
   A. 这会让你在了解当地的文化时更顺利。
   B. 这会让你在接待游客时更方便。
   C. 这样会让你更快的了解一种文化。
   D. 这样可以让你在过海关时省去很多时间。

64. His feelings as he read the letter were hardly to be defined.

A. 他看信时的感情早已限定。

B. 他看信时的心情不可名状。

C. 在他看信时他的感情几乎不能确定。

D. 在他看信时他的感情几乎可以被确定。

65. In those days a strict unwritten code governed how young men and women behaved toward each other. Members of the opposite sex never gave each other clothes as gifts, not even a sweater, well maybe a necktie or a pair of gloves. Anything else was considered much too personal. Good book. Nice wallet. Nothing more intimate than that. Young men and women certainly never took overnight trips to the beach or anywhere else, even with their steadies and the code word said, "don't call him. He's supposed to call you."

Part V Writing (25 minutes)

Directions: *This part is to test your ability to do practical writing. You are required to finish the following writing according to the information.*

说明:根据下列信息,写一封祝贺信。

你听说你的朋友玛丽下个月要结婚了,知道玛丽的家人一定为她感到高兴,你也想表达同样的感受。请你写封祝贺信,祝她拥有一个幸福的婚姻。

答 案 解 析

Part I Listening Comprehension

听力原文

Section A

1. Did you travel to Qingdao from Beijing by bus or by plane?

2. How often do you visit your grandmother?

3. Mary looks good in that new skirt, doesn't she?

4. Hi, Jason. How did you like the Fashion Show you saw last night?

5. Jim, why are you so late today?

Section B

6. M: How did your writing go this morning? Is the book coming along all right?

   W: I'm not sure. I think the rest of it will be difficult to write.

   Q: What does the woman think of her writing?

7. M: When does your father leave?

   W: He usually leaves at six, but yesterday he left an hour earlier.

   Q: When did her father leave yesterday?

8. M: How much did you pay for this used book?

W: I paid 4 dollars—half of its usual price.

Q: What is the usual price of the book?

9. M: How long can I keep the books?

W: For three weeks. You must renew the books if you want to keep them longer. Otherwise you'll be fined.

Q: Where does the conversation probably take place?

10. W: What do you think of his new novel?

M: It couldn't be better.

Q: What does the man think of the novel?

Section C

I work in a small, high-class restaurant. I've been there since **11 last March**. I was lucky to **12 get the job** because they'd had a boy before. They didn't **13 advertise** for a girl and it was a big **14 decision** for them to **15 hire** me. It's harder for a girl to be accepted because men are better able to cope physically.

答案详解

Part I Listening Comprehension

Section A

1. [答案]D

[解析]"Did you travel to Qingdao from Beijing by bus or by plane"翻译为"你从北京到青岛是坐公共汽车还是坐飞机";A"Yes, I came to Qingdao from Beijing"翻译为"是的,我从北京去青岛的";B"It is possible to travel by bus and by plane"翻译为"坐公共汽车或坐飞机都可以";C"I like both bus and plane"翻译为"我既喜欢坐公共汽车又喜欢坐飞机";D"I flew there"翻译为"我坐飞机来的"。所以根据题意选择 D。

2. [答案]C

[解析]"How often do you visit your grandmother"翻译为"你多久看一次你的奶奶";"Once a week"翻译为"一周一次"。所以根据题意选择 C。

3. [答案]D

[解析]"Mary looks good in that new skirt, doesn't she"翻译为"玛丽穿这件新裙子看起来很漂亮,不是吗"。本题考查的是反意疑问句及其回答。题中反意部分为 doesn't she,所以回答时必须用"does"的相关形式。所以根据题意选择 D。

4. [答案]A

[解析]"Hi, Jason. How did you like the Fashion Show you saw last night"翻译为"你好,杰森! 你觉得昨晚的时装表演怎么样";A"It was a waste of time"翻译为"就是浪费时间",言外之意就是觉得不好。所以根据题意选择 A。

5. [答案]C

[解析]"Jim, why are you so late today?"翻译为"吉姆,你今天为什么这么晚到";C "The traffic was terrible"翻译为"交通太糟糕了";D"The bus was on time"翻译为"公共汽车很准时",所以根据题意选择 C。

Section B

6. [答案]B

[解析]对话中"I think the rest of it will be difficult to write"翻译为"我想,剩下的部分会很难写"所以根据题意选择 B。

7. [答案]D

[解析]对话中"He usually leaves at six, but yesterday he left an hour earlier"翻译为"他通常在 6 点走,但是昨天他早走了 1 个小时"言外之意是说昨天他 5 点走的。所以根据题意选择 D。

8. [答案]D

[解析]对话中"I paid 4 dollars—half of its usual price"翻译为"我花了 4 美金——它正常价格的一半"。所以根据题意选择 D。

9. [答案]C

[解析]问题是"Where does the conversation probably take place"翻译为"这个对话很可能发生在哪";对话中"How long can I keep the books"翻译为"我能借这些书看多久";" For three weeks. You must renew the books if you want to keep them longer. Otherwise you'll be fined"翻译为"三个星期。如果你想借更久就必须来换书卡。不然你将被罚款"。所以根据题意选择 C。

10. [答案]B

[解析]问题是"你觉得这本新小说怎么样",对话中:"It couldn't be better"翻译为"不能再好了"。所以根据题意选择 B。

Section C

11. last March   12. get the job   13. advertise   14. decision   15. hire

Part II Vocabulary & Structure

Section A

16. [答案]D

[解析]agree with 在此翻译为"(气候、食物等)相宜,适合"。所以根据题意应选 D。

17. [答案]C

[解析]alike 在此翻译为"一样地,相似地"。所以根据题意应选 C。

18. [答案]B

[解析]quality 在此翻译为"质量,品质";strength 在此翻译为"力量,力气";experience 在此翻译为"经历;经验"; attitude 在此翻译为"态度"。所以根据题意应选 B。

184

19. ［答案］C

　　［解析］teach someone a lesson 在此翻译为"给某人一个教训"。所以根据题意应选 C。

20. ［答案］A

　　［解析］强调句结构是"It ＋be＋强调部分＋that／who＋其他"。强调部分指人就用 who;除此之外用 that。题中强调部分是 Japan,所以应选 A。

21. ［答案］B

　　［解析］be afraid of ＋doing 表示"害怕……"。句子的意思是"人们因为怕被袭击而不敢在晚上出门"。在这里 attack 表示的是被动,所以用被动结构,应选 B。

22. ［答案］D

　　［解析］communicate 翻译为"(思想上)沟通";issue 翻译为"发行,发布"; speak 翻译为"说(某种语言)"; spread 翻译为"传播;散布"。所以根据题意应选 D。

23. ［答案］C

　　［解析］far too 翻译为"太……"。book 可数,因此用 far too many 表示很多。所以根据题意应选 C。

24. ［答案］A

　　［解析］"It's high time"后面的从句用一般过去时表示虚拟语气。翻译为"是做某事的时候了"。所以根据题意应选 A。

25. ［答案］B

　　［解析］分词短语作定语。boy 与 sit 之间是能动关系。所以根据题意应选 B。

Section B

26. ［答案］not to know

　　［解析］pretend to do 翻译为"假装做……"。

27. ［答案］standing

　　［解析］分词作状语。People 与 stand 之间是能动关系,所以用 standing。

28. ［答案］reasonable

　　［解析］reasonable 翻译为"合情合理的"。形容词作表语。

29. ［答案］invitations

　　［解析］wedding 作定语,与 invitation 构成名词短语,翻译为"婚礼请柬"。送给很多朋友,所以用复数形式。

30. ［答案］will have learnt

　　［解析］by 引导的时间状语用完成时,next month 指"下个月",为将来时,所以用将来完成时。

31. ［答案］lively

　　［解析］very 修饰形容词,形容词修饰名词。根据句子结构,所填的词介于形容词和名词之间。所以用形容词形式 lively。

32. ［答案］heard

　　［解析］make oneself done 翻译为"让自己被别人……"。

33. ［答案］meeting

[解析] look forward to 中 to 为介词,后面用动名词或名词。

34. [答案] fortunate

   [解析] fortunate 形容词作为 be 动词的表语。翻译为"幸运的"。

35. [答案] had done

   [解析] as if 引导的句子用虚拟语气,主句是过去时,表示与过去事实相反。

Part III   Reading Comprehension

Task 1

36. [答案] D

   [解析] 推断题。peak 翻译为"顶峰,最高点"。在第二段开始介绍每个人精力顶峰的时间段不同,因此一个人如果早上没有精神,起床觉得很难,我们就可以推断出这个人精力的顶峰是在下午或是晚上。所以根据题意应选 D。

37. [答案] A

   [解析] 推断题"Much family quarrelling end when husbands and wives realize what these energy cycles mean, and which cycle each member of the family has. (当他们意识到精力周期时争吵结束)",以此可推断出他们争吵的开端是因为没有意识到精力周期的作用。所以根据题意应选 A。

38. [答案] C

   [解析] 根据"If your energy is low in the morning but you have an important job to do early in the day, rise before your usual hour"选择 C。

39. [答案] A

   [解析] 根据"Get off to slow start which saves your energy"选择 A。

40. [答案] B

   [解析] Dr. Kleitman 说没有任何科学家能对人们精力顶峰出现的时间段的不同做出解释。所以根据题意应选 B。

Task 2

41. [答案] A

   [解析] "... the plane hadn't left Spain for technical problems"翻译为,据此得知飞机是从西班牙来的。所以根据题意应选 A。

42. [答案] D

   [解析] "... the plane hadn't left Spain for technical problems"此句翻译为"飞机由于技术问题还没有离开西班牙",据此推理是飞机本身出了问题,并非因为天气、乘客,更不是因为路上的车太多。所以根据题意应选 D。

43. [答案] B

   [解析] "We waited again for a long time until late evening when we were asked to report again"翻译为"他们在候机厅里,等待着他们要乘坐的飞机的消息"。所以根据题意应选 B。

44. ［答案］D

［解析］当飞机长时间晚点,航空公司会为了表达对乘客的歉意,为乘客在候机厅送来免费的食物和水。所以根据题意应选 D。

45. ［答案］C

［解析］根据"Guess what had happened while we were asleep! Our plane had arrived and taken off again."选择 C。

Task 3

46. ［答案］a memorial building

［解析］从文章第一段最后一句话可以找到答案。

47. ［答案］unborn baby cry out

［解析］文章第一段中"... she said she had heard her unborn baby cry out. It was a sign of death"明确表明了答案。

48. ［答案］turned snow – white

［解析］从文章第二段最后一句话中可以找到答案。

49. ［答案］Aurangzeb

［解析］从文章第四段第一句话可以找到答案。

50. ［答案］1632

［解析］根据文章第一段中"In 1612, Shah Jehan married Mumtaz Mahal. Madly in love, they had 14 children over the next 20 years. But then sadness came. As Mumtaz was about to give birth to child number 14, she said she had heard her unborn baby cry out. It was a sign of death."可以推断出答案应该是 1632。

Task 4

51. (E)(F)　　52. (N)(I)　　53. (A)(K)　　54. (M)(B)　　55. (L)(D)

A——水龙头

B——厕所

C——浴液

D——香水

E——指甲刀

F——拖鞋

G——街名索引

H——浴巾

I——双人间

J——理发店

K——台灯

L——被子

M——床单

N——开关

187

Task 5

56. ［答案］Intercultural Communication

［解析］问题是"课程的内容是什么"标题已经告诉我们是 Intercultural Communication。

57. ［答案］Tuesdays and Thursdays

［解析］问题是"你在什么时间上课"回答问题时,用的是"On...and..."由此可以看出让我们回答的是具体在哪两天上课,而在文章中有"CLASS MEETS ON TUESDAYS AND THURSDAYS"。

58. ［答案］ninety five minutes

［解析］问题是"课要上多长时间"而依据文章中的 TIME：from 3：15 to 4：50 可以计算出课上 95 分钟。

59. ［答案］Beyond Language

［解析］问的是："上课时你要带什么书"文章中已经说明"TEXTBOOK：Beyond Language"。

60. ［答案］1：00 to 2：00 on Wednesdays

［解析］问题是"如果你想上这门课,你要什么时间报名"。文章中也说明 OFFICE HOUR：1：00 to 2：00 on Wednesdays；这里 office hour 翻译为"工作时间"。

Part IV   Translation—English into Chinese

61. ［答案］B

［解析］"...and they often placed in the graves with the dead"这里的 they 指的是 containers；with 翻译为"与……一起",据此可以看出,这些容器是与尸体一起埋在坟墓里,而不是用来装尸体。

62. ［答案］A

［解析］passengers 翻译为"乘客"；except 翻译为"除……以外"；American citizens 翻译为"美国公民"。

63. ［答案］D

［解析］the Customs 翻译为"海关"。

64. ［答案］B

［解析］本句正常的结构和语序是"His feelings were hardly to be defined as he read the letter."hardly 翻译为"几乎不"；as 翻译为"当……时"；defined 翻译为"下定义,解释,说明"。

65. ［译文］那个时候有不成文的条例严格规范男女间的行为举止,异性间不能互赠衣物,甚至毛衣。领结扣手套或许还可以。其他诸如好书、质地优良的钱包都被列为私人物品,没有比这更能表示亲昵的东西了。年轻男女不应到海滩或别的地方外宿,哪怕是和自己的男女朋友去。规定是"不要给他打电话,该让他打给你"。

Part V Writing

参考答案

July 8 , 2007

Dear Mary,

    I heard that you will get married next month. I know that all your family must be very excited, and as your friend, I feel the same.

    I wish you will be happy and have a wonderful marriage.

    With best wishes.

Yours Sincerely,
XXX

Test 13

Part I Listening Comprehension (15 minutes)

Directions: *This part is to test your listening ability. It consists of 3 sections.*

Section A

Directions: *This section is to test your ability to give proper answers to questions. There are 5 recorded questions in it. After each question, there is a pause. The questions will be spoken two times. When you hear a question, you should decide on the correct answer from the four choices.*

1. A. I like it very much.
   C. I am right.
   B. I am a student.
   D. I got up too late this morning.

2. A. China.
   C. English.
   B. My mother.
   D. Computer.

3. A. They are out of fashion.
   C. They are fifty dollars.
   B. They are blue.
   D. They are too large.

4. A. She likes planes.
   C. She flew there.
   B. She is in Wuhan now.
   D. She likes Beijing.

5. A. It's a bit hot here.
   C. It's cloudy in my hometown.
   B. I like to be here.
   D. It is beautiful here.

Section B

Directions: *This section is to test your ability to understand short dialogues. There are 5 recorded dialogues in it. After each dialogue, there is a recorded question. Both the dialogues and the questions will be spoken two times. When you hear a question, you should decide on the correct answer.*

6. A. Bookshop
   C. Furniture Shop
   B. University
   D. Street

7. A. 7:00
   C. 8:00
   B. 7:30
   D. 8:00

8. A. Tom is in hospital.
   C. Tom is going to the hospital.
   B. Tom is going to the school.
   D. Tom is a doctor.

9. A. No, he didn't.
   B. Yes, he did.

C. No, but he would let her know that night. D. He refused.

10. A. Traveling.
    B. Staying home.
    C. Going to the school.
    D. Reading.

Section C

Directions: *In this section you will hear a recorded passage. The passage is printed on the test paper, but with some words or phrases missing. The passage will be read three times. During the second reading, you are required to put the missing words or phrases on the blanks according to what you hear. The third reading is for you to check your writing. Now the passage will begin.*

These days, people who do manual work often ___11___ far more money than people who work in ___12___. People who work in offices are frequently referred to as "white-collar workers" for the ___13___ reason that they usually wear a collar and tie to go to work. Such is human ___14___, that a great many people are often willing to sacrifice ___15___ pay for the privilege of becoming white-collar workers. This can give rise to curious situations.

Part II Vocabulary & Structure (15 minutes)

Directions: *This part is to test your ability to use words and phrases correctly to construct meaningful and grammatically correct sentences. It consists of 2 sections.*

Section A

Directions: *There are 10 incomplete statements here. You are required to complete each one by choosing the appropriate answer from the 4 choices marked A, B, C and D.*

16. The policeman said that the young man was _____ for the accident.
    A. responsibility
    B. recent
    C. responsible
    D. result

17. —The fish were _____ yesterday, but they are all died today, why?
    —Maybe they were lack of oxygen.
    A. life
    B. love
    C. alive
    D. lovely

18. Never in his whole life _____ such a stupid thing.
    A. did he do
    B. has he done
    C. he has done
    D. he did

19. It's time you _____ your membership dues.
    A. paid
    B. pay
    C. will pay
    D. to pay

20. Whenever you _____ your mind, please tell me.
    A. change
    B. exchange

C. make
D. changeable

21. He soon _____ from failure, and promised to work harder than before.

A. got across
B. got through
C. got over
D. got away

22. Jack is very sad; everyone went to the zoo _____ him.

A. besides
B. against
C. for
D. but

23. I have five other courses _____ Computer.

A. besides
B. exception
C. except
D. beside

24. Every suitcase is _____ with your clothes; I can't find an empty one.

A. find
B. fine
C. full
D. filled

25. Mary, as well as Lily, _____ Japanese very hard.

A. study
B. has studied
C. studies
D. had studied

Section B

Directions: *There are 10 incomplete sentences here. You should fill in each blank with the proper form of the word given in the brackets.*

26. If the team members hadn't helped me, I (tumble) _____ in a stream.

27. (see) _____ from the air, the island is a sleeping girl.

28. More and more Chinese people are spending spare time _____ (learn) English for the Olympic Games in 2008.

29. My uncle's _____ (marry) is destined to fail.

30. She looked at me with _____ (adore) in her eyes.

31. I've been looking forward to _____ (travel) in China for a long time.

32. The tourist guide suggested that everyone _____ (carry) too much luggage.

33. I made up my mind _____ (study) in France.

34. Professor Wang is a _____ (respect) person.

35. It's an excellent cell phone, but it has its _____ (advantage).

Part III Reading Comprehension   (40 minutes)

Directions: *This part is to test your reading ability. There are 5 tasks for you to fulfill. You should read the reading materials carefully and to do the tasks as you are instructed.*

Task 1

It's that time of year when we pack up our bags and head to the beach for the day to enjoy those warm sunrays and the refreshing sound of the lapping water.

Here are some helpful tips to make your day at the beach fun and keep you looking fashion fresh all day and all the way home.

First, before you leave home, if you've got long hair, pull it into a high pony tail or fun knot. Use some funky hair accessories that will stay in place when you're swimming.

Second, slather yourself in sunscreen before leaving the house, and then toss the sunscreen in your bag so you can reapply after a swim or every few hours. Don't let yourself turn into the lobster of the day.

Why not get something fun and fashionable to keep you looking fashion fresh? Make sure you've got all the daily essentials in your bag—sunglasses, sunscreen, a good book, a floppy hat, some lip gloss, and any other makeup touch ups you'll want. If you plan to wear eye makeup, make sure it's waterproof. Stay away from heavy foundations. If you must apply something, use a bronzer moisturizer. It's also a good idea to bring lip balm with an SPF15 to protect your lips. It never hurts to put some moisturizer in the bag. Include a snack and plenty of fluids. It's important not to get dehydrated(使脱水).

My favorite beach look is this. And what's perfect is that it keeps me looking fashion fresh throughout the day and takes me right into the evening.

36. The word "tips" in the first sentence of the second paragraph means _____.
    A. clothes   B. words   C. tour   D. clues
37. Which one of the following sentences is TRUE? _____
    A. The author told us to bring as many things as you can.
    B. Before you leave the house, it is no use wiping the sunscreen.
    C. It is very important to make yourself not to get dehydrated.
    D. A big bag is not necessary for you.
38. If you want to go to the beach , what should you prepare for your hair? _____
    A. Some funky hair accessories.   B. Mirrors.
    C. Sunglasses.   D. A good book.
39. Which of the following is essential in your bag in the article? _____
    A. Chair.   B. Sunglasses.
    C. Shirt.   D. Coat.
40. Which one is the best title for this article? _____
    A. Look Fashionable At The Beach!   B. Beautiful Beaches!
    C. Traveling Around The World!   D. Vocations On The Beach!

Task 2

5 Steps to Becoming a Better Net worker

We all have places to go and people to impress (or at least get them to remember us!). Unfortunately, no one ever teaches us how to mingle with a crowd and leave an impression. Here are five steps to becoming a snazzy networker in your own right.

1. You don't have to be an Extrovert: Most people think that the best net workers are the

extroverted bubbly types. Not at all! Some of the best networkers I know are actually introverts. Why? Because they are usually better listeners. At events where everyone is trying to talk, a genuine listener stands out from the crowd. People remember those who listen to them.

2. Wear a Scarf:... or a wild tie or a bold necklace. You don't have to consider yourself stylish, but do pick one item to wear that allows you to stand out.

3. Do Something Nice: Doing something nice for people is always appreciated and remembered.

4. Keep in touch with the people you meet. It is best to email someone two days after a conference or an event. They will still remember you, but will also have had enough time to unwind and catch up on other Business.

5. Be a Hub: A hub is a connector. Find a way to connect people with what they need and you will be valued.

41. If you want to be a good networker, you should _____.
   A. not dress up smartly
   B. do something nice
   C. not see the people you met anymore
   D. keep talking when you are with friends

42. Which of the following is TRUE? _____
   A. Listening to others is better than talking in some circumstances.
   B. You should introduce to everyone you don't know.
   C. Not emailing someone is a good way.
   D. You don't have to keep in touch with the people you met.

43. "INTROVERTS" are the kind of people who _____.
   A. are good at communicating with people
   B. are export-oriented
   C. always talk to others
   D. are good listeners

44. What is this passage talking about? _____
   A. How to be a good leader.
   B. Several ways to do business.
   C. How to be a successful net worker.
   D. How to keep in touch with people.

45. Which one of the following is mentioned in the Paragraph One? _____
   A. Be a nice person.
   B. Be a connector.
   C. Be a good listener.
   D. Be a talkative person.

Task 3

Beijing has an extensive public transportation network. Subway and City Rail with high speed trains running at intervals of 3 to 5 minutes are the fastest public transportation in the city. There are more than 60 thousand taxis in the city. Public buses are the cheapest means of transportation which cover the entire city.

The starting fare of public buses is 1 Yuan in the city and 2 Yuan in the suburb areas. It is also a good idea to buy a Public Transportation Card which charges a starting fare of 40 cents per trip. You need to pay a deposit of 20 Yuan and prepay a certain amount to use the Public Transportation Card just like any Beijing citizen. When you leave Beijing, just return the Card at any card sale counter and the deposit will be refunded to you. The Public Transportation Card can also be used in Subway and City Rails but no discount on the ticket fares will be given.

1. This passage is talking about Beijing's ___(46)___.

2. ___(47)___ and ___(48)___ are the fastest public transportation in the city.

3. If you want to go to the suburb areas, you have to pay ___(49)___ Yuan.

4. There are ___(50)___ taxis in Beijing.

Task 4 *The following is a list of terms. After reading it, you are required to find the items equivalent to (与……同) those given in Chinese in the list below.*

A. —— Sailing

B. —— Weightlifting

C. —— Artistic Gymnastic

D. —— Baseball

E. —— Cycling

F. —— Athletics

G. —— Judo

H. —— Wrestling

I. —— Shooting

J. —— Boxing

K. —— Table Tennis

L. —— Volleyball

M. —— Badminton

N. —— Tennis

O. —— Fencing

P. —— Swimming

Q. —— Diving

example：游泳（P）　　　　　　　　　　乒乓球（K）

51. 艺术体操 （　）		射击　（　）	
52. 羽毛球　（　）		柔道　（　）	
53. 举重　　（　）		田径　（　）	
54. 摔跤　　（　）		网球　（　）	
55. 跳水　　（　）		自行车（　）	

Task 5

Directions: *Read the following letter carefully. After reading it, you are required to complete the statements that follow the question (No. 56 through No. 60). You should write your answers briefly on the blanks correspondingly.*

Jacob Warren

Objective: motivated business school graduate seeking a marketing assistant position to help develop and implement marketing communications projects

Education: 1999—2003 Seattle University

Bachelor of Science in Business Administration

Marketing major

Experience: 2004—present World Marketing Company Portland, Oregon marketing assistant

—created media kits to enhance sales presentation

—conducted market research on industry trends in the software field

Skills: Fluent in French

Experienced in conducting market research

Analytical in approach to problems

Confident public speaker

56. What is this passage?

It is a _____.

57. What did Jacob Warren study in the university?

Jacob Warren studied _____.

58. What does Jacob Warren want to apply for?

Jacob Warren wants to apply for a position as a _____.

59. Which university did he study in?

_____.

60. Which language can he speak?

_____.

Part IV Translation—English into Chinese (25 minutes)

Directions: *This part numbered 61 through 65 is to test your ability to translate English into Chinese. After each sentence of number 61 to 64, you will read four choices of suggested translations. You should choose the best translation.*

61. The English language has a vivid saying to describe this kind of phenomenon.

A. 语言中有活泼的表达方式和处境。

B. 英语中有很说法来说明这种情况。

C. 英语中有一个生动的说法来形容这种现象。

D. 英语语言有着很生动的活力。

62. Much as we may pride ourselves on our good taste, we are no longer free to choose the things we want.

  A. 尽管我们可以自夸自己的鉴赏力如何敏锐，但我们已经无法独立自主地选购自己所需的东西了。

  B. 尽管我们以自己的鉴赏力感到很自豪，但也无法买到所需要的东西。

  C. 尽管我们的品味有限，但仍然能买到所需要的东西。

  D. 尽管我们自己的鉴赏力很敏锐，但我们再也不买我们不需要的东西了。

63. The sense of humor is mysteriously bound up with national characteristics.

  A. 这个国家的所有人都有种幽默感。

  B. 这个国家的人的性格缺乏幽默感。

  C. 幽默感与民族的关系密不可分。

  D. 幽默感与民族有着神秘莫测的联系。

64. No one suspected that there might be someone else on the farm who had never been seen.

  A. 谁也没有怀疑农场里有个露过面的人。

  B. 谁也没想到农场里竟会有一个从未露面的人。

  C. 谁也没看到农场里有个从没露过面的人。

  D. 谁也不认识这个从没出现过的人。

65. With the sub-tropical climate, Hong Kong has an annual average temperature of around 23℃. During the hot and damp summer, you're advised to bring the umbrellas, take the sunstroke precautions. As soon as you enter Hong Kong, you'll unconsciously integrate yourself into its fast-pace life and fully appreciate various conveniences of commercial civilization. Hong Kong Disneyland and Ocean Park shall be your ideal destinations to find a relaxed mind.

Word-reference: sub-tropical 亚热带的   sunstroke 中暑

Part V　Writing　(25 minutes)

Directions: *This part is to test your ability to do practical writing. You are required to finish the following writing according to the information.*

说明：根据下列信息，以计算机管理系的名义写一份通知。

内容如下：计算机管理系邀请著名软件工程师张先生来我校讲座。讲座内容为现代计算机管理模式，时间定于 11 月 12 日晚上 6：00—8：00。地点在多媒体演讲厅。希望本系学生前往听讲。落款为计算机管理系。通知日期为 2006 年 11 月 11 日。

答案解析

Part 1　Comprehension listening

听力原文

Section A

1. Why are you so late for class?

2. Who's your favorite person?

3. Excuse me, how much are these clothes?

4. Did your sister travel to Beijing from Wuhan by train or by plane?

5. What's the weather like here?

Section B

6. W: I want to buy a book about writing, where can I find the books?

   M: They are over there.

   Q: Where is the conversation probably taking place?

7. W: I'm late for the meeting. It's already 8:00.

   M: No, the clock is half an hour fast. Don't hurry.

   Q: What's the time now?

8. W: What's the matter with Tom?

   M: He had a car accident, and he is in hospital now.

   Q: What do we learn from this conversation?

9. W: Would you like to go to the theatre with me on Sunday?

   M: Well, I don't know. Can I tell you tonight?

   Q: Did he receive the woman's invitation?

10. W: What shall we do this summer vocation?

    M: How about traveling instead of staying at home.

    Q: According to the man, what's he going to do?

Section C

These days, people who do manual work often **11 receive** far more money than people who work in **12 offices.** People who work in offices are frequently referred to "as white-collar workers" for the **13 simple** reason that they usually wear a collar and tie to go to work. Such is human **14 nature,** that a great many people are often willing to sacrifice **15 higher** pay for the privilege of becoming white-collar workers. This can give rise to curious situations.

答案详解

Part I Listening Comprehension

Section A

1. ［答案］D

   ［解析］题目问："你为何上课迟到"，选项 D"I got up too late this morning"翻译为"我早

上起来晚了"其他选项不符合题意。所以根据题意应选 D。

2. ［答案］B

   ［解析］题目问："谁是你最喜欢的人"，B 选项翻译为"我的母亲"。所以根据题意应选 B。

3. ［答案］C

   ［解析］题目问："这些衣服多少钱"。C 选项翻译为"它们五十美元"；A 选项为"它们已经过时了"；B 选项为"它们是蓝色的"；D 选项为"它们太大了"。所以根据题意应选 C。

4. ［答案］C

   ［解析］题目问："你妹妹从北京到武汉旅游是选择坐火车还是飞机"。A 选项翻译为"她喜欢飞机"；B 选项翻译为"她现在在武汉"；D 选项为"她喜欢北京"；C 选项翻译为"她坐飞机过去"。所以根据题意应选 C。

5. ［答案］A

   ［解析］题目是询问天气情况。A 选项表示天气有点热；B 选项翻译为"我喜欢在这"；C 选项翻译为"我的家乡现在是多云的天气"。D 选项翻译为"这很美。"所以根据题意应选 A 选项。

Section B

6. ［答案］A

   ［解析］对话中女士询问关于写作的书在哪。题目问："对话在哪发生的"。B 选项翻译为"大学"；C 选项翻译为"家具店"；D 选项翻译为"街道"；A 选项翻译为"书店"。所以根据题意应选 A。

7. ［答案］B

   ［解析］女士说："已经八点了，我开会要迟到了"，男士说"别担心，钟快了半个小时"，题目问："当时是几点"。B 选项翻译为"七点半"；所以根据题意应选 B。

8. ［答案］A

   ［解析］题目问"我们从这段对话中得到什么信息"。由对话中女士问"汤姆出什么事了"，男士回答"他出了交通事故，现在在医院"，A 选项翻译为"汤姆现在在医院"。所以根据题意应选 A。

9. ［答案］C

   ［解析］女士问"你星期天可以和我去剧院吗"，男士回答"晚上再告诉你"，题目问"他接受邀请了吗"。C 选项翻译为"她晚上才能知道"，所以根据题意应选 C。

10. ［答案］A

    ［解析］女士问"我们暑假干什么"，男士回答"去旅游如何"。A 选项翻译为"他可能去旅游"，所以根据题意应选 A。

Section C

11. receive   12. offices   13. simple   14. nature   15. higher

Part II   Vocabulary & Structure

Section A

16. ［答案］C

　　［解析］responsibility 是名词,翻译为"责任";recent 是形容词,翻译为"最近的,近来的";responsible 是形容词,翻译为"有责任的,负责的";result 翻译为"结果"。be responsible for 翻译为"对什么负责",为固定用法。所以根据题意应选 C。

17. ［答案］C

　　［解析］life 为名词,翻译为"生命";也可作形容词表示"生命的";love 为动词,翻译为"喜爱";alive 是形容词,翻译为"活着的,有活力的(暗含有死的可能,但还活着)";lovely 为形容词,翻译为"可爱的"。根据题意应选 C。

18. ［答案］B

　　［解析］这道题测试的是部分倒装的用法,当句子的开头出现 never,seldom 等表示否定的词时,后面的句子要用部分倒装,即助动词提前。根据时态应用现在完成时。所以正确答案为选项 B。

19. ［答案］A

　　［解析］考查虚拟语气的用法,It's time…句型中,从句用虚拟式,从句中谓语动词用过去式。A 选项为动词的过去式,B 选项为动词原形,C 选项为将来时态,D 选项为动词不定式。正确答案为选项 A。

20. ［答案］A

　　［解析］change 翻译为"改变";exchange 翻译为"交换";make 翻译为"做,成为";changeable 是形容词,翻译为"可变的,多变的"。change one's mind 为固定搭配,翻译为"改变主意"。正确答案应为选项 A。

21. ［答案］C

　　［解析］get across 翻译为"讲清楚,被理解";get through 翻译为" 到达,完成";get over 翻译为"克服,恢复过来";get away 翻译为"离开,出发"。根据题意,正确答案应为选项 C。

22. ［答案］D

　　［解析］besides 翻译为"除……之外(还有)";against 翻译为"反对";for 翻译为"因为,对于";but 翻译为"除了(某人)没有"。根据题意,正确答案应为选项 D。

23. ［答案］A

　　［解析］besides 翻译为"除……之外(还有)";exception 翻译为"例外,除外";except 翻译为"除了";beside 翻译为"在旁边";根据题意,正确答案应为选项 A。

24. ［答案］D

　　［解析］be filled with 翻译为"装满,填满",是固定搭配;full 翻译为"满的,装满的";与之搭配的短语是 be full of,翻译为"装满,填满";其他两个选项不符合题意。根据题干内容,正确答案应为选项 D。

25. ［答案］C

[解析]as well as 是状语,对前面的主语起修饰作用,翻译为"与……一样",句中谓语动词取决于前面的主语,故用单数形式。C 选项为动词 study 的第三人称单数形式。A 选项是动词原形,B 选项是现在完成时态,D 选项是过去完成时态。正确答案应为选项 C。

Section B

26. [答案]would have tumbled

[解析]此题考查的是虚拟语气的用法。在虚拟语气中,表示与过去事实相反,从句用"if + 主语 + had + 过去分词",主句用"主语 + should / would / could/might + have + 过去分词";表示与现在事实相反,从句用"if + 主语 + 动词的过去式(be-were)……",主句用"主语 + should / would / could/might + 动词原形";表示与将来事实相反,从句用"If + 主语 + were to(should) + 动词原形",主句用"主语 + should / would / could/might + 动词原形"。此题表示的是与过去事实相反。tumble 翻译为"跌倒"。

27. [答案]Seen

[解析]本句的主语为非生命的 island,与 see 有被动关系。所以用过去分词构成过去分词短语表示被动。see 为动词表示"看",需变成它的过去分词形式 seen。

28. [答案]learning

[解析]"spend time + V-ing"形式为固定搭配,表示花费时间做某事。

29. [答案]marriage

[解析]句子缺少主语,marry 翻译为"结婚",为动词,需变成名词作主语。

30. [答案]adoration

[解析]adore 翻译为"崇拜",为动词,需变成名词与 with 构成介词短语。

31. [答案]traveling/travelling

[解析]"look forward to + 动名词/名词"为固定搭配,翻译为"期望,盼望做某事"。

32. [答案](should) not carry

[解析]虚拟语气。本题考查的是在表示愿望、请示、命令等意义的动词后的宾语从句中要用虚拟语气的用法"(should)+ 动词原形"。同样的动词还有 demand, insist, recommend, intend, advise, decide, ask, request, order, propose, command 等。

33. [答案]to study

[解析]make up one's mind to do sth.'决定做某事"。study 为动词翻译为"学习"。需变成不定式。

34. [答案]respectable

[解析]respectable"受人尊敬的;值得尊敬的"。respect 翻译为"尊敬",为动词,需变成形容词修饰后面的 person。

35. [答案]disadvantages

[解析]词形变换题。advantage 翻译为"优点,有利条件",为形容词,需变成否定形式。

Part III Reading Comprehension

Task 1

36. ［答案］D

［解析］clue 翻译为"线索,提示";clothes 翻译为"服饰";words 翻译为"词语";tour 翻译为"旅游"。根据题意,正确答案为选项 D。

37. ［答案］C

［解析］题目问的是哪个选项是正确的。文中第五段最后一句话提到"It's important not to get dehydrated.(不要让自己脱水是非常重要的。)"所以 C 选项是正确的。A 选项文中没有提到;B,D 选项错误。

38. ［答案］A

［解析］文中第三段"Use some funky hair accessories that will stay in place when you're swimming"提到最好带些头发装饰品。A 为正确答案。

39. ［答案］B

［解析］在文中第五段"Make sure you've got all the daily essentials in your bag—sunglasses..."提到必带的物品。只有 B 选项中的太阳镜被提到,其他三个选项均未被提到,因此选项 B 为正确答案。

40. ［答案］A

［解析］本文的主要内容是谈如何在沙滩上时尚以及给出的几点建议。因此选项 A 是最符合题意的答案。

Task 2

41. ［答案］B

［解析］文中第三点"Do Something Nice：Doing something nice for people is always appreciated and remembered"中提到"要做一些好事"。其他三个选项都是错误的。所以选项 B 为正确答案。

42. ［答案］A

［解析］文中第二点提到,在某种情况下,你应该做一个好听众,这样人们就会记住细心听别人说话的听者。根据"...People remember those who listen to them"A 选项为正确答案。

43. ［答案］D

［解析］introverts 本意为"性格内向,不善言辞的"。选项 A 翻译为"善于与人交流的人";选项 B 翻译为"性格外向的人";选项 C 翻译为"经常与他人说话的人";选项 D 为"善于倾听的人"最符合题意。

44. ［答案］C

［解析］本文第一段中提到"Here are five steps to becoming a snazzy networker in your own right"根据文章大意,只有 C 选项是正确的。其他都未提及。

45. ［答案］C

［解析］本文第一段"...Because they are usually better listeners..."提到"要做一个好

Task 3

46. ［答案］transportation

［解析］在文中第一段第一句话"Beijing has an extensive public transportation network."中可以找到答案。

47. ［答案］Subway

［解析］在文中第一段第二句话"Subway and City Rail with high speed trains running at intervals of 3 to 5 minutes are the fastest public transportation in the city."中可以找到答案。

48. ［答案］City rail

［解析］在文中第一段第二句话中可以找到答案。

49. ［答案］2

［解析］在文中第二段第一句话"The starting fare of public buses is 1 yuan in the city and 2 yuan in the suburb areas."中可以找到答案。

50. ［答案］more than 60 thousand

［解析］在文中第一段第三句"There are more than 60 thousand taxis in the city."中可以找到答案。

Task 4

51. （C）（I） 52. （M）（G） 53. （B）（F） 54. （H）（N） 55. （Q）（E）

A——帆船

B——举重

C——艺术体操

D——棒球

E——自行车

F——田径

G——柔道

H——摔跤

I——射击

J——拳击

K——兵乓球

L——排球

M——羽毛球

N——网球

O——击剑

P——游泳

Q——跳水

Task 5

56. ［答案］resume

［解析］从整篇文章可以看出,这是一份求职简历。

57. ［答案］marketing

　　［解析］在文中第二段 education 一栏中可以找到所学的专业是 marketing。

58. ［答案］marketing assistant

　　［解析］从文中第一段第一句话"seeking a marketing assistant position"可知答案。

59. ［答案］Seattle University

　　［解析］从在文中第一段第一句话"1999—2003 Seattle university"可知答案。

60. ［答案］French

　　［解析］从文中最后一段第一句话"Skills：Fluent in French"可知答案。

Part IV　Translation—English into Chinese

61. ［答案］C

　　［解析］vivid 翻译为"生动的"；saying 翻译为"说法"；phenomenon 翻译为"现象"。

62. ［答案］A

　　［解析］taste 翻译为"品味,鉴赏力"。no longer 翻译为"不再,再不干某事"。

63. ［答案］D

　　［解析］the sense of humor 表示幽默感。be bound up with 表示"与……联系在一起"。

64. ［答案］B

　　［解析］"suspect"翻译为"怀疑,感到质疑"。

65. ［译文］香港属于亚热带气候,年平均气温在 23℃左右。夏季炎热以防中暑。天气潮湿,请备好雨具。你只要一踏进香港,便会不由自主地融入到快节奏的生活当中,同时尽享商业文明带来的种种便利。香港的迪斯尼乐园和海洋公园,是人们放松心情的大好去处。

　　［解析］destination 翻译为"目的地,终点"；convenience 翻译为"方便,便利"。

Part V　Writing

参考答案：

　　英文通知首先要包括 notice,而且每个字母要大写。放在通知的正上方。内容包括时间、地点、事件以及所要通知的对象。表达要准确、简洁。必须写上写通知的日期以及写通知的人或单位。

Sample

NOTICE

Nov 11th, 2006

　　Mr. Zhang, the famous software engineer, will give a lecture on Modern Computer Management Model at 6:00p. m. on Nov 12. The two-hour lecture will be held in the multi-media lecture room. Students of Computer Management Department are invited to attend the lecture.

Computer Management Department

Test 14

(2006 年 6 月高等学校英语应用能力考试真题试卷)

Part I   Listening Comprehension   (15 minutes)

Directions: *This part is to test your listening ability. It consists of 3 sections.*

Section A

Directions: *This section is to test your ability to give proper answers to questions. There are 5 recorded questions in it. After each question, there is a pause. The questions will be spoken two times. When you hear a question, you should decide on the correct answer from the 4 choices marked A), B), C) and D) given in your test paper. Then you should mark the corresponding letter on the Answer Sheet with a single line through the centre.*

Example: *You will hear*:

You will read: A) I'm not sure.

B) You're right.

C) Yes, certainly.

D) That's interesting.

From the question we learn that the speaker is asking the listener to leave a message. Therefore, C) Yes, certainly is the correct answer. You should mark C) on the Answer Sheet. Now the test will begin.

1. A. So do I.   B. Thank you.   C. Yes, I like it.   D. Yes, of course.
2. A. Yes, it is.   B. Yes, I have.   C. I like the city.   D. It's a famous city.
3. A. My pleasure.   B. Not at all.   C. Nothing thanks. D. Sure.
4. A. I often drink tea at home.   B. No, thanks.
   C. Not likely.   D. No problem.
5. A. Thank you.   B. It's important.   C. Yes, I will.   D. No, it isn't.

Section B

Directions: *This section is to test your ability to understand short dialogues. There are 5 recorded dialogues in it. After each dialogue, there is a recorded question. Both the dialogues and questions will be spoken two times. When you hear a question, you should decide on the correct answer from the 4 choices marked A), B), C) and D)*

205

given in your test paper. Then you should mark the corresponding letter on the Answer Sheet with a single line through the centre.

6. A. A business plan.   B. A working schedule.
   C. A computer problem.   D. A computer class.
7. A. She's a manager.   B. She's a secretary.
   C. She's an engineer.   D. She's a teacher.
8. A. A list.   B. A product.   C. A contract.   D. A book.
9. A. In a post-office.   B. In a restaurant.   C. At a airport.   D. At a railway station.
10. A. Anytime today.   B. This morning.   C. Next afternoon.   D. Tomorrow morning.

Section C

Directions: *In this section you will hear a recorded short passage. The passage is printed in the test paper, but with some words or phrases missing. The passage will be read three times. During the second reading, you are required to put the missing words or phrases that you hear on the Answer Sheet in order of the numbered blanks according to what you hear. The third reading is for you to check your writing. Now the passage will begin.*

Modern technology has a big influence on our daily life. New devices are widely used today. For example, we have to ___11___ the Internet every day. It is becoming more and more ___12___ to nearly everybody. Now it's time to think about how the Internet influences us, what ___13___ it has on our social behavior and what the future world will look like. The Internet has ___14___ changed our life; there is no doubt about that. I think that the Internet has changed our life in a ___15___ way.

Part Ⅱ   Vocabulary & Structure   (15 minutes)

Directions: *This part is to test your ability to use words and phrases correctly to construct meaningful and grammatically correct sentences. It consists of 2 sections.*

Section A

Directions: *There are 10 incomplete statements here. You are required to complete each statement by choosing the appropriate answer from the 4 choices marked A), B), C) and D). You should mark the corresponding letter on the Answer Sheet with a single line through the centre.*

16. My impression of the service in the hotel was that it had really _____.
    A. improved   B. implied   C. imported   D. imagined
17. The policeman stopped the driver and found that he _____ alcohol.
    A. drinks   B. has drunk   C. is drinking   D. had drunk
18. There are three colors in the British flag, _____ red, white and blue.

A. rarely   B. namely   C. really   D. naturally

19. I can't find the key to my office, I _____ have lost it on my way home.

    A. would   B. should   C. must   D. ought to

20. David has _____ much work to do that he is staying late at his office.

    A. such   B. so   C. very   D. enough

21. I tried hard, but I couldn't find the _____ to the problem.

    A. solution   B. help   C. reply   D. demand

22. _____ writing a letter to the manager, he decided to talk to him in person.

    A. Due to   B. Because of   C. As for   D. Instead of

23. As far as I'm concerned, I don't like _____ in that way.

    A. to be treated   B. to treat   C. treated   D. treating

24. Lisa was busy taking notes _____ Mark was searching the Internet for the information.

    A. until   B. unless   C. while   D. if

25. There was a heavy fog this morning, so none of the planes could _____.

    A. get through   B. take off   C. pull out   D. break away

Section B

Directions: *There are also 10 incomplete statements here. You should fill in each blank with the proper form of the word given in the brackets. Write the word or words in the corresponding space on the Answer Sheet.*

26. Of all the hotels in the city, this one is the (good) _____.

27. Yesterday they received a written (invite) _____ to a dinner from Mr. Black.

28. That new film is worth (see) _____ for the second time.

29. Next week we (sign) _____ the sales contract with the new supplier.

30. (general) _____ speaking, he is a person that you can trust.

31. The new machine ought to (test) _____ before it is put to use.

32. If your credit is good, you will be allowed (use) _____ the credit card.

33. It will be very (help) _____ if each member presents his or her own opinion at the meeting.

34. The number of sales people who have left the company (be) _____ very small.

35. It is well-known that sports will (strength) _____ the friendship between nations.

Part III   Reading Comprehension   (40 minutes)

Directions: *This part is to test your reading ability. There are 5 tasks for you to fulfill. You should read the reading Materials carefully and do the tasks as you are instructed.*

Task 1

Directions: *After reading the following passage, you will find 5 questions or unfinished statements, numbered 36 through 40. For each question or statement there are 4 choices* *marked A), B), C), or D). You should make the correct choice and mark the corresponding letter on the Answer Sheet with a single line through the centre.*

Dear Sir or Madam,

The MDC Company was established in 2001 and in four short years has become one of the most successful companies in the market place. For this, we are pleased, proud and grateful.

We are pleased because our customers have confirmed our belief that if the products we offer are new, exciting, innovative (有创意的) and of excellent quality, they'll be purchased.

We are proud because we know we are a company that keeps its word to its customers; that guarantees that any product can be returned within 30 days if it proves to be unsatisfactory in any way; and that always lets our customers know if there is to be a delay in delivery.

We are grateful to customers like you, because you confirm our beliefs that good service and quality result in satisfied customers. Without you, there would be no reason for us to be pleased or proud. We thank you for your orders and for giving us the opportunity to be of service to you.

Our special summer catalogue is at the printers and should be in your home soon. We hope that you will be pleased with new selections.

Yours faithfully

John Brown

36. From the passage we can learn that MDC Company always _____.

A. keeps its promise

B. provides the same products

C. sells its products at a low price

D. delivers its products without delay

37. MDC Company believes that its customers are satisfied because the company _____.

A. give them opportunities to order

B. provides good service and quality

C. guarantees the quickest delivery

D. sends new catalogues to them

38. The customers will be informed if _____.

A. the product can't be delivered on time.

B. the product is out-of-date and unsatisfactory.

C. the company doesn't accept the returned product

D. the company can't send a new catalogue on time.

39. The purpose of this letter is to _____.

A. tell the customers about the quality of their products

B. express the company's thanks to the customers

C. prove the excellent service of the company

D. inform the customers of a new catalogue

40. What can we learn about the company? _____

208

A. It has the largest number of customers.

B. It is grateful for its employees' efforts.

C. It is successful in the market place.

D. It charges the least for its services.

Task 2

Directions: *This task is the same as Task* 1. *The* 5 *questions or unfinished statements are numbered* 41 *through* 45.

Unlike Britain, the US does not have a national health care service. The government does help pay for some medical care for people who are on low incomes and for old people, but most people buy insurance(保险) to help pay for medical care. The problems of those who cannot afford insurance are an important political subject.

In Britain, when people are ill, they usually go to a family doctor first. However, people in America sometimes go straight to an expert without seeing their family doctor first. Children are usually taken to a doctor who is an expert in the treatment(治疗) of children. In Britain, if a patient needs to see a specialist doctor, their family doctor will usually recommend a specialist.

Doctors do not go to people's homes when they are ill. People always make appointments to see the doctor in the doctor's office. In a serious situation, people call for an ambulance(救护车). In America, hospitals must treat all seriously ill patients, even if they do not have medical insurance. The government will then help pay for some the cost of the medical care.

41. Some medical care is paid by the U.S. government for _____.

    A. people living in the country   B. non-government officials

    C. people with insurance   D. the poor and the old

42. Most people in the United States buy insurance _____.

    A. to pay for their own medical care

    B. to help to live on their low incomes

    C. to improve the national health care service

    D. to solve one of the important political problems

43. What do British people usually do when they are ill? _____

    A. They go to see their family doctor first.

    B. They go to see a specialist doctor first.

    C. They call for a specialist doctor.

    D. They call for a family doctor.

44. In America, seriously ill patients will _____.

    A. be treated if they have an insurance

    B. make an appointment with a specialist only

    C. receive treatment even without insurance

    D. normally go to see an expert for treatment

45. Which of the following would be the best title for this passage? _____

A. Types of Doctors in the United States.

B. Health Care in the United States and Britain.

C. Treatment of Sick Children in the United States.

D. Medical Insurance in the United States and Britain.

Task 3

Directions: *The following is an advertisement. After reading it, you should complete the information by filling in the blanks marked 46 through 50 **in not more than 3 words** in the table below.*

Thanks for using Metro(地铁)

Clean. Modern. Safe. And easy to use. No wonder Metro is considered the nation's finest transit (公交) system. This guide tells how to use Metro, and the color-coded map on the inside will help you use Metro to get all around the Nation's Capital.

Metro-rail fares

Each passenger needs a fare-card. (Up to two children under 5 may travel free with a paying customers.)

Fares are based on when and how far you ride. Pay regular fares on weeks 5:30—9:30 a. m. and 3:00—7:00 p. m.. Pay reduced fares at all other times.

Large maps in each station show fares and travel times. Please ask the station manager if you have any questions.

Fare-card machines are in every station. Bring small banknotes because there are no change machines in the stations and fare-card machines only proved up to $ 5 in change (in coins). Some machines accept credit cards.

A Transit System Metro
Features of the system : 1) __46__ , 2) modern, 3) safe, and 4) __47__
Fares for weekends: __48__ fares
Place showing fares and travel times : large maps in __49__
Change provided by fare-card machines: up to $ __50__

Task 4

Directions: *The following is a list of signs for public attention. After reading it, you are required to find the items equivalents to those given in Chinese in the table below. Then you should put the corresponding letters in the brackets on the Answer Sheet, numbered 51 through 55.*

A. —— Buses Only

B. —— No Parking

C. —— No Standing

210

D. —— Police Cars Only

E. —— No U-Turn

F. —— No Admittance

G. —— No Entry By This Door

H. —— One Way Street

I. —— One Lane Bridge

J. —— Admission By Ticket Only

K. —— Admission Free

L. —— Keep Away

M. —— House To Let

N. —— Keep Order

O. —— Wet Paint

P. —— Line Up For Tickets

Q. —— No Posting of Signs

R. —— Seat By Number

S. —— Wheelchairs Only

Example：（Q）请勿张贴　　　（C）禁止停车候客

51.（　）禁止停车	（　）禁止掉头
52.（　）此门不通	（　）不得入内
53.（　）房屋出租	（　）单行道
54.（　）排队购票	（　）凭票入场
55.（　）公交专用道	（　）对号入座

Task 5

Directions：there are two business letters here. *After reading it, you are requited to complete the answers that follow the questions (No. 56 through No. 60). You should write your answers in no more than 3 words on the Answer Sheet correspondingly.*

Letter 1

June 10, 2006

Dear Sir or Madam,

　　Last night the central heating system that you installed（安装）in our factory exploded. The explosion caused a great deal of damage and our stock of fashion clothes has been completely ruined.

　　We must insist that you replace the heating system immediately and pay for our damaged stock, valued at ＄400,000.

　　We look forward to your reply.

Yours faithfully,

Bill Black

Assistant Manager

211

Letter 2

June 15, 2006

Dear Mr. Black,

We are writing in connection with the recent explosion at your factory.

We would like to point out that we have been manufacturing heating systems for over 25 years and we have never had a complaint before. We have asked a surveyor to find out the cause of the explosion.

We are hoping that we can provide you with a satisfactory answer soon.

Yours sincerely,

Mary Miller

Service Manager

56. What happened in the factory last night?

The central heating system _____.

57. What was the damage caused to the factory?

The stock of _____ was ruined.

58. How much was the stock valued at?

It was valued at _____.

59. What did Bill Black demand in his letter?

To replace _____ and pay for the damage.

60. What has been done by the heating system supplier?

_____ has been asked to find out the cause of the accident.

Part IV Translation-English into Chinese (25 minutes)

Directions: *This part, numbered 61 through 65, is to test your ability to translate English into Chinese. Each of the four sentences (No. 61 through No. 64) is followed by four choices marked A), B), C) and D). Make the best choice and write the corresponding letter on the Answer Sheet. Write your translation of the paragraph (No. 65) in the corresponding space also on the Composition/Translation Sheet.*

61. All in all, the ABC Company offered me the experience to advance my career in China.

A. 总而言之,ABC 公司使我有了工作经历,我要在中国发展我的事业。

B. 总而言之,ABC 公司的历程有助于我实现在中国发展事业的目标。

C. 总而言之,ABC 公司使我有了在中国拓展我的职业生涯的经历。

D. 总而言之,ABC 公司的历程使我认识到我应该在中国发展事业。

62. We are confident that we will get rid of those difficulties since the government has agreed to give us some help.

A. 由于政府已经同意给予我们一些帮助,我们有信心克服那些困难。

B. 自从政府同意给予我们帮助以来,我们才下了脱贫致富的决心。

C. 政府同意给我们一些帮助,因此我们要下决心直面困境。

212

D. 我们有信心克服困难,争取政府同意给我们一些资助。

63. Both late sleepers and early risers find the fixed hours of a nine-to-five workday a problem.

   A. 早起的和晚睡的人都发现了问题,应该把早9晚5的工作时间定下来。

   B. 早起的和晚睡的人都发现了早9晚5这种固定工作时间带来的问题。

   C. 早起的和晚睡的人都认为早9晚5这种固定的上班时间有问题。

   D. 早起的和晚睡的人都认为应该把工作时间定为早9点到晚5点。

64. Not surprisingly, many scientists predict that such changes in the climate will probably result in hotter days.

   A. 毫不奇怪,许多科学家都预计气候的这些变化可能会导致天气变暖。

   B. 毫不奇怪,许多科学家认为这样的变化可能会导致热天更多。

   C. 许多科学家对于气候变化和炎热天气所产生的后果毫不惊讶。

   D. 许多科学家都认为天气变暖会改变气候,这并不令人怀疑。

65. We are glad to welcome our Chinese friends to this special Business Training program. Here, you will have a variety of activities and a chance to exchange ideas with each other. We hope that all of you will benefit a lot from this program. During your stay, please do not hesitate to speak to us with questions or concerns. We believe this will be an educational and enjoyable program.

Part V   Writing   (25 minutes)

Directions: *This part is to test your ability to do practical writing. You are required to write a Memo according to the instruction given in Chinese below. Remember to do the writing on the Composition/Translation Sheet.*

说明: 假定你是销售部经理 John Green，请以 John Green 的名义按照下面的格式和内容给本公司其他各部门经理写一个内部通知。

主题: 讨论 2006 年度第三季度 (the 3rd quarter) 销售计划

通知时间: 2006 年 6 月 16 日

内容: 本部门已制定 2006 年第三季度的销售计划。将于 2006 年 6 月 19 日下午 1:00 在本公司会议室开会,讨论这一计划。并希望各部门经理前来参加。如不能到会,请提前告知本部门秘书。

Words for reference: 告知   notify   提前   in advance

SALES DEPARTMENT

MEMO

DATE:_____

TO: _____

FROM: _____

Time: _____

SUBJECT: _____

_____

_____

答案解析

Part 1　Comprehension Listening

听力原文

Section A

1. Excuse me, can I see your boss?
2. Is this your first trip to Beijing?
3. Is there anything you want me to do?
4. Would you like another cup of tea?
5. Will you attend the meeting this afternoon?

Section B

6. W: I've tried everything, but my computer still doesn't work.

    M: Let me have a look at your computer.

    Q: What are they talking about?

7. M: Mrs. Smith, have you got any work experience?

    W: Yes, I have been a secretary for five years.

    Q: What do you know about the woman?

8. W: Mr. Yang, have you brought a price list with you?

    M: Yes, here you are.

    Q: What does the woman want?

9. W: Would you like to see the menu, Sir?

    M: Oh, yes. What is today's special food?

    Q: Where does the conversation most probably take place?

10. W: What time should I check out if I leave the hotel tomorrow?

    M: Anytime tomorrow morning.

    Q: When will the woman check out?

Section C

Modern technology has a big influence on our daily life. New devices are widely used today. For example, we have to **11 deal with** the Internet every day. It is becoming more and more **12 useful** to nearly everybody. Now it's time to think about how the Internet influences us, what **13 effect** it has on our social behavior and what the future world will look like. The Internet has **14 totally** changed our life; there is no doubt about that. I think that the Internet has changed our life in a **15 wonderful** way.

答案详解

Part I Listening Comprehension

Section A

1. ［答案］D

　　［解析］题目问"打扰了,我可以见一下你的老板吗"。"Can I …"用于提出要求,翻译为"我能……",回答对方请求的客气用法只能是 D 选项 "Yes, of course. (当然可以)"故选 D 选项,其他选项不符合题意。

2. ［答案］A

　　［解析］"Is this your first trip to Beijing"翻译为"这是你第一次去北京旅行吗",回答用 A 选项"Yes, it is. (是的)"。

3. ［答案］C

　　［解析］问题翻译为"有需要我做的事情吗"。选项中只有 C 选项"Nothing, thank you(没有,谢谢你。)"符合题意。其他选项答非所问。

4. ［答案］B

　　［解析］询问建议题。"Would you like another cup of tea? (再来一杯好吗?)",答语中只有 B 选项"No, thanks. (不了,谢谢)"为委婉谢绝的说法,其他选项不符合题意。

5. ［答案］C

　　［解析］问题翻译为"你今天下午要参加会议吗"。只要听清"will you …"就可以判断出答案为选项 C "Yes, I will"翻译为"是的,我要参加"。其他选项都不符合题意,且答非所问。

Section B

6. ［答案］C

　　［解析］由对话中女士说"我已尽力了,但是电脑仍无法正常工作",男士则说"让我看一下你的电脑",可知两人谈论的是有关电脑的问题。

7. ［答案］B

　　［解析］"关于那位女士我们知道什么",只要听清女士的回答"I've been a secretary for 5 years"就不难判断出答案为 B 选项 "她是一名秘书"。

8. ［答案］A

　　［解析］问题问"那位女士要什么"。根据女士询问男士的话"have you brought a price list with you"可知她想要 A 项"A list"。其他选项不符合题意。

9. ［答案］B

　　［解析］问题问"这个对话很有可能发生在哪"。根据男士说的 menu 一词与女士所说的 special food 可推断出对话很有可能发生在一家餐馆里。故选 B 项。

10. ［答案］D

　　［解析］问题问"那位女士什么时间办理退房手续"。根据男士的回答"明天上午任何时间"可知应选 D 项"Tomorrow morning",其他选项不符合题意。

Section C

11. deal with   12. useful   13. effect   14. totally   15. wonderful

Part II Vocabulary & Structure

Section A

16. ［答案］A

［解析］import 翻译为"进口"；imagine 翻译为"想象"；imply 翻译为"暗示"；
improve 翻译为"提高"，其他选项都不符合题意只有 A 选项"improved"与题意最
符合。

17. ［答案］D

［解析］宾语从句的时态要与主句一致。所以只能选 D 项"had drunk"，表示过去的
过去，其他的选项时态均不正确。

18. ［答案］B

［解析］rarely 翻译为"很少地，难得地"；really 翻译为"真正地"；namely 翻译为"那就
是，即"；"naturally"翻译为"天然地，非人为地"；根据句意，只有 B 选项"namely"符合
句意。

19. ［答案］C

［解析］表示对过去已发生的事进行肯定推测用"must ＋have done"句型。

20. ［答案］B

［解析］so/such... that... 翻译为"如此……以至于……"，是结果状语从句连词。so
修饰形容词；such 修饰名词。根据句子意思和结构，选项 B 为正确答案。

21. ［答案］A

［解析］本句考查名词的含义。Solution 翻译为"方法，解决问题的途径"；help 翻译为
"帮助，协助"；reply 翻译为"应答，答应"；demand 翻译为"要求"。根据题意，只有 A
选项"solution"符合题意。

22. ［答案］D

［解析］due to 翻译为"因为，由于"；as for 翻译为"至于，对……而言"；because of 翻译
为"因为，由于"；instead of 翻译为"代替，而不是"。根据题意可知应选 D 项"instead
of"。

23. ［答案］A

［解析］本句考查时态的运用，根据句意主语 I 与 treat 是被动关系，其他动词形式不
构成被动结构。只能选 A 项。

24. ［答案］C

［解析］until 表示"直到……"；unless 翻译为"除非"；while 表示"而"；if 引导条件
状语从句。因此只有 while 放在句中合适，表示转折含义。

25. ［答案］B

［解析］本题考查几个短语的含义。get through 翻译为"通过"；take off 翻译为"飞机

起飞"；pull out 翻译为"车离站，离开"；break away 翻译为"某人离开，逃离"。根据题意只能选 B 项。

Section B

26. ［答案］best

　　［解析］此句考查形容词的最高级用法。句首有 of，表示两者以上的范围。空格前有定冠词，根据形容词比较级和最高级用法的规则此处要用 good 的最高级形式 best。

27. ［答案］invitation

　　［解析］根据句子结构和题意，a 修饰名词。written 是过去分词相当于形容词，应该修饰后面的名词。所以将 invite 变为名词形式 invitation。

28. ［答案］seeing

　　［解析］本题考查的是动名词的用法。句中动词词组"be worth + V – ing"形式翻译为"干……是值得的，值得干……"，动名词作宾语。

29. ［答案］will/ shall sign 或 are going to / are to sign

　　［解析］根据时间状语 next week 判断本句应用将来时态，表示按计划、安排要做某事。可用 will/shall + 动词原形；又可用 be going to + 动词原形；也可用 be + 不定式，表示将来，所以本题答案可以多选。

30. ［答案］Generally

　　［解析］speaking 在本句中是现在分词形式，仍具有动词的特性，所以需要副词修饰。general 的副词形式是在其后 + ly 构成。

31. ［答案］be tested

　　［解析］动词 test 与主语 the new machine 之间应是被动关系，所以应用被动式"be + tested"。前面 ought to 是情态动词，后面跟动词原型。所以正确答案为"be tested"。

32. ［答案］to use

　　［解析］根据题意 allow 翻译为"允许"，其用法有"allow to do sth"和"allow sb. to do sth"故本题应用 use 一词的不定式结构。

33. ［答案］helpful

　　［解析］very 修饰形容词，同时 be 动词后应用形容词形式作表语，所以用 helpful。

34. ［答案］is

　　［解析］本句的主语为"the number of"短语，即指"……的数量"为单数名词。所以谓语动词应用单数 is。

35. ［答案］strength

　　［解析］根据题意和句子结构，will 后面要跟动词原形。名词 strength 的动词形式为 strengthen，所以答案为 strengthen。

Part III　Reading Comprehension

Task 1

36. ［答案］A

[解析]根据文中第三段首句"We are proud because we know we are a company that keeps its word to customers",中的 keeps its word 与选项 A keeps it promise 意义一致,所以 A 为正确答案。

37. [答案]B

[解析]根据文中第四段第一句话"We are grateful to customers like you, because you confirm our beliefs that good service and quality result in satisfied customers"判断 B 选项为正确答案。

38. [答案]A

[解析]由文中第三段最后一句话"... and that always lets our customers know if there is to be a delay in delivery"翻译为"如果我们不能按时发货,我们会通知我们的客户。"与选项 A 意思一致,所以选 A。

39. [答案]D

[解析]本题考查学生综合理解能力。纵观全文内容,作者写这封信的目的是 D。即原文最后一段"Our special summer catalogue is at the printers and should be in your home soon. We hope that you will be pleased with the new selection."因此应选 D 项。

40. [答案]C

[解析]本题问"关于这家公司,我们通过文章了解到了什么?"根据文章第一段第一句话"... one of the most successful companies in the market place"判断,A,B,D 三项内容在本文并没有明显的论据来证明这三项是正确的,只有选项 C 被提及,所以 C 为正确答案。

Task 2

41. [答案]D

[解析]由第一段第二句话"The government does help pay for some medical care for people who are on low incomes and for old people."判断,选项 D 为正确答案。

42. [答案]A

[解析]由第一段第二句话"···but most people buy insurance(保险)to help pay for medical care."判断选项 A 为正确答案。

43. [答案]A

[解析]由第二段第一句"In Britain, when people are ill, they usually go to a family doctor first."可知答案为 A 项。

44. [答案]C

[解析]由短文第三段倒数第二句"In America, hospitals must treat all seriously ill patients,even if they do not have medical insurance."判断选项 C 与该论述含义一致。所以 C 为正确答案。

45. [答案]B

[解析]本题考查学生的综合概括能力。阅读全文可知大部分文章都在谈论英国与美国的医疗福利。所以本题最佳答案为选项 B。

Task 3

46. [答案]clean

[解析]文章第一段第一句话就谈到了地铁的特点"干净、现代、乘车简便",所以本题应填 clean。

47. [答案]easy to use

[解析]答案在第一段第一句话。

48. [答案]reduced

[解析]文中 Metro-rail fares 一栏中谈到"Pay regular fares on weekdays 5：30—9：30 a. m. and 3：00—7：00 p. m.。Pay reduced fares at all other times."所以本空应填 reduced。

49. [答案]each station

[解析]根据文中 Metro-rail fares 一栏中的第三条"Large maps in each station show fares and travel times."可知本空应填 each station。

50. [答案]5

[解析]根据文章倒数第二句"fare-card machines only provide up to ＄5 in change（in coins）"可以得知正确答案为 5。

Task 4

51. （B）（E）　52.（G）（F）　53.（M）（H）　54.（P）（J）　55.（A）（R）

A——公交专用道

B——禁止停车

C——禁止停车候客

D——警车专用道

E——禁止掉头

F——不得入内

G——此门不通

H——单行道

I——独行桥

J——凭票入场

K——免费入场

L——请远离

M——房屋出租

N——保持秩序

O——油漆未干

P——排队购票

Q——请勿张贴

R——对号入座

S——轮椅专用道

Task 5

56. [答案]exploded

[解析]从第一封信第一句话中可以找到答案。

57. [答案]fashion clothes

   [解析]从第一封信第一段第二句话中可以找到答案。

58. [答案]$ 400,00 / 400,000 dollars

   [解析]从第一封信第二段中可以找到答案。

59. [答案]the (heating) system

   [解析]从第一封信第二段中可以找到答案。

60. [答案]A surveyor

   [解析]从第二封信第二段最后一句话中可以找到答案。

Part IV Translation—English into Chinese

61. [答案]C

   [解析]要注意不定式短语 to advance my career in china 在此作定语修饰 the experi-
   ence；all in all 固定词组翻译为"总而言之"；offer 翻译为"提供"。根据全句的意思，
   正确答案为 C。

62. [答案]A

   [解析]since the government has agreed to give us some help 是由 since 一词引导的原因
   状语从句，翻译为"由于……"；同时主句中又有一个 that 引导的补语从句，补充说明
   前面的 confident。are confident 翻译为"有信心"；get rid of 翻译为"克服，摆脱"；agree
   to 翻译为"同意"。纵观全句正确答案为 A。

63. [答案]C

   [解析]主语是由 both …and 连接的两个名词。find sth. a problem 翻译为"认为……
   有问题,不合理,存在问题"；fixed hours 翻译为"固定时间"；nine-to-five workday 翻译
   为"早9晚5的工作时间"。根据全句的意思,正确答案为 C。

64. [答案]A

   [解析]本句翻译时注意以下表达法的翻译。result in 翻译为"导致……"；not surprisingly 翻译为"毫不奇怪"；predict 翻译为"预计"；hotter days 翻译为"天气变暖"。根
   据全句的意思,正确答案为 A。

65. [译文]我们非常高兴地欢迎中国朋友参加这次商务培训专修班/项目。在这里,你们
   将参加各种活动并且有机会相互交流。我们希望,你们大家都会从培训项目中得到
   收获。在各位逗留期间,如有问题和困难,请告知我们。我们相信这次培训既有意义
   又轻松愉快。

   [解析]a variety of 翻译为"各种各样的,各种……"；during your stay 翻译为"在你逗留
   期间"；business straining program 翻译为"商务培训项目"；hope 一词后跟一个由 that
   引导的宾语从句；hesitate 翻译为"犹豫"；前加 do not 表示祈使句,翻译为"请(直接)
   告知"；enjoyable 翻译为"令人愉快的,可享受的"。

Part V Writing

SALES DEPARTMENT

MEMO

DATE: June 16th, 2006

TO: Director / Manager of every department

FROM : John Green, Sale Manager

Time: 1:00p. m. June 19th, 2006.

Subject: Discuss the sales plan for the 3rd quarter of 2006

This department has made a sales plan for the 3rd quarter of 2006. It is going to hold a meeting to discuss it in the manager of every department will attend. If you cannot be present, please notify our secretary in advance. Thank you.